# YOUNGEST GUNSLINGER

## CHARLIE BARNETT

CB061412a

www.gateswoodbooks.com

ISBN- 978-0615538297

# Chapter 1

Pa and I lived alone in a run-down old home place that we had planned to fix up when spring came. We had bought the old place a little over a year ago after we saw an ad in a northern newspaper. Course, he and I still lived in Ohio at the time. We purchased the spread for a song and sung it ourselves, you might say. We couldn't wait to move out here, hoping to leave the drab past behind. With what little we could take, he and I headed out for our new future. My pa had wanted to go west for as long as I could remember, even before Mother died. After Ma passed, it seemed his druthers got the best of him. Pa sulked for a while and I couldn't blame him, because he had lost the one thing he really loved. I could tell he was looking forward to that new baby.

It was hard on a boy my age, trying so desperately to replace the love that a loving wife and baby could give. I remember the day Pa read the ad in the newspaper, "Go west young man". As young as I was, I felt a new spirit radiating from my pa. I could actually see new hope gleaming in his eyes. With this new courage he was trying desperately to live again; I was hoping what little encouragement I could give would help.

Pa borrowed enough money from my Aunt Becky Jointer, his only sister and kin, that he knew of. My ma said Aunt Becky had married into money as a teenage girl. Uncle Tom Jointer was a clothing manufacturer; he hob-nobbed with the Paris designers to make his fortune. Of course, Uncle Tom had died years before and some other fellow had swept Aunt Becky off her feet. And wouldn't you know he moved into her big mansion. What a mistake that was I heard.

It didn't take me long to find out that it gets nearly as cold in the Oklahoma Territory as it does in the state of Ohio. Somehow, I had taken on the job of keeping the wood box full of wood in the house, without even volunteering for the job. Our woodpile was in the back yard along with the smokehouse an' chicken-houses. I finished chopping a good armload of kindling and started up the back steps. I knew to watch my step, because the steps were barely hanging on to the old house. It was one of Pa's 'get-around-to-it' projects.

One of my pa's talents was that he could look at the sun as it sank into the west and literally tell if it was gonna be a cold night or not. I had some doubt, but could never prove him wrong. Pa said his granny taught him how to tell when he was a young boy back in Ohio. Along in this same conversation he would tell me to watch the fuzzy-wuzzy worm in the fall - if it grew long hair it was going to be a very cold winter. This I had to think on.

I was about ready for some warm weather to come along myself; chopping wood was not my cup of coffee - or was it tea? Anyhow, as I stood there at the foot of the steps chewing on a splinter, I heard horse hooves in the front yard. I thought it a bit unusual for this time of evening. I guessed they rode up, unbeknownst to me, while I was chopping and gathering up an arm load of fire wood. I stopped in my tracks and trained my ear to listen...then I heard a man's voice call out to my pa.

"Fred! We need to see you out here." Now as young as I was, it just sounded like trouble to me. There was anger and hostility in the man's voice. I quickly dropped my armload of wood. Like a scared rabbit running to hide, I dropped to my all-fours and started crawling under the old house. I stopped just before I reached the front porch. The old dwelling was a wood frame board and batten house; it was built high enough off the ground so I could crawl under it with ease.

We owned two ol' Dominick chickens that insisted on nesting under the house. We also owned two blue-tick hounds that slept under there as well. The sun was almost down, and under the house it was dark as pitch. I stopped just before I reached the front porch and listened again. I could hear the men still talking to my pa.

I could tell Pa was standing right above me in the doorway; some grit was sifting through the cracks in the old board floor.

"Where's the boy?" I heard one of the men ask in that harsh tone of voice. I could tell Pa had a lot on his mind because he wasn't himself today. I also knew my pa was expecting trouble when he lied about me being gone.

"He's spending the night over at Josh Turner's house. That's a friend of his." I guess that was the last word I ever heard my pa utter. When I heard the three shots ring out, I was certain my pa was standing in the doorway right over where I was lying on my stomach. I heard a loud thud on the floor right above me. Then drops of blood starting dripping though the cracks of the boards.

"Check the backyard and the barn!" a voice called out, "Fred may be lying about the boy." I could only see the hooves of the horse that galloped toward the barn. I could see the boots of another man as he dismounted and started around the west side of our house. The cowboy was toting a lantern and wearing a pair of fancy boots. What really caught my eye were those odd-looking spurs he was wearing.

Without making a sound, I began to back up to where the two dogs had their bed. It was wallowed out big enough to bury a small horse. Thank goodness, they had gone off hunting by themselves tonight. Pa had been going into town most every night; and everyone, including the dogs, had to fend for themselves.

I didn't lose any time hiding myself as I slid down in the hole. The stench was terrible, but I thought it was better than getting my head shot off.

"You better check under the house, Calvin," the same rough voice cried out in the front yard, "the boy might be hiding under it." The man with the fancy boots was in the backyard by now. I was looking over the rim of the hole. I watched as he stooped down and waved the lantern under the house, trying to see if anything was moving. I knew to lay as still as possible in the hole. I don't think I even breathed until I saw the man get up and start back around front.

"Ain't no one under the house, Boss," I heard a man say about the time the man rode from the barn. "The boy ain't in the barn neither."

As they rode off, I knew I needed to remember what I had seen and heard. The only names that were mentioned were Calvin and Boss. I didn't know any Calvin or Boss. But I made dad-gum sure they were gone before I crawled out from under the house. My pa loved to read and had left a coal oil lamp burning on his makeshift desk in the living room. It gave enough light for me to see as I knelt down to check Pa. He was sprawled out right in the doorway. I thought he was still breathing. I was might-near out of breath myself, huffing and puffing. The thought of him being dead or dying never crossed my mind. Without losing any time, I ran to the barn and hitched up our bay to the buggy.

It was all I could do to load Pa in the back of the buggy. I was only fourteen going on fifteen, but strong as an ox and big for my age. I thank the Lord for the full moon that night; it was giving off ample light. I managed to get Pa loaded into the back of our buggy, still thinking he was alive. I hopped onto the buggy seat and started for town. Silver Springs wasn't but about six miles as 'the crow flies.' Our bay was picking 'em up and putting 'em down. There wasn't any grass growing under the buggy that night. On the way, I would call out to Pa now and then, hoping he had come to and would answer me.

As I rode along, many things came to my mind, I wondered if Pa knew what he was getting into when he read that real-estate ad in our Ohio newspaper. It was too late now to turn time back. I was doing all I knew to do, and that was to get Pa to the doctor and get him well.

Of course, the doctor was gone to bed by the time I arrived in Silver Springs. The doctor and his wife, Mrs. Mildred, lived on the edge of town in a small, white, wood-framed house. The woman's touch was prevalent. There had been flowers planted everywhere, but the harsh Oklahoma winter had taken its toll. I pulled up to the white picket-fence and found the gate hard to open.

I beat on the door several times hoping to get Doctor Fletcher's attention.

"Hold your horses, I'm coming," a voice rang out from the back part of the house. I heard footsteps jarring the floor as someone hurried through the house. I waited patiently while hearing several locks flipping and clicking; then the door opened.

"My lord, what is it? I was almost asleep!" Doc Fletcher exclaimed, squenching his eyes and pushing his specks up on his nose.

"Is that you, Wolf, what in tar-nation is going on?"

"My pa's been shot, Doctor Fletcher. I got'em out here in the buggy; we are sitting right in your front gate."

"Well, come on, Wolf, and we'll take a look-see." The doctor was carrying a lantern, huffing and a puffing along the cobblestone walk. The first thing the doctor did was unbutton Pa's shirt; he took a look at his chest, holding the lantern high.

"How many times did your pa get shot, Wolf?" the doctor asked, looking around at me.

"I only heard three shots fired. I was under the house and it was getting dark when Pa got shot."

"This will come as a blow, Wolf, your pa is dead. Whoever killed him was a sharp shooter and probably a fast gun. All three bullet holes in his chest can be covered with a silver dollar.

"You mean Pa is dead?" This couldn't be, I thought.

"I'm afraid so, Wolf; and we might as well carry your pa's body on down to the undertaker. I personally think you and I need to do it tonight. Old man Jerd Coggins is the undertaker and he can fix your pa up; you need to bury your pa sometimes tomorrow." I nodded and we climbed on up in the buggy and started down the muddy road to the funeral parlor.

"How old are you now, Wolf?" the doctor asked before we reached the funeral parlor.

"I'm just fix'in to turn fifteen. Pa and me have been out here little over a year now."

"Yes, and everybody in Silver Springs told your pa not to buy that piece of property when you all moved out here from Ohio."

"Who do you think would want to kill my pa?" I asked, holding the lantern for the doctor.

"Don't ask, Wolf, but everyone south of your spread has had a gut full of your pa...he could be a real horse's ass when he wanted to be."

I knew what Doctor Fletcher was talking about.

"It's all about the water rights, but my pa didn't break any laws or hurt anybody, did he?"

"No, he didn't break any law, but he kept a few others from doing it. His motto was, 'water ain't for sale'. He was the only one that would let the drovers cross his spread and let their cows drink water for free."

"I know it. Our creek was the last good watering hole before the cows reached the stockyard in Abilene."

"It wasn't your pa's friends that killed him, it was his enemies. And if the truth was known, it was probably the gutless bastard that owned the ranch just south of you."

"You mean the man that owns the saloon in town?" I asked.

"Same man, but you will never prove it. Why do you think your pa got that land dirt cheap? My lord, he bought it for half the price land was selling for at the time. As far as I know, the last two men who owned that spread met with an accident of some sort."

"The man that sold my pa the spread moved back East."

"Same difference, Wolf. He sold out, and moved back east before he was killed. He knew what side his bread was buttered on."

"Let me tell you here and now, Doctor Fletcher, the men that killed my pa is gonna get their bread buttered, if it's the last thing I do."

"Now, Wolf, you will get yourself killed just like your pa. It's a wonder they didn't kill you when they shot your pa tonight."

"The men couldn't find me, they looked everywhere. Pa told them I was spending the night over at Josh Turner's house. He's a friend of mine; his family moved out here about the same time we did."

"Well, you need to stay in town the rest of the night and we'll bury your pa before dinner tomorrow. Here is a bit more advice, you need to sell the few cattle and horses you have, and go back east...Don't you have an aunt that lives somewhere in Ohio you can live with?"

"But you don't understand, Doctor Fletcher, this was pa's dream, moving out west."

"Your pa's dream has got 'im killed... is that what you want?"

"As pa would say, 'That's hitting below the belt,' ain't it?"

"That was a bit low, Wolf, but I don't believe you know who you are dealing with out here. These men are paid killers." I knew the doctor was right, but going back to Ohio was not an option. We were sitting at his front gate and he started getting down from the buggy.

"You need some help, Doctor?" I asked, seeing he was having a difficult time in getting down.

"No Wolf, I got my legs in gear now. I'll see you tomorrow at the funeral home."

I drove on down to the local livery stable that belonged to Kermit Travick. I didn't see him anywhere so I went ahead an unhitched my horse, leaving the buggy parked out in front. I led the horse under the tin shed and found an empty stable. I made my way up in the hay bales and found a warn place to spend the night, with a mother cat and dozen kittens, give or take a few. I smelled like dogs but we got along right well.

# Chapter 2

By morning I smelled like a horse covered with six sweaty saddle blankets, and was ready for some fresh air. The cat and all her kittens had departed during the night…I couldn't much blame 'em.

As I started down to the diner at the end of town, I thought how Pa and I had eaten there many times after we came west from Ohio. There was a thin coat of ice on the horse trough which I broke to wash the sleep out of my eyes. I dried my face and hands on a corn sack someone had left hanging on the pump handle. As I passed the general store, Mr. Grimes was bringing out some horse collars and wash-pots and setting them on the board walk.

"Sorry to hear about your pa, Wolf. Jerd Coggins just came by and broke the news. About what time do you plan to carry his remains up to boot hill?"

"Don't really know, Mr. Grimes. I am going to the diner to get me a mouthful of breakfast before I go to see Jerd Coggins about my pa."

"Something I have been wanting to ask you for a long time, how did you get the name Wolf stuck on you? I know your ma didn't name you that."

Since it was a sad day, maybe Mr. Grimes was trying to cheer me up. "I'm afraid my mother didn't name me Wolf, my real name is Bob. But my mother did start calling me Wolf before she passed on.

I guess it was the children at the school I went to in Painesville, Ohio. I was in the second grade, as I recall, and it was the first day of school. I came that morning with the whooping cough, barking like a dog, but sounding more like a wolf, the teacher said. Everyone just died laughing, and since my last name was Mann, naturally the class started calling me Wolfman. Soon man was eliminated and I was just plain Wolf."

"Well, now I know, let me ask you something else, Wolf. Now that your dad is gone, do you have any plans for the future, or is too soon for me to ask?"

"All that is on my mind right now is how I'm gonna get the men that killed my pa. Now let me ask you something, Mr. Grimes; you sell spurs in you store don't you?"

"Yes, do you need a pair?"

"No, but what kind of spur has the wheel part of the spur flat, rather than up straight as normal?" I asked.

"That is called a side rowel spur. Mostly trick riders wear them; I don't even sell a spur like that."

"Do you know of anyone around town that you've seen wearing a pair of side rowel spurs?"

"I can't say that I have. Why are you asking?"

"Well, whoever killed my pa was wearing a pair of side rowel spurs. I was under the house but I saw his fancy boots and the spurs he was wearing. And something was causing a strange odor in the air when I came out from under the house."

"Strange odor as in gun powder. or something else?" asked Mr. Grimes.

"No, I know what smoke from gunpowder smells like, but this odor was more like tobacco smoke with a very distinctive smell – almost sweet-smelling."

"There is only one man in Silver Springs who smokes rum-maple flavored tobacco, and that is Huey Black, the man that owns the saloon in town. I believe one of his bodyguards once rode and shot a pistol in a Wild-West Circus, or that is what I was told."

9

"Mr. Grimes, I sure do thank you. You've been a big help this morning." He went back in the store, and I moseyed on down to Faye's Diner. I looked to see if I had money, because I didn't want to be embarrassed before a bunch of people for not having any money.

Now wouldn't you like to know who was eating breakfast in there? You guessed it...Huey Black and his two bodyguards. They didn't notice me at first so I ordered some hash browns and eggs from Miss Faye, and went across the diner and took a seat. I never made direct eye contact with any of the three men, and never let on that I knew that these three hoodlums were the ones who shot my pa. I made it up in my mind that I was gonna be this bunch's worst nightmare, until they paid for killing my pa.

Faye brought my breakfast over with a steaming cup of coffee.

"Jerd Coggins was over early this morning and said somebody shot your pa last night." I was watching out the corner of my eye like a chicken, never moving my head. I saw Huey Black and the other two men look my way. Miss Faye talked like she was raised around a saw-mill.

"Yeah, I was over at Josh Turner's house and missed the whole thing, and I'm glad I did."

"Does anybody know who it was?" Miss Faye asked, wiping her hands on her apron. I could tell she was taking the killing as hard as I was.

"I don't have a clue. Some said my pa had a few enemies, but just as soon as I can sell our few cows and a horse or two, I am going back to Ohio and live with my Aunt Becky."

"Wolf; that might be the smartest move you ever made in your entire life. Try to get into one of them eastern colleges and get a good education, while you are young." I can tell you one thing, what Miss Faye was saying went in one ear and out the other. I didn't say anything, but my plan was to become a gun-slinger, and my goal was to become the fastest gun in the west.

Now I didn't want to arouse any suspicion, but I shore wanted to see what type of spurs these no-good polecats were wearing. I never looked their way, but when Huey Black finished his breakfast he took a pipe out of his coat pocket and fired it up. He blew a few smoke rings and soon the diner smelled just like our front yard last night. One down and two to go, I thought. As fate would have it, the trio got up from the table and came walking straight toward me. Old man Huey Black was leading the pack of buzzards. I kept my cool and kept right on eating like nothing had happened.

"I couldn't help but hear what Miss Faye said about your pa. He seemed to be doing so well with his spread. I also heard you say you were going to sell out and go live with your aunt in Ohio."

"Yes sir, that is my plan as of now," I answered, without even looking up. I was thinking to myself if I had a gun I would kill him right where he stood. I was sitting no more than three feet from the man that shot my pa. Yeah, he stood there in his freshly pressed black suit, and his highly polished boots; while my pa was over in the morgue in a pine box.

"I know this is not the time to discuss business, son, your pa being deceased and all, but after the funeral, come see me. I will give you a good price for your animals and your ranch." I thought the nerve of this son-of-a-bitch was enough to gag a maggot.

"That's right neighborly of you, sir, I'll give it some thought." That's when I thought about the spurs and looked down at the feet of the men standing to one side. I had just taken a bite of my eggs, and nearly choked. There he stood in his fancy boots and side rowel spurs, with a Colt hanging low and tied to his leg.

I wondered who did the actual shooting - the man with the smelly pipe, or the man with the fancy spurs. Don't matter, I thought, as the trio turned and left the dinner, they all need a good killing anyhow.

While I was finishing my breakfast, Miss Faye came over to clear the table. "You know who that was, Wolf?" she asked, as I took my last sip of coffee and set my cup down.

"Yes! That was the rattlesnakes that killed my pa last night." I thought Faye was gonna drop the tray of dishes on the floor, as she looked all around.

"Wolf! Don't say something like that. Do you know who runs this town?" I might not be but fourteen, but this got my dander up, whatever that means.

"Yes! I am."

11

"You are... Wolf, you don't know what you're saying. You're just upset and I can't blame you." Miss Faye shook her head and just stood there, as if she was feeling sorry for me. I had done paid for my breakfast, and I flipped a quarter on the tray Miss Faye was holding.

"No! No! Wolf, you don't have to tip me," she said, looking very surprised.

"I know Miss Faye, but I own Silver Springs, Oklahoma Territory. Didn't I just get through telling you?" Miss Faye twisted her mouth, turned, and walked off.

It was still early, but I thought I would walk on over to the general store and kill some time before the funeral. After all, it was right on the way to the funeral parlor. The door was wide open although it was a bit nippy this morning, and I eased on in the store. As I began to look all around, I heard a voice over behind some sacks of feed.

"Come on around, Wolf, and take the load off." I made my way, without knocking something over and breaking it, to where Doctor Fletcher and Mr. Grimes were sitting. I didn't quite know whether to roll up my britches legs or sit down. I could tell the two were getting caught up on the town's gossip.

"I was just telling Doc, what this town needs is a sheriff."

"And I can tell you what he probably said," I retorted, as I pulled up a chair and sat down backwards in it. "He wouldn't last as long as a snow-ball in Hades." Both men went to laughing, and Mr. Grimes slapped the table.

"That's exactly what Doc said, and sad to say, it's the truth."

"I know I'm only fourteen years old, but this town of Silver Springs is not owned by a bunch of snakes like Huey Black." I was still fed up with the way this town bowed down to the murdering bunch over at the Silver Slipper Saloon. Doctor Fletcher and Mr. Grimes were not ever going to cross this buzzard; they had families and wives to consider.

"I don't have anything to consider, now that Pa is gone."

Both Doctor Fletcher and Mr. Grimes looked at me as if I had lost my mind. "What did you say, Wolf?" Mr. Grimes questioned.

"I guess I was just daydreaming. But why hasn't someone done something before now?" I asked - with an attitude a mile long.

"Your pa tried to do something, Wolf, and look what it got him!" It took all I could to keep from breaking down right in front of Doctor Fletcher and Mr. Grimes. I guess they would have understood, since I'm only fourteen years old.

"It's about time we need to climb the hill, don't you think, Doc?" Mr. Grimes remarked as he stood.

"I reckon, it's going on ten o'clock. We are going with you Wolf; Doc and I thought a lot of your pa, and let us say here and now we are very sorry about the whole thing."

"That's right, Wolf; and if we can ever do anything, for you, please let us know." Mr. Grimes added, and then they headed for the front door.

"I guess you two and Miss Faye are the only friends I have in Silver Springs, now. I reckon I'll be leaving as soon as I can sell our few cattle and the horses," I said, walking between Doctor Fletcher and Mr. Grimes.

"What about the ranch and house?" Doc asked, looking at me.

"Well, them too. I'll probably never be back here in Silver Springs anyway," I said.

"Well, after what happened, you may have some trouble selling the land," Mr. Grimes commented.

"I don't know about that. That rotten buzzard, old man Huey Black done approached me about my property while I was over at breakfast this morning."

"I told you, Doc...Huey Black would wind up with the whole valley; now he can charge for all the water," Mr. Grimes acknowledged.

"Go ahead and sell him your spread, Wolf, you will probably save another life," Doc said.

"No one will blame you, Wolf. Get what money you can and go back East and finish school."

The hearse was already at the grave site when we walked up. Mr. Jerd Coggins was waiting for someone to help him unload my pa's body. The grave was already dug, and I guess Mr. Jerd Coggins thought more of the townsfolk would attend my pa's funeral. He motioned for the two darkies who had dug the grave to come help with the casket. They were sitting behind the only bush on the hill, trying to stay warm. The north wind had picked up and it was downright cold.

Mr. Grimes opened up a small Bible he had brought with him; he read some scripture, then said a few kind words. The five of us lowered the pine box into the deep, dark hole. The two darkies did have respect. They waited until we turned to leave before they started throwing dirt on the casket.

It seemed that my pa deserved more in life than this; but out here in the West it's a hard life, to say the least. My pa lost his wife as she was giving birth to his daughter. Now he had lost his life, trying to protect me and his property.

"I'll make it up to you, Pa, you wait and see."

We were about halfway down the hill when Doctor Fletcher spoke up, "Wolf, I don't think you are in danger as long as Huey Black thinks you are going to sell out to him. I know you are going back to your home to pack up."

"The only thing I'll be packing when I get home is a few of my clothes and my pa's six-gun." Doctor Fletcher looked at Mr. Grimes and shook his head. It was like they disapproved of my foolishness.

"Don't worry, gentlemen, when I come back to Silver Springs, whenever that will be, I'll be the fastest gun in the world."

"I believe you will, Wolf, and we'll be waiting."

I didn't see Doctor Fletcher and Mr. Grimes for several days, until I returned to Silver Springs later. I eased on over to the livery stable after the funeral and hitched my buggy and said goodbye to Kermit Travick. As I started to leave, I spied a black horse standing in the back lot behind the livery stable. I got out of the buggy and went inside. Kermit Travick was a pretty good blacksmith, if I do say so. He was just fixing to beat on a horseshoe.

"How much do you want for that black horse behind the shop?"

"I don't think you want that stud, he stays too fired up all the time." Now I don't know why, but it was just like something was telling me to buy that horse.

"Well, is that bad? I don't know anything about horse flesh."

Kermit Travick put his horseshoe back in the forge, laid his hammer down and walked over to the water bucket. "No, it's not a bad thing. You just got to let him know who is boss. You have got to ride him or he'll ride you."

"Do you think I could handle him if I really tried? He's not mean is he?" I started back to the lot and Kermit Travick followed me.

"You ain't serious about that powerhouse are you, Wolf? That's a high dollar horse," Kermit Travick said, as he and I propped up on the corral fence.

"My lord, Mr. Kermit, the more you say about that horse the worse I want him. If you will put a price on that bad boy I'll ride him home." I could see myself splitting the wind on that solid black stallion.

"What are you going to do with your buggy and that bay you have hitched up?"

"Well, since I'm going to buy the black horse from you, I don't need my buggy and the bay. I don't think for one minute you'll have any trouble getting shed of Pa's fine buggy," I said, still admiring the black horse.

"You're not suggesting we trade my black horse for your buggy and your horse?"

"Like I said, I don't need the buggy or the horse."

"Wolf, my buddy, I'm not going to take advantage of you; your rig is worth more than the black horse." Mr. Kermit Travick opened the gate and we walked over to the horse. Like he said, the horse was right spirited, but stood proud.

I eased over to where the horse was sanding.

"Can he run?" I asked, putting my arm around the horse's neck and my face against the horses' long jaw.

"Can he run, you asked? Now I can say something good about this horse... I have never seen or owned a horse any faster in my fifty years, beating on horseshoes."

"Look at this, Mr. Kermit, I believe he likes me." As he and I turned to walk off the black horse nuzzled me on the back and followed me to the corral gate.

"I tell you what I'll do, Wolf, we can swap and I'll give you fifty dollars cash." By this time, we were inside the office part of the blacksmith shop. Mr. Kermit also sold saddles, bridles and other horse-related supplies.

"How much will you take for that black saddle lying over there, Mr. Kermit?" I walked over and patted the saddle, and thought how good it would look on my black horse.

"How bout fifty dollars, and I will throw in a black bridle to match the saddle," Mr. Kermit said, walking over to the saddle.

"Could you throw in that dark blue saddle blanket hanging up there on that hook?"

"You are driving a hard bargain, Wolf, but I believe I can let it go" he said, laughing under his breath.

"If you are happy Mr. Kermit, I'm tickled to death. I bet'cha there ain't many fourteen-year-old boys that will be sporting a fine animal and rigging like I've got." I was going by the general store as soon as I sold some of my cattle, and buy me a black hat and boots to match.

Mr. Kermit wrote me out a bill-of-sale for my horse and helped me saddle my prized possession. We adjusted the stirrups and I was soon on my way home.

# Chapter 3

I had to pass the cemetery on my way out of town although it was a ways off the road and high up on a hill. I was about even with the graveyard when something caught my eye. Now curiosity killed the cat and all them cats got the best of me so I turned off the road and started toward the cemetery. Before I reached my pa's grave site I could tell there was a woman kneeling at the head of his freshly dug grave.

I got off my horse and started over to the woman who was bitterly weeping. She looked up quickly, somewhat surprised.

"Wolf, it's you," she said as she began to dry her eyes and regain her composure.

"Yes ma'am, Miss Faye, it's me."

"Wolf, I thought a lot of your pa. Over the last few weeks he and I had made a few plans. We were going to tell you this week."

"Miss Faye, you wouldn't think less of me, or think I'm a little kid if I cried some over my pa, would you?"

"Come here, Wolf, and kneel next to me." Faye put her arms around my neck and that's all it took. I guess this was when reality took its toll. I would never see my pa ever again because he was under this pile of red clay. I don't know how long I cried...both me and Miss Faye. I was pretty much tuckered out when I got up and helped Miss Faye up from the ground. We stood and hugged each other for the longest time.

"So you and Pa were thinking about getting hitched?"

She nodded and wiped her face on the handkerchief she was holding. "Yes, he and I had grown very fond of each other. We had something in common; your pa and I had both lost a mate. It's sad living alone, Wolf, I loved my husband very much but we must go on living. Neither your pa nor I was over the hill." Miss Faye broke down again and pulled me close. I had done give Pa up, and my crying was over. It was like you had turned off a kerosene lamp; Miss Faye stopped crying, stepped back, and lit up like new snow on a cedar tree.

"You know what, Wolf," her eyes were sparkling, "you can come and live with me! After all, I was might-near your ma."

"Now Miss Faye, I'll do some thinking on it," I said.

"I could sure use some help. My ma still lives with me and you could help with the milking, and chopping wood. Why, I would even pay you, Wolf."

"I'm still thinking, Miss Faye. You've even got a place for my horse, and plenty of pasture room."

"That's right, Wolf, and I'll do all the cooking, and you'll have your own room and feather bed; and you can come and go as you see fit."

"Miss Faye! I'm through thinking..."

"Well..."

"You got yourself a boarder." This seemed to cheer Miss Faye up and she grabbed me again. I thought my crying was over, but she reminded me so much of Mama that the tears flowed again.

"I'm so glad you brought some flowers and placed on Pa's grave; he would have liked them." I had just thought Miss Faye's crying was over.

"You loved Pa, didn't you?" Evidently I said the wrong thing. Miss Faye quickly turned and fell across Pa's grave and began to scream and pound on the dirt with her balled up fists.

"Why, Lord? Why me, Lord? You knew I was carrying Fred's baby."

Now this was a hard pill to swallow. I wondered, would this baby be my brother or sister even though Miss Faye and Pa weren't married yet? I was ashamed even to ask. Maybe I'd let that sleeping dog lie, and open that keg of nails later. I gently took hold of Miss Faye's arms and lifted her to her feet.

"Come on, let's go," I whispered, leading her over to my horse. Miss Faye regained her composure and dried her eyes.

"Now, Blackie, you stand still till I can get in the saddle."

"What did you say, Miss Faye?" I asked, waiting to get on my horse, also.

Miss Faye turned to face me, "Wolf, you may have to help me. I don't remember the last time I rode a horse."

"What did you call my horse?" I questioned, holding the stirrup for Miss Faye.

"I told this beautiful horse to stand still for me to get on."

"Yeah, but you called him a name." I was thinking that would be a good name.

"I called him Blackie, is that not his name? I'm sorry." I swung my leg over and sat right behind Miss Faye.

"Well, it is now. You just named my horse. Get up, Blackie!" I said, gently kicking him in the ribs.

"Do you have a cold, Miss Faye? I can't help noticing you holding your handkerchief to your nose."

"Oh no, Wolf...but do you take criticism well?"

"Now Miss Faye, you using them big words... remember I'm only fourteen; and I've never had much schooling, you know."

"You mean criticism? That's when someone tells you something that you may not agree with. Would you get mad?"

"Now Miss Faye...I don't rightly know. You see what I mean?"

"Well, Wolf, here's an example; what if someone told you they couldn't tell whether you smelled like a horse or a dog?"

"You know, Miss Faye, I guess I wouldn't mind; they could very well be talking about me. If it wasn't for the holes the dogs wallowed out, I would be pushing up daisies this morning, and if it wasn't for a dozen sweaty horse blankets, I would have froze to death last night."

"You have lost me along the way, but I hope this is all in the past. And if you will, pull up right in front of the general store, I'm going to buy you some decent clothes."

"Now Miss Faye, I will pay you back just as soon as I sell my cows." I guessed now I could get my black outfit and become a gunslinger.

"I'm not worried about the money, Wolf; I'm worried about when you come in the house. Mama would turn up her nose and wonder who let the dogs in the house." We both slid off Blackie, I tied him up to the hitching rail, and we headed inside.

"I didn't think you had any dogs to get in the house, Miss Faye."

"I need to run on over to the diner and check on the girls. I left them by themselves fixing dinner. We'll talk about the dogs tonight, Wolf."

I reckon Mr. Grimes heard us jabbering out in front of the store. He walked out on the porch to see what all the commotion was about.

"How are you this morning, Mr. Grimes?" Miss Faye asked.

"Doing right well, Miss Faye, iffen I can win over this gout in my big toe. By the way, I didn't know you owned a horse. He shore is a fine un."

"Oh, this is Blackie, and he belongs to Wolf...said he bought him from Kermit over at the blacksmith shop; and speaking of Wolf, he is going to get some new clothes. Put the charges on my ticket. Then, if you will, send him next door to the barber shop and have Rooty give him a grown man's hair cut - not something that looks like someone used a bowl. "

"Now, you just listen to her, Wolf!" he teased.

"You take a good hot bath before you put on your new clothes. Did you hear all of that?"

"Yes Ma'am, I shore enough did!"

"Then, come on over to the diner and we'll have dinner together. When I pass by the barber shop I'll tell Rooty you will be over soon."

"Wolf, I didn't think I would see you again before you drug off to Ohio." Mr. Grimes and I eased back into the store, and I started looking around.

"Wolf, the shirts and pants are over this way. I just got in a good shipment of clothes, in your size, I believe.

I picked up a solid black shirt and gave it the eagle eye, as Pa would say. "You reckon this 'un will fit me?"

Mr. Grimes held the shirt up to my shoulders and down my arms. "It will be perfect, Wolf," he proclaimed.

"Then I'll take both of them," I answered, picking up another shirt.

"But they are both just alike, Wolf!"

"I know, I'm going to be a fast gun; and they always wear black. Now what about some black pants?"

Mr. Grimes took a ribbon looking thing that had numbers up and down it and pulled it around my waist. "Step over this way, Wolf. You said you wanted black, well, we are in luck. These will match your shirts."

"That's fine, give me two pair."

"I reckon you want both pair black, too?" Mr. Grimes asked, putting both pair in the sack with the shirts.

"I also want a pair of fancy black boots, a black hat, and a black belt with a large silver buckle."

"I figure you'll need a black gun belt, as well?"

"Now, Mr. Grimes, you are reading my mind. I'm going home tomorrow and pack my other stuff and Pa's six-guns. Then I'll come back by the store and get a holster." I walked over to where a black coat was hanging. "Boy, this is nice!" I took it off the hanger, "I'll bet it's warm, too."

"That's a nice coat, Wolf, and it is warm. I have one at home just like it. I'm throwing in some long-handles and socks and you should be all set for your trip to Ohio."

"Mr. Grimes, I have kinda put that trip on the back burner for now. I'm gonna be boarding over at Miss Faye's house until I sell my cattle and property. She says she needs some help with her ma and the diner."

"Now I can understand that, Wolf. You don't need to be living by yourself for a while, especially just after your pa's death. Did you pick you out a hat yet?"

We walked over to a rack that held a dozen or more hats, and I spied just what I wanted; it had a wide band with silver conchas end to end, and it fit like a glove.

"You may need to try on the boots and see if they fit before you leave the store, Wolf. There is nothing more irritating than a boot too tight - except maybe a toothache."

I sat down on an apple box close by and Mr. Grimes handed me a black boot. I slid off a brogan that had seen its better day and reached for the boot.

"Wolf, you might want to put on your new socks to try on your new boots, seeing neither you nor your Pa ever darned socks."

I was soon prancing around like a peacock in my new boots. "They fit fine, Mr. Grimes. I think I'll just wear them over to the barber shop since I got 'em on."

I thanked Mr. Grimes for the help and started on over to see Rooty Picket at the barber shop. Now Rooty Picket hadn't been in Silver Springs long. He was shore nuff a damn Yankee from Boston. At times I couldn't understand anything he said. I had been to his shop a time or two with Pa.

You might say I got the whole treatment, even the soap smelled good; it beat the devil out of the lye-soap Pa made. Course, that had cured the mange on our blue tick in less than a week.

I stood before a full length mirror in the back room where I had taken my bath. I just stood for a minute or two admiring myself. All I needed was a pistol, a holster tied to my leg, and a few shooting and fast draw lessons. I put my hat on and screwed it down tight. I could have fooled the governor. Yes-sir-ree-bob, I said to myself, I'm gonna be a bad dude when I strap on Pa's pistol.

I thought it was about time to get on over to the diner for some lunch, so I headed back through the barber shop.

"You are a mighty fine looking young man," Rooty Picket said.

I stopped and looked at him as he was cutting a man's hair. "Well, thank you very much, sir, you are looking at the next world's fastest gunslinger." The man sitting in the barber chair grunted and started laughing. "You got a problem, do you, mister? What's wrong with being the world's fastest draw?"

"Nothing, I guess, but you are going to have to take the title from me...I'm the world's fastest man with a pistol."

I quickly sized the man up. All I could see was his face and his boots as he was covered with a striped cape. I nearly choked when I saw he was wearing side rowel spurs.

I thought I would change the subject since I wasn't wearing a pistol - and probably couldn't hit the side of a barn even if I was in the barn.

"Where did you get those side rowel spurs, mister?" I asked, backing up to take a good look.

"I bought them in Chicago years ago."

"I'll bet you did some trick riding when you was younger." I could tell the man was lost for words, he was probably wondering how a young boy not even dry behind the ears knew so much about side rowel spurs and trick riding.

"Do you still do some trick riding?"

"My name is Calvin, and you are Wolf, Fred Mann's son. No, I don't do any performing anymore. How would you like to have my side rowel spurs?"

Me, wearing the spurs of the man that killed my pa?

"Yes sir, Mr. Calvin, I would sure like to have them because they are so different."

Many things began to bombard my mind: Was Calvin's conscience bothering for killing a man with a son only fourteen? Would giving me the spurs make amends in some way? Was I going down the same road that he went when he was my age...becoming a killer? I'd never thought about it that way. When you carry the title as a fast gun you're sure to be challenged - and it is either put up or shut up. Man or mouse, there's more to this gun slinging business than I'd thought.

I was still standing in the middle of the barber shop when Rooty Picket finished up with Mr. Calvin. He paid for his haircut, walked over and sat down on a makeshift couch covered with cow hide and started taking off his spurs.

I eased over and sat down beside Mr. Calvin. "You weren't joshing about the spurs was you, Mr. Calvin?"

I never will forget the look on Mr. Calvin's face when he handed me the pair of side rowel spurs. "Son, I'm not a good person, I have even killed innocent men, but I won't go to hell for lying." He quickly arose and headed for the door.

"Thank you, Mr. Calvin," I said.

He never said a word or even looked back at me. I went ahead and put on my spurs and pranced around in the barber shop listing to the jingle.

"What do you think, Mr. Rooty?"

He stopped and propped up on his broom. "If I hadn't seen it with my own eyes, I wouldn't have believed it. Wolf, do you know who that man was? He's a paid killer, hired by that cut-throat Huey Black."

Yes, I knew who he was but I wasn't gonna let on and blow my cover. If anybody in this town had any idea I knew who killed my pa, my life wouldn't be worth a plug-nickel.

I guess I took Miss Faye by surprise when I walked into the diner. Lunch was over and she and the two girls were cleaning up the place. The diner only served two meals - breakfast, and the noon meal.

"My lord, Wolf, come here and let me look at you!" She turned to the other girls, Margie and Elie Mae, "Ain't he something? And just to think, Wolf is going to be living with me," Miss Faye said, coming over and hugging me up.

I had to admit, I didn't quite know how to respond to this hugging business. After all, I was only fourteen. Could this be the starting of a love affair on her part? The way Miss Faye introduced me... 'He's moving in with me.' For crying out loud, when Miss Faye gets big as a barrel just who do you suppose people will think the daddy is? Just thinking, visiting my Aunt Becky Joiner may not be such a bad idea after all!

Miss Faye took off her apron and she and I took a small table over in the corner next to the kitchen. Talk about service! Elie Mae and Margie swallowed us up. You would have thought I was a king. Neither Margie nor Elie Mae was much older than me, and the way they were taking on over me, I wasn't used to the like. And what was so good or bad - call it what you want - I could get used to this life. Two good-looking young ladies swooning over me, and Miss Faye was a good looker herself.

"Miss Faye, it's still early and I'm thinking on riding out to the home place and feeding up - maybe get the rest of my clothes."

Miss Faye reached over and took my hands and with the softest smile and sweetest voice said, "You be carefully now, Wolf, darling."

You see what I mean? This darling stuff messed with my mind. I needed to be on that stagecoach heading east very soon.

I thought I would swing by Josh Turner's house beings I was this close. I wanted to show him my horse, and mention that my pa had been shot. When I rode up, I caught both Josh and his pa sitting on the front porch spitting and a whittling. Josh was whittling, and his pa was doing the spitting.

"Fine looking horse flesh you're riding, boy," Mr. Turner said, spitting a stream of tobacco juice half way across the yard.

"His name is Wolf, Pa," Josh scolded, laying his stick and knife down by his straw bottom rocking chair.

"I come by to tell you folks my pa has been shot, and I'm moving back East with my Aunt Becky." This got Mr. Turner's attention.

"Whatcha gonna do with the cows and horses you got?"

"I guess I'll have to sell them. I sure can't take 'em with me to Ohio," I said sliding out of the saddle.

"How much are you gonna be asking fer 'em?" Mr. Turner asked, letting another streak of tobacco juice fly. "I'd sure would like to have them breed cows y'all got, son, but I'm barely making it."

I started to tell Mr. Turner he could sell that stick his son was whittling on. Can you believe it? Here it was nearly two o'clock in the afternoon and these two were sitting on their butts with dry corn hanging in the field. Pa done said it; both Josh and his pa had a streak of laziness a mile long.

# Chapter 4

"I tell you what I'll do, Mr. Turner, iffen I can sell my land for a good price, I'll let you have my stock for market value, and you can pay me when you get able."

"Now, Wolf, that is right neighborly of you."

"I believe Pa had five or six plug norses hanging around, you can have them too. I done traded the bay and the buggy for Blackie, standing there."

"Reckon when you will sell the land, Wolf?" Mr. Turner asked, letting another stream of tobacco juice slide across the grassless yard. He nearly hit a hound dog that was so poor he would have to lean up side of the house to bark.

"I plan on looking up ole man Huey Black and selling out to him," I said, as I mounted my horse.

"You are not serious, are you, Wolf?" Mr. Turner asked, nearly choking on his tobacco juice.

"Serious as a cougar eyeing a longhorn. Why do you ask?"

"Well, he's been trying to get that piece of property for years and he's finally done it, and if the truth were known he had something to do with your pa being shot."

"You reckon so?" I asked, acting as dumb as a sack of Oklahoma river bottom rocks. "How can I prove it? You and Josh sitting there know good and well Silver Springs has no law; and if they got a sheriff Huey Black would have him killed within a week."

I left Mr. Turner and Josh just like I found them, sorrying away, sitting on the front porch. I took a short cut and was at the ranch before a cat could lick her kittens. I guess the only change I saw, Pa wasn't there.

The locks never worked on that old house, so I just walked on in as if I had never been here before. I eased over where Pa's pistol was hanging on a deer antler nailed to the wall. This, as I recollect, was the first time I had really ever looked at Pa's pistol. I took it off the wall and flopped it around me. Naturally, it was too large, but not much. Pa was not a huge man but, he was raw-boned and hard as nails.

I knew Pa always kept a leather awl over at his desk... he was always punching holes in something. Without too much fanfare, I adjusted the holster and tied it to my leg. As I laid the awl back on the roll top desk I noticed a three page letter with an envelope that was addressed to Aunt Becky Joiner. I folded the letter and stuck it in the envelope to carry it with me. I thought I would let Miss Faye read it to me tonight, because Pa couldn't write no better than I could read. I went ahead and packed the few clothes I had, along with a picture of Ma and the letter, in a grip. I wanted to get back to town before dark, so I lit out, thanking God for the new coat. Mr. Grimes was right, it was really warm.

I reckon I was half way to town when I spotted a figure of a man up ahead. He started flagging me down, so I stopped to see if I could be of some assistance. That was my first mistake. He didn't look dangerous to me; all he was carrying was a grip like mine.

"Can I help you in some way, mister?" I asked, waiting on his sad story about how his horse had died or how he was robbed and left for dead.

"You sure can, sonny, I need your horse."

"But, mister, you don't understand......."

"I understand, boy! You are the one that don't understand."

28

This is when he drew his pistol and pointed it right at me. Now I might not be but fourteen, and don't read or spell good, but I'm not stupid. I dismounted as if I had already been shot out of the saddle.

"You're smarter than you look, boy, he said as he mounted Blackie, holding his grip close to him. He looked down at me and smiling like a jackass eating briars replaced his pistol in his holster and started riding away.

Now, thank goodness for the long coat; it hid my gun rigging. I quickly drew my pistol and pointed right at him. I wasn't going to start off being called a back shooter so I cocked the pistol and held it with both hands. Drawing a fine bead on the back of his head I yelled out, "Hey, mister!" He was no more than a few yards away when he turned and looked straight at me. I pulled the trigger. He and the grip hit the ground like a sack of Idaho spuds.

I eased over to where the man was lying and took hold of the reins of Blackie, who seemed a little skittish... the strange rider and the gunshot...no wonder. I saw right off this man wasn't going anywhere. I had shot him right between the eyes. But what was even stranger, the grip lying on the ground had come open in the fall and money covered the ground.

As I poked all the big bills back in the bag, the thought came to me that this man, whoever he was, had robbed a bank somewhere and ran his horse to death trying to get away from the law. I tied his grip and my grip together, threw them behind the saddle and headed for Silver Springs as fast as I could. I didn't stop until I got to the morgue. I caught Jerd Coggins, the funeral director, coming out of the funeral parlor and told him what had happened a few miles back down the road. I asked if I could help in any way. He assured me that he could take care of the matter.

Course, I didn't tell him everything. I didn't tell him I had a bag full of money tied to my horse. The diner was closed when I rode by so I went straight on over to Miss Faye's big house. I fed and stabled my horse. Then I went to the back door and knocked two or three times and waited. It was near freezing by now. Finally, I heard footsteps coming through the big house.

"Thank God you're safe, Wolf. Mother and I had begun to worry about you - it getting dark and all."

"It sure is nice and warm in here," I said, taking off my heavy coat.

"Give me your coat, and let me introduce you to Mother, then I'll show you to your room."

Miss Faye led the way and I followed with the two grips. Mrs. Pittman was sitting by the big fire place in a huge straw bottom rocking chair. I set the two bags down and went over to shake Mrs. Pittman's hand.

"A friend of Faye's is a friend of mine." She pulled me down, hugged me and gave me a kiss. I guess this hugging thing was hereditary among these folks.

"It's so good to meet you, Mrs. Pittman," I said, backing up to the roaring fire.

"It good to have you living with us, Wolf, and I'm so sorry about your pa. Faye has told me all about you wanting to be a fast gunslinger. Sometime I'll tell you about my first boyfriend; he was a gunslinger."

"Did you and he think about getting hitched?" I asked.

"Oh yes! But he didn't live long enough." I thought wryly - this will make me sleep better tonight.

"Come on, Wolf, let me show you to your room. We can come back and gab later before we turn in." It was a beautiful room, something I wasn't used to. "Can I help you unpack?" she asked.

"Oh no, I can manage, but I do want you to read a letter for me."

I took the letter out of my bag and gave it to her. Then I went back in by the fireplace. I was biding my time to tell Mrs. Pittman and Miss Faye about killing the man who was stealing Blackie. I decided that I'd wait until after I got the letter read. The three of us were enjoying the fire, but I was anxious to know what the letter said. Miss Faye took a wing-back chair near her ma and pulled a milking stool-looking contraption up in front of the fireplace for me to sit on, since I had been out in the cold all day.

I handed the letter to Miss Faye and watched carefully as she took the three sheets of paper out of the envelope and laid it to the side. She unfolded the pages and began to read: 'Dear Becky, It's been over a year since I seen you, and might near that long since you have written me. I can't talk; I don't write either. Wolf and I are doing well as can be expected. Wolf is growing like a weed, and near tall as I am. I'm hoping for a good spring this year. It looks like all of my brood cows will drop a calf; that's like money in the bank. I haven't forgotten the money I borrowed from you to buy the ranch. How are you and your new husband making out? I know he will never take Tom's place, but I hope you are happy.

Becky, dear, I have good and bad news and I will give you the good news first... I have met a wonderful lady since I come to Silver Springs. We both have lost our first loves and are trying to make up for lost time. As you know it's been over two years since I lost Vivian and the baby. Faye tells me she has been living alone for that long, or longer. I'm not one to pry but she is the most loving and caring person I have ever met.'

Miss Faye choked up and held the letter to her chest. Mrs. Pittman and I waited, not saying anything until she could regain her composure.

'I think she loves me and she comes from a very good family, Faye lives with her mother, Mrs. Pittman, who is a wonderful person. Faye owns and runs Faye's Diner in Silver Springs. From all indications, she is doing quite well but working too hard. She has two young ladies to help her out. For the last few months, she and I have been seeing lots of each other. I have put Wolf on the back burner, so to speak, and haven't even told him of our love affair.'

Miss Faye stopped reading, and I thought she was going to fold the letter up. Instead she looked right at her mother and twisted her mouth.

"Mother," Faye remarked "you might as well know now, you will know soon enough. I was wondering how to tell you I'm with Fred's child." Well, you could have heard a pin drop. "I have already told Wolf..."

Mrs. Pittman never said a word but she smiled. Miss Faye went on with the letter. 'Faye told me the other night she was carrying my baby and this was something she always wanted. I thought I was over the hill, but Faye reminded me she was only thirty-eight. Needless to

31

say, this altered our plans somewhat. But we both agreed this could be a new start for both of us.'

Miss Faye took a big breath and scrunched her shoulders. "I'm glad that is over, in a way, but I must go on." Miss Faye found her place in the letter and went on reading.

'Now, Sister Becky, that was the good news. What I'm about to tell you in this letter, keep it to yourself for now.' Miss Faye stopped reading the letter, and started to fold it up and reached for the envelope.

"What are you doing?" asked Mrs. Pittman.

"Mother, I feel like I'm pilfering and eavesdropping or putting my nose into someone's private life." Miss Faye looked over my way trying to make a decision one way or the other. "What about it, Wolf, do you want me to keep reading?"

Just then a strange feeling came over me, as if to say, 'tell her to keep reading.' Pa was trying to tell us something even after his death.

"Go ahead, Miss Faye. I believe Pa wants to tell us something we don't know!"

"All right, here is the last page."

I began to give a close ear now, and I noticed Mrs. Pittman perked up, too.

'Dear Sister, I love you very much, but this may be the last word you ever get from me. My life is being threatened. Huey Black and his hired killers are out to get me this time. It's not the water on my property he wants anymore. I found out yesterday, from two surveyors that I ran into down on my south forty, that the railroad is coming right down this valley.' Miss Faye stopped and looked up at Mrs. Pittman and me, nodded, and started back reading. 'Now, Becky, I'm not predicting my future, but... if anything happens to me, I'm giving you all rights to be the guardian over Wolf, until he is twenty-one years old.

As you know, the last three people that owned this homestead met with an accident, or got run off... I do want to pay you, but...'

"But what, Miss Faye?" I questioned. Mrs. Pittman rose up in her chair.

"That's it," said Miss Faye, folding the letter back up. I heard Mrs. Pittman clear her throat, and caught her gaze.

"Wolf, do you want the advice of a wise old woman?"

I looked over at Miss Faye and she nodded.

"Yes Ma'am, if you got some to spare."

Mrs. Pittman started laughing, nearly out loud. I thought to myself, what in tar-nation is so funny...Pa is dead, and Miss Faye is about to drop a young'un. Plus, Mrs. Pittman has one foot in the grave and the other on a banana peel. And I done went and killed a man dead as a door nail.

"Yes, ma'am, if you got some good advice I sure would like to hear it, and what's so funny?"

"Well, you listen and listen good; what I say is very important. In the morning before your shirt tail touches your back, you need to find ole man Huey Black, and if you ever put up the poor mouth, this is the time...tell that murdering buzzard you want to sell your ranch and move back to Ohio as quick as you can. Take anything he will offer you for the land. Have him write you out a bill of sale and you make sure to sign and date it."

"But, what is so funny?" I asked.

"Well, when you sell old man Huey Black your property, you have just pulled the wool over his eyes. He is so greedy and carried away with owning your pa's ranch he has forgotten the legal aspects of selling and owning land. The deed that he will have is signed by a fourteen-year-old boy and is not worth the paper it is written on."

"But what about when he sells the land to the railroad?" I asked.

"It is not legal. It is not his land to sell. Your Aunt Becky in Ohio can get a good lawyer and get every bit of your land back. Ignorance is no excuse in the sight of the law. My husband was very intelligent when it came to the law. He worked as a land assayer for over thirty years."

"Then you know what you're talking about," I replied.

"Oh yes! This is why the crooked lawyers and gutless judges have jobs. One doesn't need a gun now-days to rob someone, they can do it with just ink and pen. I would think this is where the cliché originated: 'The pen is mightier than the sword,' wouldn't you?"

"You two can sit here and yak while I fix us a bed time snack." Miss Faye suggested, heading off to the kitchen.

"I'll bet you have seen lots of corruption in your day, Mrs. Pittman."

"You don't know the half of it, Wolf. This world is just prone to be bad in spite of itself."

I thought this would be a good time to tell my new family about the man I had killed earlier. I was just fixing to tell Mrs. Pittman about what happened when someone knocked on the front door.

"I'll get it," Miss Faye yelled out from the kitchen.

We sat patiently, waiting with an attentive ear, wondering who it could be. The wait was short as Miss Faye unlocked and opened the door.

A strong male voice echoed through the big house. "Is it possible that I may speak with Wolf Mann? Mr. Jerd Coggins said I may find him here."

"And you are?" we heard Miss Faye ask.

"I'm so sorry, ma'am...I'm David Brooks, a Pinkerton Agent."

"Won't you step inside, Mr. Brooks? That cold wind is frightful this afternoon; this big house is so hard to keep warm. You'll find Wolf right this way."

I believe the Pinkerton Agent's visit surprised us all, especially me. At the time, I had no idea it had something to do with the man I had killed earlier.

There stood a heavy-set man in a three-piece pinstriped suit. He wore a bow tie and derby hat. The big man quickly held out his hand. I arose, walked over and shook his hand.

"I'm mighty proud to shake the hand of the man that took down Jeff Dobbs...this notorious outlaw has been dodging the Pinkertons and the Texas Rangers for over five years. He has maimed, mutilated and murdered over sixty men - that we have record of."

I looked over at Mrs. Pittman and Miss Faye. Their mouths were wide open and their eyes big as saucers. I never got a word in edge ways.

"Mr. Wolf, I guess you know there is a five thousand dollar reward for Jeff Dobbs, dead or alive. If you will meet me over at the bank when they open in the morning, I have permission to write you a certified check from the railroad."

Well, needless to say, I had a lot of explaining to do after the Pinkerton Agent left. As we sat eating our supper snack, I was bombarded with questions from Mrs. Pittman and Miss Faye. All I can say is that these two ladies had fallen in love with me, and were bound and determined to keep me safe from all harm. I had two bosses now instead of one.

"I make a motion we all 'hit the sack.' You know what time I open the diner in the morning. As I see it, we all have a big day ahead of us tomorrow," said Miss Faye, stretching as she stood up.

"Let me ask a favor and a question all at the same time."

Miss Faye stopped and turned around to face me.

"If everything goes well tomorrow, and I sell my property to old man Huey Black before the stage runs...would it be okay if I go to Ohio to see my Aunt Becky?" As the old saying goes, 'their feathers just dropped'.

"Will you be staying long? Miss Faye asked sadly.

"Yes, you know we'll miss you, Wolf," said Mrs. Pittman.

"Not long. I want to deliver this letter, and make sure our guardian arrangement is in order. It's no telling what a mess we will go through getting my land back, along the money from the railroad coming through my property."

Miss Faye looked at her mother and smiled. "I guess we can spare you for a while, Wolf."

'Early to bed, and early to rise, makes one healthy, wealthy, and wise'...Pa would quote time and again. I ain't all that wise but I consider myself healthy - and if you call five thousand dollars wealthy - two out of three ain't bad for a fourteen year old boy.

# Chapter 5

I rolled and tumbled the better part of the night; being in a strange bed and having killed a man didn't help matters. I guess it was meeting with old man Huey Black and dickering over the money situation for my ranch that really bothered me.

For a minute I didn't know if I was dreaming or just hearing voices...

"Wolf, Wolf," I heard a soft voice calling.

I rolled over and looked all around. "Is that you, Lord?" I asked, trying to wake up.

"No, it's Faye. Can I come in? It's time to get up." Now I don't mind telling you, it had been a long time since I was awakened by a woman, especially a beautiful woman in a silk night gown, sitting on the side of my bed.

"I pressed your clothes for you this morning, Wolf, darling."

"Miss Faye, you don't need to take on over me like you do."

I will never forget what she said as I nearly broke down; I knew then how much she loved my pa. "But you don't understand, I don't have anyone to take on over any more."

What could I say to encourage her and make her life worthwhile?

"I hope you have me a little sister soon," I said, taking her by the hand.

"Oh, do you really?" Miss Faye exclaimed, so encouraged. "Do you think it will be a girl?"

"What do you want?" I asked.

"Let us pray for a girl, I already got me a man." She leaned over and started hugging and kissing me; and I'll admit - I loved it. "Come and walk with me over to the diner; I'll fix you a good breakfast with steaming hot coffee. I'll be ready to leave soon." With those words she dashed out of my room.

When we arrived Elie Mae was already at the diner, with coffee ready and two big wood heaters roaring. I noticed a few early rising cowboys had taken up residence at a table and were sipping coffee. There even sat Jerd Coggins, drinking a cup of coffee while waiting on breakfast.

"Can I join you this morning?"

He seemed a little surprised but nodded. "By all means, pull up a chair, Wolf. Did the Pinkerton Agent get up with you last night?"

I was just sitting down when Elie Mae sashayed over with a steaming mug of coffee for me. "Good morning, Mr. Wolf," she said in a flirting tone of voice, "Miss Faye said she'd have your breakfast in a jiffy."

"Sorry for the interruptions, Mr. Coggins...but yes, he found me over at Miss Faye's house a fixin' to eat supper."

"Tell me now, Wolf, where did you learn to draw and shoot like you did, as young as you are? Did you know the reputation this notorious outlaw Jeff Dobbs had when you pulled down on him?"

"No sir, Mr. Coggins. I had never seen this man, or even heard of him, before last night. The Pinkerton Agent told me he had maimed, mutilated and murdered over sixty men that the Pinkerton Agency has record of."

"Well I can say one thing, Wolf; you did the area west of the Mississippi river to South California a favor when you turned Jeff Dobbs' lights out. Let me run; I have a thousand things to do today. I see your breakfast is coming."

I was well into my breakfast when Margie came in and headed straight for my table. "What is all this I hear about you, Mr. Wolf Mann?"

I thought to myself, news travels fast in Silver Springs. "What in the world are you referring too, Margie?"

"As if you don't know..." Margie did a little soft-shoe as she pranced back into the kitchen, looking over her shoulder;.

I figured the bank was open by now, and thought I would mosey on over and see if Mr. David Brooks was waiting on me. As I opened the diner door to leave, I heard a voice coming from the kitchen.

"Wait! Wait up, Wolf!" Here came Miss Faye with her arms stretched out to me. As usual, I braced myself and made ready for a big hug and kiss.

"Was you going to ease out and not say good-bye to me, Wolf Mann?"

"I'm so sorry, Miss Faye; I guess I had too much on my mind this morning, selling my land and all." Miss Faye rolled her beautiful eyes, and twisted her mouth.

"Well... I forgive you this time, but try not to let it happen again." Then here came another hug and kiss.

"I promise it will not happen again, and before you tell me, I will be careful today."

"Well, you just better. Mother gave me strict orders to look after you today. And she also said for you not to be shooting anyone else if you can help it."

"I promise, I promise, Miss Faye, now give me another hug, I must run."

As I approached the bank, shore enough, there was the Pinkerton Agent, David Brooks, talking to Archie Dykes. He was the owner, editor, chief cook and bottle-washer of our local newspaper, the *Silver Springs Gazette*. There wasn't much to the thing, but it gave the merchants a place to advertise.

"Good morning, Wolf, I was just filling in your local newspaperman on Jeff Dobbs. This outlaw has been vandalizing and man-slaughtering innocent people over this territory long enough."

"Good morning, Wolf, it looks as if we'll have something to write about this week, thanks to you."

"Well, thanks to both you gentlemen, but Mrs. Pittman told me last night too much publicity will go to your head," I said, already feeling like I was something special. All I done was shot the man who was stealing my horse, for Pete's sake; that is a hanging crime to begin with, Pa would say.

"I don't know about you, Mr. Brooks, but I think Wolf needs all the glory he can get. The reward is a good gesture along with a full page write-up in my paper. Would you mind coming by my office this morning and giving me some details, Wolf?"

"I will, Mr. Archie. Let me get my money in the bank first, so Mr. Brooks can get on with his rat killing."

I had no trouble changing my dad's account over to my name, since everyone knew he was dead. Mr. Flynn, the owner, was delighted to have my five thousand dollars in his bank.

Before Mr. David Brooks, the Pinkerton Agent departed, he gave me some fine ideas how I could pursue an occupation as a gunslinger and noted fast gun. He suggested I could stay within the realm of the law by being a bounty hunter. Within a few months I would find out that in my new job as a bounty hunter, I would be about as popular as a tax collector.

I had to go right by the general store to get to old man Hugh Black's office.

"Hey! Wait up a minute." I turned and saw Mr. Grimes waving me back to the store.

"I got something for you, Wolf, come on in the store and I will get it for you." I hadn't ordered anything, as I recollected.

"Come this way."

I followed him back to where the guns and ammunition were kept. There, lying on the glass counter, was a fancy black gun belt and holster.

"Well, what do you think Wolf?  It's yours."

"You just giving it to me?" I asked.

"That's right. See if it fits." I took Pa's rigging off and put the fancy holster on, tying it to my leg.

"You put the icing on the cake, Mr. Grimes, I like it."

"Well, Wolf, it's a present from the whole town, for what you did. You managed to rid our land of a parasite that had been plaguing our parts for years."

"I sure do thank you, Mr. Grimes.  This is the nicest present I ever received. By the way, I was headed over to old man Huey Black's office to sell my ranch, and then if I have time I'm catching the stage up to Calvert, and ride the train to Ohio."

"A word of advice, Wolf, don't let that old skin-flint beat you out of your land. And I'm not going to ask where you got those side rowel spurs you're sporting."

"Well, I won't tell you, Mr. Grimes, but a man was wearing these spurs the night he put three holes in my pa's chest - in a pattern the size of a silver dollar." Mr. Grimes didn't look surprised.

"When I get back from Ohio, I'm gonna call this man out on Main Street and empty Pa's pistol into his heart, with a pattern the size of an Indian Head penny."

Mr. Grimes, still not looking surprised, replied, "And I believe you will, Wolf."

Old man Huey Black's office was in the saloon, on the top floor just above the stairs.  The rest of the rooms the whores used, at least, that's what Pa had said.

I walked in like I owned the joint.  It was as empty as last year's bird nest.  Course, it was early. The bartender was polishing shot glasses, and some slut was over by the piano practicing a song. As I eased by her, I noticed the poor thing looked like she had slept in her dress, not to mention, she couldn't carry a tune in a syrup bucket.

It was for sure one couldn't slip up on old man Huey Black the way these stairs squeaked. I knocked on the hardwood door.

"Come in," a strong voice vibrated through the door. I made my entrance and stood in front of his big mahogany desk.

"Well, if it isn't the Wolf Mann, in person!" He smiled and leaned back in his big easy chair.

"That's right, sir, you got me pegged."

"I hear you are the youngest gunslinger in Silver Springs."

"You heard wrong, sir; I'm the youngest gunslinger in the world." I looked around the office. His two bodyguards were sitting over at a table playing cards.

"I hear you are mighty fast with that Colt, Wolf Mann."

"Not bad, I suppose, I chalked me up a varmint yesterday."

"And not a bad varmint; from what the boys were telling me earlier."

"You know the old saying, the bigger they are, the harder they fall. But I'm not here to discuss the shooting and the crying, moaning and dying, an' the fellow with the switch blade knife. I want to sell my ranch before the stage runs today. I'm going to visit my Aunt Becky in Ohio."

"You are at the right place, and since you are receiving that big reward, I should be able get your spread at a good price." Old man Huey Black smiled like a goat gnawing on a briar as he leaned back putting his hands behind his head.

"Now that I have received that five thousand dollar reward... and since the railroad is a fixin' to come right through my property... I don't need to sell my land. You have a fine day." As I turned to leave, old man Huey Black stumbled all over himself trying to get up.

"Wait! Wait! Wolf, let's not be too hasty. Just name your price."

I knew right then, I had this bunch over a barrel. "Let me see...I believe my pa gave Walter McNay a dollar and a dime for that spread; if you will double that I will be packed and ready to leave for Ohio at three o'clock."

Mr. Black fumbled through the mess on his desk and came up with a legal document and shoved it over to me to sign.

"You put the amount in the space and have your two men witness it and give me a copy; then I will sign it."

In a flash he found a duplicate copy, and with a piece of carbon, we were set.

"We are going over to the bank, ain't we? After all, I need to get the money before I leave for Ohio."

"The boys and I were just leaving for the bank when you came in. We'll be right behind you," he said, putting on his coat.

I thought to myself - if I loved liars I'd turn around and hug that polecat's neck.

I had already had dealings with Mr. Curtis Flynn this morning when I deposited my reward check in his bank. He was still in his office and I walked straight on back as the others followed. Of course, he knew Mr. Huey Black, but I wasn't sure about the other two polecats. The office was getting crowded now and Mr. Flynn started to get up.

"Keep your seat. This is not a hold up," I cheerfully quipped, and everyone laughed. "Mr. Huey Black is purchasing my ranch and I'm going back to Ohio."

Mr. Flynn sat back down and Huey Black passed him the make-shift deed, which he scanned quickly. "What about the animals? They are not on here."

I guess Mr. Flynn was looking out for my interests, seeing I was so young. I explained, "Mr. Black ain't concerned about that handful of poor cows and a couple of plug horses. Besides, they are already spoken for."

"As far as I can tell, it looks good to me. You men sign on the dotted line and I will notarize it and transfer the money over to Wolf's account." As the others left the small office, Mr. Flynn caught my gaze, slightly cocked his head, twisted his mouth, and said, "You just jilted that old cuss - and good enough for him. But how, in the name of God, did you get that much money out of that old miser?"

"You may keep this under your hat, but there is a railroad coming through Silver Springs, and it will split my property right through the middle."

"Wolf, that was a bold statement. Do you have proof of that?"

"Yes, I do. Pa talked to the railroad surveyors the day he was killed, and that's all I can say."

I kept out enough money to make my trip to Ohio and pay my bill over at the general store. I also bought a few snacks, accordingly. I told Mr. Flynn I would see him when I got back.

The girls had been busy buying luxury items for my trip as well. I told Mr. Grimes about the railroad coming to Silver Springs. They had stopped serving the midday meal when I arrived at the diner, so they all had time to come over and give me a hug and a kiss. I knew Miss Faye was going to start something with Elie Mae and Margie. She ought to have known - whatever she does, they copy. A while ago, Elie May had kissed me right in the mouth - and she never even looked to see if anybody was watching. And take Margie...she gets too close to me when she hugs.

Miss Faye finally took a break and came over to where I was sitting at a small table near the kitchen. "You've made up your mind to go to your aunt's, haven't you?"

"I guess so, Miss Faye. I need to get this chore over as soon as I can, before the railroad comes through Silver Springs."

"I know what you're saying, but I'm just going to miss you, Wolf." I thought for a minute she was going to start crying.

"You want to go to Ohio with me?"

"Don't tempt me, Wolf, darling!"

"But Elie Mae and Margie can run the diner while you're gone."

"Elie Mae and Margie would run this place in the ground in two days, but thanks for the thought. Maybe we can do something when you get back from your aunt's house after the baby comes."

"That was a very good dinner and, by the way, I paid off Mr. Grimes at the general store. Did you notice my new gun rigging? Mr. Grimes said the town gave it to me."

"It's very nice, Wolf, but I hate guns. They have killed both men I ever loved. I am glad you are so good with your pistol and that you can protect yourself. The girls in the kitchen are saying you are the fastest gun in the whole West."

I figured people would believe anything they wanted to. If some real fast gun actually called my bluff, I would be better off throwing my pistol at him. For Pete's sake, I had fired a pistol one time - and now I was the fastest gun in the whole west?

"It's getting late, Miss Faye, and I still have two more chores to do before getting on that stage. I'm gonna let Kermit Travick keep Blackie, so he will be no bother to you. You have enough worry with this diner. And I want to say goodbye to your ma before I leave. I also want to thank her for the good advice on selling my land."

"Did you get a good price for it?" Miss Faye asked.

"Good price! I received twice as much as Pa paid a year ago."

Faye seemed so excited. "Could I ask how you managed that," she inquired.

"Yes! I snatched my pistol out of my holster and rammed about two inches of the barrel up his ugly nose, then threatened to blow his head off."

Miss Faye quickly looked all around. "I'm sure glad Elie Mae and Margie didn't hear that, Wolf. They are full of lies already."

I got up to leave, waiting for the big hugging and kissing thing to start. I noticed Elie Mae and Margie were waiting to get their licks in before I left the diner to get on the stage. I eased around to the door of the kitchen, where the girls were busy. Miss Faye was right behind me, ready to attack.

"Well, ladies! My departure is near, and I must say farewell." The girls stripped off their aprons (I was glad that was all) and literally became unruly, right along with Miss Faye. When the girls got through hugging and kissing me and let me go, I had two cricks in my neck, and thought I would have to go change my slobbery shirt.

I hated to part with Blackie so soon; during the few days we had been together, a bond had formed between us. I knew Kermit Travick would take good care of him while I was in Ohio. Before I left the livery stable, I noticed Mr. Kermit eyeing the Colt hanging on my side.

"The other day when you and that outlaw, Jeff Dobbs, had that shoot out, did you draw and fan your 1873 revolver, or cock your revolver and pull the trigger?" Mr. Kermit asked.

"I don't follow you," I said.

"Let me see your revolver," he requested. I flipped the thong off the hammer and handed Mr. Kermit my pistol.

"Did you say you wanted to be a fast draw?" Mr. Kermit asked. "Then tell me how you drew your pistol, cocked it and beat that outlaw to the draw?"

What Mr. Kermit was asking all made sense now. "Mr. Kermit, what everybody is saying happened, is not what happened. What you hear and read and what folks are telling is not the truth. Yes, I do want to be a fast draw. But what really happened is when I went home and packed my clothes, I strapped on Pa's gun rigging before I started back to town. I did look to see that it was loaded. Well, I was about three miles from town when I spotted a man standing in the road. As I drew near, he flagged me down. Now, I'll be frank with you, I didn't know who he was or what he had done. I could tell he took a quick gander at me, and saw I was no more than a 'shirt-tail boy' as pa would put it. 'Can I help you in some way?' I asked. And then he said he wanted to borrow my horse. 'My horse isn't for loan,' I told him. And that's when he pulled his pistol and pointed it at me. Now, don't get me wrong, I love my horse, but he ain't worth getting shot over. Well, I unloaded myself, along with my grip, faster than a cobra strikes.

He was also carrying a grip, and he assumed I wasn't armed... my long coat covered my gun. Well, like taking candy from a baby, he replaced his pistol in his holster, hung his grip on the saddle horn, and took another look at me, standing there like a wooden Indian. He stepped in the stirrup, mounted Blackie, and started riding away.

I quickly drew my pistol and pointed it right at him. I'm not starting off being called a back shooter. I cocked the pistol and held it with both hands - drawing a fine bead on the back of his head. I yelled out, 'Hey, mister!' He was no more than a few yards from me when he turned and looked straight at me. I pulled the trigger and he and the grip hit the ground like a sack of Idaho spuds.

I eased over where the man was laying and took hold of the reins of Blackie, who was skittish. I saw right off this man wasn't going anywhere; I had shot him right between the eyes. Now, Mr. Kermit, you can tell this story any way you see fit, but this is the way it happened." I didn't know whether he believed the story or not.

"Come with me," he directed, and we I went into the office part of the building where he began to disassemble my pistol like he knew what he was doing. I didn't say anything.  It seemed he was concentrating on the hammer of my Colt. I watched as he pulled out a drawer on an old desk.  Mr. Kermit shuffled around and pulled out a piece of metal that looked a lot like the hammer on my Colt. "You know what this is?" he asked, holding up a piece of blued metal.

I took a step closer and stretched my neck. "It looks a lot like the piece you removed from my pistol."

"That right. It's a hammer for an 1873 single shot Colt revolver. But notice! The thumb tab is higher... I'll show you. He carefully reassembled my pistol and replaced the six cartridges. "Let's step out the back door." I followed close behind. "You watch this now, Wolf," Mr. Kermit instructed, pointing the revolver toward a clay bank. He was holding the pistol with his right hand, about belt high. Using the palm of his left hand, he began to fan the pistol, as he brushed the hammer off with the trigger held back. Six times he did this, and six times the pistol belched smoke, lead, and flame into the clay bank of dirt.  It was hard to count the shots; it was more like a loud roar. "Now what did you think about that?" Mr. Kermit asked, handing the pistol back to me. "The barrel may be hot."

"I can see you certainly know how to unload a single action Colt in a hurry!" I exclaimed, taking the pistol and checking the barrel to see if it really was hot.

Mr. Kermit started laughing. "Always remember this, Wolf; it may save your life one day.  It ain't how fast one can shoot, it's hitting the target by shooting fast."

I took a good look at the pistol and saw the extended hammer made a difference. "Where did you come up with this idea?" I asked, still giving my pistol a second look.

"To tell you the truth, it wasn't my idea, Wolf. Lots of the fast gunslingers say this gives them the edge over the other shooter. But

46

to tell you where I first heard about this trick, a drifter rode into town about seven or eight years ago. He pulled in here and tied up at the hitching rail outside. I was watching him out of the corner of my eye; you can't be too careful these days you know. He looked all around, then up at my sign, and eventually strolled in here like he knew where he was going. I spoke to him and he began explaining to me what he wanted. Well, to make a long story short, I do a little gun smithing on the side and had extra parts for guns, especially for the 1873 Colt. I told him I would use my hammer, in case I messed it up. He laid a twenty dollar gold piece on the anvil sitting there, said he would be back later to get it. It was a slow day and I didn't have anything else to do but earn that gold piece. So, I heated up the forge and started to work, brazing a piece onto the hammer. I got to admit, it turned out better than I thought. Sam Colt would have been proud of me. I heard a disturbance and some shooting down at the saloon but thought nothing about it. It's not uncommon to hear shooting around this town."

"Mr. Kermit, I hope you finish this story before the stage runs." We both started laughing.

"Well, it can't run until I hitch up four fresh horses."

"You know, Mr. Kermit, I slam forgot about that."

"It was like I said, I heard a disturbance and some shooting down at the saloon, and in about an hour or less Jerd Coggins pulled up outside, leading a horse behind his hearse..

'Wonder if you can hold this horse till I can get in touch with the next of kin of the young cowboy lying back there?' I opened the door of the hearse and saw it was the same man I had just fixed the hammer for...I don't guess he had the edge. I found out later he had gotten into a gunfight with one of Huey Black's men."

I studied the stage schedules (printed in the leading newspaper) closely when I bought my ticket. I learned that some stages ran daily, with the exception of Sunday. Others, only three days a week...Monday, Wednesday and Friday. Some left only once or twice a week for isolated parts of Oklahoma. I also learned that many stage drivers liked to leave early in the morning; a coach might depart at 4 A.M.. and certainly by 7 A.M. Drivers wanted to have as much daylight travel as possible since night travel was unsafe. Most drivers avoided night trips, however, a night traveler would be fortunate to have a full moon on a clear night..

Mr. Kermit had the horses hitched and ready to exchange when the stage pulled up. I had also learned that stations were located every ten to fifteen miles along the stage routes. At each station the horses would be changed. When the stage arrived, the tired horses would be unhitched. Fresh ones, already harnessed, would be hitched in their places - the changes made in one or two minutes. Silver Springs was not a full service stop; but it had toilet facilities for both men and women.

Meals were served at the stations. Many also had sleeping accommodations. Even a brief stop would permit passengers to relax. Travelers could get out of the stage and stretch and drink fresh water. The stage still had five hours of daylight before reaching Centerville, Oklahoma, where the stage stop had food and sleeping accommodations.

As I boarded the stage, no one got on or off, but there were two elderly ladies and a middle-aged man already on the stage. It was cold inside the coach and they were bundled up pretty good. I sat on the seat with the man, and the ladies sat facing us in the back of the stage. No one actually spoke, just nodded and smiled. This was the second time I had ever ridden a stage. The first was when Pa and me came to Silver Springs and took the ranch. At times I think it was a year wasted, and what did we have to show for it? Well, Pa didn't have anything to show for it. He loved me, and them old brood cows, and a few horses.  He dreamed of a big ranch one day. Without fail, he was up before daybreak, rain or shine, never sick. I believe the last four mouths before he got shot were the happiest I had seen him, since Mother had died giving birth to my little sister.

# Chapter 6

It was a good road between Silver Springs and Centerville, and the driver, facing that cold air, was letting the new team slip. We would be at our destination about dusk dark if things went well.

"Are you going far, young man?" one of the ladies asked.

"Yes. I'm going to Ohio to visit my Aunt Becky Joiner. My name is Wolf."

"Now that's rather a strange name. My name is Gertrude Perry and this is my older sister, Rachael Baits. We are also going to Ohio."

The older sister just smiled not saying anything. I guess we had gone five or six miles on up the road and it seemed to be getting colder.

"You know the Lord, young man?" the younger sister asked.

"Yes Ma'am, He is God," I answered, changing positions in the seat.

There was a long pause..."Do you know much about God?" she asked.

"Yes Ma'am! He wrote the Bible." I'm glad she changed the subject for that's about all I knew about the Bible. We did go to church before Ma died but it seemed that Pa blamed God for her dying. Then we moved to Silver Springs, and Pa put God on the back burner since there was no church or preacher within miles.

I began to get a strange feeling about the man sitting beside me. First of all, he never said a word or even smiled. He was wearing a black suit and small rimmed, black hat that he kept pulled down over his eyes. His collar was pulled together up around his neck. His boots were shined to a T and you could tell he had never worn spurs on these boots. I finally got a good look at his hands. At first glance I could tell they had never been introduced to a Georgia Stock or an ax handle.

I know it's wrong to draw an opinion about folks too quickly, but this man sitting beside me was a snake in the grass, you know what I mean? I'd never seen him, didn't know him from Adam's house cat, but he looked like a river boat gambler with his thin, black mustache. Pa said he would never cultivate something under his nose that grew wild between his legs.

It was dusk dark now but Centerville was in sight. The town was lit up like a candle-lit Christmas tree and I could hear the ragtime pianos in the distance. I was wanting to get a bit of sleep and something to eat.

The stage driver let it be known that the stage would depart at five o'clock the next morning. "I hope to be in Springfield before dark tomorrow," he announced, before we flushed like quail. Great cities and towns boast fine hotels, inns, and taverns.

I was cocked and primed and ready to go at five o'clock. So were the two old ladies and the man I didn't like. Another young lady passenger, by the name of Ruth Allen, announced she was going back East to teach and also let it be known - to excuse her French - she'd had a gut full of the wild, wild, West. I couldn't help but notice that the male passenger had become jumpy and jittery, even wringing his hands at times. I don't think anyone else even noticed it. Maybe I just had it in for this gentleman with his thin, black mustache and beady eyes.

I guess we might have been an hour or more into our trip. It was full daylight now and the stage was near a crawl. I could tell we were going up a steep hill. The air was still cold and crisp... it was then I heard a voice... other than the driver hollering at the horses as he popped the whip.

"Hold up there, mister, and no one will get hurt!"

The voice overpowered the beating of the horse hooves as they came to a stop. I quickly stuck my head out the side window to see what was going on. And to my surprise there sat a man on horseback, pointing a double barrel shotgun at the stage driver.

"Throw down your scatter gun, driver, now your side arm."

The driver obeyed every command; I found out the stage line doesn't hire fools.

"Now that strong box you got there in the boot!"

I watched as the metal strong box hit the ground and rolled to one side.

"Now, tell every one to get out of the stage."

"You, there in the stage, you heard the man!"

The man with the thin black mustache and beady eyes stepped to the ground first. "There is no one in the stage but three women and a teen-aged boy, mister."

The man on the horse rode over to the strong box and dismounted, still holding the shot gun. He surveyed the driver and stage; everything looked normal. I was still sitting in the stage with the women, who were scared half to death.

The robber rolled the strong box over to get a good shot at the lock. Taking a step back, he cocked the shotgun and blew the lock to kingdom-come. Now, strange at it may seem, when the outlaw saw the money, he literally threw the shotgun down beside the strong box and began putting the stacks of bills in his saddlebags. I thought to myself, this is my chance. The outlaw was in full view and the man with the black mustache and beady eyes had his back toward me.

When I unbuttoned my coat and put one knee in the seat, I heard oohs & aahs coming from the ladies; they were sitting across from me lined up like butter-beans in a pod. I quickly made a grim face - putting my finger to my lips and slightly shaking my head. Then I drew my pistol. As I brought my Colt up, using both hands, I cocked it and drew a fine bead, hoping I wouldn't miss. The man was absolutely obsessed with packing the money in his saddlebag. When he turned, I yelled out: "Hey mister!" He looked right at me and I pulled the trigger. Money flew everywhere.

But what I didn't expect - the man with the black mustache and beady eyes had a Derringer up his sleeve. He spun around quickly and the little gun filled his hand. He pointed it right at me and fired. It missed me by an inch; I held the trigger back on my 1873 single action and fanned it until the noise stopped and the gun was empty.

The driver was the first to get to the man with the black mustache and beady eyes. He was lying flat on the ground, face up, wearing a light blue shirt. By this time, I had loaded my pistol and jumped out of the stagecoach and walked up to the man the driver was examining.

"Five shots right through the heart, sonny!" He did a double take and looked back at me. "Good lord! You're Wolf Mann, the fast gun from Silver Springs."

I nodded and took a few steps over to the other man who had money still clenched in his hand and a round hole right between his eyes.

By this time, the young lady that was fed up with the wild, wild west walked up to me. "Is there anything I can do, Mr. Wolf?"

I looked at the driver. "Do you mind if the young lady gathers up the money and puts it back in the strong box?"

"My name is Ruth Allen," she said, and she started picking up the stacks of bills and replacing them in the strong box.

The driver was brushing the dirt and dust off his pistol and checking his double barrel to see if it was all in one piece after hitting the ground. "Wolf Mann," he said, "son, you are a one man army. Now what are we going to do with these two desperadoes?"

"The way I see it, we can tie the man with the three eyes on his horse and tie the horse behind the stage. And the man with heart trouble, we can throw him on top of the stage. I don't think we need to worry about the flies blowing them - as cold as it is."

We finished that chore in ample time and were ready to go. The driver thanked Miss Ruth Allen for helping with the money. As we started to get on the stage I spied the little Derringer lying half covered in the dirt.

"Miss Ruth, would you be so kind as to hand me that little Derringer lying there?"

She smiled and reached down and picked up the little derringer, then handed it to me as she stepped into the stage.

"I thank you very much for the Derringer, Miss Ruth. I always wanted a boot pistol."

She sat down by me giving the elder ladies plenty of room. I heard the whip pop and we were on our way.

"Mr. Wolf, that wasn't my Derringer to give away."

"But didn't you find it lying back there in the road nearly covered up with dirt?"

"Yes sir, but I didn't actually find it."

"Find it now, or find it later, if we had left it there somebody would have found it sooner or later, and it might as well be you, sooner - than later."

"We didn't do something dishonest, did we, Wolf?"

I shook my head. "No! Who is going to complain, the man on top of the stage?"

I noticed Miss Ruth was cold, and not dressed for this weather; and the stage was going northward all the time.

"You ladies wouldn't be offended if Miss Ruth sat closer to me, would you? It looks like she is a fixing to have a chill."

They shook their heads and I opened up my warm coat and she scooted over. I put my arm around her, trying to cover us both with my coat.

I could tell the two elder ladies were covered with several quilts and faring very well. As a matter of fact, they began to snore.

"You know something, Mr. Wolf? While I was putting all that money back in that strong box, you and the driver was busy with the bodies and not noticing me - I was so tempted to hide a stack of the hundred dollar bills in my bosom and not tell anyone."

We were warm as a fresh baked cat head biscuit now, and felt at ease with each other. "Well, why didn't you do it? Probably nobody knows exactly how much money is in that box to begin with," I said, moving around and pulling Miss Ruth a little closer.

"I thought about that, too, Mr. Wolf, it was just money. I know it belongs to someone somewhere, doesn't it? It's not like the little Derringer; the man who owned it is dead. Like I said, it was so tempting - since I don't know where my next meal is coming from."

"I take it you have no money?"

"That's right, no money, no home, no clothes, no folks, and no where to go when I get off this stage," Miss Ruth answered in a breaking voice.

I began thinking, but didn't want to pry.

"Mr. Wolf, life hasn't been good to me; it's been root hog or die poor all my life." There was a long silence then she began to sniff. "I've even thought about ending it all...I can, you know."

I just sat there, listening. The two old ladies were still sound asleep.

"I wake up each morning hoping this day will be better than yesterday, but it never is. Mr. Wolf, this has been going on for twenty-years. Course, I lived with my granny for most of it." She stopped talking and I thought she had gone to sleep.

Our driver had pushed the horses pretty hard, and was trying to make up for lost time. He probably wanted to get rid of the two bodies. According to the route schedule I was given when I bought my ticket, there should be a stop just up ahead

"We should be stopping soon," I said to Miss Ruth. "This should be a right good size town. We came through here, Pa and me, but that's been a year or so ago. By the way, let us not forget to give the briefcase to whoever we give the dead man's body to." It was lying on the seat over to the side of us.

"Mr. Wolf, do you have any extra money?" Miss Ruth asked, looking at me with the saddest eyes.

"Yes, I've got plenty of money. Why do you ask?"

"Would you buy me something to eat when we stop?"

Now that got to me and I even wondered how long had it been since she might have eaten. "Would you hand me the man's briefcase you found?"

She looked as if she was being tricked again but handed me the rather large briefcase. My luck, it was locked so I reached in my pocket for my knife.

"What do you think you are doing?" Miss. Ruth asked, rather loudly.

"I'm opening the briefcase for the man upstairs."

"Well, he might not want you opening his briefcase."

"That's dumb, Miss Ruth, he don't know what he wants. He's dead."

She was more anxious to see what was in the briefcase than I was.

"What do we have here? Pictures of river boats and saloons, and women with hardly any clothes on!" Miss Ruth was helping me to check out everything. "And look at this."

"It's a book," I said, still looking in secret spaces.

"Yes, a book on how to cheat at five card stud. Well, I just do declare! And look at the number of decks of cards he has."

"But look at this stack of twenty dollar bills you found." I handed them to her to put in her pocket.

"Now, Mr. Wolf, don't start that stuff with me. I'm trying to be honest. This will be the second time I've been tempted today."

"Didn't you just get through telling me you have never had a good day?"

She nodded.

"Well, I'm gonna make sure your luck will change for you, and this will be a good day for you. Now, start throwing the decks of cards out the window, then tear all the pictures in small pieces and let them fly."

Miss Ruth did as she was told and sat back down close to me. "What now?" she asked, smiling.

"You start calling me Wolf, and I will call you Ruth. This man that owns this briefcase is a no good, low down drifter that has cheated cowboys and poor farmers out of money. He took food off tables and milk out of babies' mouths. He's stole shoes off little children's feet with his scheming, rotten, cheating ways all across this country. Now you put this roll of money in your grip and never mention it ever again; is that clear?"

"Yes sir, and thank you very much, 'specially for the warm body."

"Didn't you say you were a school teacher?" I asked, wrapping her back under my coat,

"Well kinda, but I failed at that miserably, like everything else I ever tried."

I thought: it's no wonder this poor soul never has a good day.

"I want to hire you as my personal secretary. I will pay you well, and I promise you will like the job."

"Could I ask what you do, Wolf?" She sounded encouraged; her voice was more cheerful.

"Here lately I've been killing lots of folks. I'm hoping that will slack up soon."

I could tell that remark threw her off guard by the way she looked over at me. "You don't need a secretary, you need a priest."

"I'm not a priest person. Do you have anymore remedies?" I asked, as I pulled the canvas back and threw the brief case out the window.

"Was you serious about the secretary job?"

"Serious as a heart attack. You said you needed a job, or was I hearing wrong?"

"No, Wolf, you was hearing right, but I don't know If I will get used to killing folks."

"Silly, killing is not my job. They just turn up and want to get shot. I'm going to be a bounty hunter and work with the law."

"So you need a secretary. I'll use my fingernail file to put notches on you pistol grip," Ruth uttered with a smirk.

"Will you forget about the killing for one minute? There is just some folks that need killing, and, by the way, we are coming into Spark Grove, Missouri."

The stage pulled up at the relay station. Again, the driver informed the passengers he would pull out at five o'clock sharp, rain or shine.

"If you would, Ruth, see if you can wake the two old ladies. Maybe we can be of some help to get them inside out of this cold weather."

We were in luck. The town was small, but had a hotel and a café. The driver came around to where I was standing with Ruth.

"You want to walk over to the sheriff's department with me, Wolf?"

I looked at Ruth and pointed to a clothing store nearby. "While the driver and I walk over to the sheriff's office you go and get you some clothes and a warm coat and I will meet you in the café in a few minutes," I instructed her.

"What is your name?" I asked the driver, as we started across the muddy street.

"Emmet Boswell, and I been looking at horses' asses for near forty years, sonny."

"I am pleased to meet you, Mr. Emmet. If you would, could you do the talking to the sheriff? I just ain't good at that kind of stuff."

"I'd be glad to, Wolf, and that was some sporty gun handling you executed on them two polecats this morning, I may add."

# Chapter 7

When we finally got the door open and walked in, the sheriff was sitting at his desk with his feet propped up, about three sheets in the wind.

"Got ya some business on the stage across the street. I'm Emmet Boswell, the stage driver, and this young fellow is Wolf Mann, the fast gun from Silver Springs, Oklahoma."

The sheriff didn't lose any time getting up shaking my hand. "Pleased to meet you, Wolf, and to shake the hand of the man that turned out the lights of Jeff Dobbs. Why, that scoundrel has robbed the bank here in town two times. I'm Sheriff Loral Hardy."

"We got two dead'uns over at the stage relay - one on top of the stage and the other skunk tied over his saddle. Look up there, Wolf, at that reward poster; ain't that the varmint you gave a headache? If it is, you have become a thousand dollars richer."

I took a closer look. "I believe you're right; that's the outlaw tied on the horse."

Sheriff Hardy sent his deputy after the funeral director to come and get the two bodies. The sheriff identified the men and said I was entitled to the reward. He also mentioned that the man with the thin, black moustache might have a price on his head. He would check it out come morning. The strong box received a new padlock and was locked in the sheriff's office till morning.

I found Ruth in the café nibbling on a free soda-cracker, and starving to death from the smell of a porter house steak being fried by someone in the kitchen.

"Now if you ain't something!" I barked, giving Ruth the eagle eye, "new coat, new jeans, and new cowboy boots."

"These are cowgirl boots," she said, jabbing a menu under my nose. "For Pete's sake, Wolf, let's order our food... I feel faint."

I motioned for the waitress to come over. I think Ruth ordered one of everything on the menu. The conversation between us came to a squelching halt as a fork gave her right hand some exercise. I love to eat, but this gal put me to shame. I would have been embarrassed if anyone had been watching.

She and I were finishing up our supper when she looked up and caught my gaze. "You know, Wolf, this is the best day of my life. I have never met anyone just like you in all my twenty years."

"Now don't you start heating up your branding-iron, Miss Ruth; you are talking to a rolling stone, and I ain't planning on gathering no moss for a long, long time."

A big smile came upon her face. "Well, I weren't planning on corralling you just yet, Wolf. I can wait."

"By the way, have you counted that stack of twenties that was in the briefcase? I'm receiving a thousand dollars for killing that outlaw and I'm gonna give you half of it for helping me. There might be a reward on the other feller that shot at me with the derringer."

"Yes, I counted the wad of bills, and it was seven hundred dollars. That's the most money I have ever seen or held in my hand at one time."

Ruth and I took a room for the night in the hotel and were ready to get on the stage after a good breakfast the next morning. I could tell something was not kosher when we started to board the stage. The sheriff, and Emmet Boswell, our driver, were apparently waiting for me to show up. Emmet moved his head in a come on over here motion.

"Go ahead and get on the stage," I said to Ruth. "Let me see what the sheriff wants." I eased on over where the sheriff and our driver were standing.

The sheriff was first to speak up. "Wolf, we have trouble brewing! It has to do with the man you killed yesterday - the one y'all hauled in here on top of the stage." I nodded that I did remember and the sheriff went on with his dilemma. "Well, he has a brother living here in Sparks Grove who was expecting him in on the stage last evening, but not dead."

I thought to myself - I done went and stepped in my mess-kit. "Does he know that his brother is dead?" I asked.

"Oh yes, when he drove in from out of town to pick him up, it was late but he headed straight for my office. I answered his questions, but he went into a rage, and said he was going to kill you. I did persuade him to wait until morning to settle up with you. Now, Wolf, he is a mean man and as sorry as his brother you killed. I never have got enough on him to arrest 'im but I do know he had rustled cows from out of state many times. And speaking of the devil, here he comes. Wolf, I don't know what to say."

I turned and watched as he was coming straight toward me - like a purple marten to a gourd. It was still cold as a well diggers butt and I was standing there with my hands in my pocket fumbling with the little Derringer, thinking how I had cleaned and reloaded it last night before I went to bed. He never broke stride but walked up within five feet of me.

"Are you Wolf Mann?"

I nodded and cocked the little Derringer, and held the hammer back with my thumb.

"I'm going to kill you........"

But before he and I had time to debate the issue, I quickly came out of my pocket, pointed the gun right at his heart and pulled the trigger. I think it surprised Emmet Boswell and Sheriff Hardy more than the man I had just shot through the heart. His eyes became large and rolled back in his head; blood began to drip from his lips as he wilted like a daylily and tumbled to the muddy street. I blew the smoke out of the little Derringer, put it back in my pocket and turned back around. Both the driver and the sheriff were standing looking at each other, with their mouths wide open .

"You about ready to pop the whip and look at some horse asses?" I referred my question to the driver.

"Don't Wolf need to stick around and sign some papers or something?" the driver asked the sheriff.

"No! Please! Get him out of Sparks Grove as quick as you can - before he kills somebody else. My lord! We'll be planting folks all day around here as it is now."

We had one more team change and time to eat some lunch and if things went well, the driver said we would pull into Springfield, Missouri about four o'clock. This is where we all would catch the train east. And for one, I was tired of the bumpy ride and cold weather. Wasn't much being said. I guess they were scared to say anything; I might up and shoot them. Do the math...I've killed four men this week and the week ain't over.

"Penny for your thoughts," said Ruth, fumbling with her new coat.

"I'm afraid you don't want to know. Besides, it will cost you more than a penny."

There was only the two old ladies and us on the stage when we arrived at the Clear Creek relay station. The lady at the relay station had the grease rolling and the chicken cut up ready to fry; and there on the table sat a big bowl of mashed potatoes and brown gravy with hot rolls steaming hot coffee.

"Are you still hungry, Ruth?" I asked, helping the two ladies get seated.

"Not as hungry as I was last night."

"Well, we are going to see the bright lights and hear the loud music in the modern day city of Springfield in a couple more hours. I will hate to leave good company but I will be heading back west. And thanks to Wolf, we have a strong box to deliver." Mr. Emmet Boswell said, taking a big gulp of coffee. He set his cup down and looked over my way. "Don't forget to pick up your reward at the bank when we get there."

I was sitting beside him at the table, and thanked him for all he had done. "It was a learning experience - if I do say so myself." I added.

Before Ruth and I went to bed, we took a bath...near bout freezing to death. She and I changed clothes and made ourselves warm and comfortable. We began to talk because the train wasn't to come through Springfield until about nine or ten o'clock.

"Now, what about yourself?" I asked, flopping down in a chair next to Ruth, who had occupied the couch.

"You mean my life's story?" she asked, sticking her feet under a blanket. I nodded and grunted. "Well, it's rather boring if you ask me. My younger days I try to forget. I was pushed from pillar to post never knowing where I belonged. I played with my doll and hoped I would have something to eat when I got hungry."

"Well, that sounds like a normal child to me," I said, holding up my end of the conversation.

"I suppose it was, but there was always something missing, and I have thought on this many times - and even now it crosses my mind. I didn't have a mother or father like all the other children in school. I lived with one of my aunts for a while; I must have been nine or ten. I never thought what I wanted to be...I had no one to share my vision, if I even had one. I saw changes in my life and my aunt was tired of me. I heard her many times saying, 'just another mouth to feed around here.'

I guess, to pass the time, I began to read, and I read most every thing I could get my hands on. This is when I moved in with my grandma on my mother's side of the family. Just so happens she was an avid reader and it seemed we had something in common. We shared our books and the stories we read."

"I take it you were not happy then, in some way."

"Wolf, there was still that void, even though my granny sent me to a good school, it seemed so temporary, as if I was in a vacuum of some sort. As she would say at times: I had nothing to get my teeth into."

"Wasn't you pretty much up in age by now?"

"Oh, yes. I was out of school and Granny wanted me to go to college, but here is the bad part, the poor thing had no money and had let the bank take what little she had, including the very house we lived in. Can you believe that!" Ruth exclaimed with an attitude.

"I can believe anything, this day and time. Me and my pa got beat out of our ranch. So what happened next?"

"Oh, well! It was bound to happen - as in every other story - girl meets boy, boy meets girl, they fall madly in love, get married, move into a big house, raise a family, and live happily every after."

"I take it that something is missing out of this story?"

"Oh yes, I was only eighteen when Granny passed on; during the rigamarole of settling the estate and all her affairs, I met this man old enough to be my daddy. Well, he fell madly in love with me, and I fell madly in love with his money and big house."

"When did the marriage and family take place?" I asked, scooting around in my chair.

She did the same, and continued the story, "I found out, after a month, he didn't have a pot to pee in or a window to throw it out of. The big house was his mother's... and I was to her...just another mouth to feed."

"So you left him and never got married?"

"No, we never got married! But where was I to go? He was providing food and a bed, by hook or by crook. He got this offer from a friend of a friend to run a saloon in a town in North Texas. I was to teach school and we were to live happy every after." Ruth shrugged her shoulders and twisted her mouth.

"I can see it didn't work out, for you are sitting here on the couch telling me a sad story. So what about his dream?"

"Wolf, he had a dream alright. The town didn't even have a school, so he suggested I tie a mattress on my back and make a living for him and me. I told him I would and we began to celebrate. I got him drunk as a skunk and took his money, caught an early morning stage, and here I sit. I did leave out one thing."

The curiosity got the best of me and I had to ask. "What about the family? You lived together for a while."

"He couldn't have children, and I thank the Lord for that every day; I don't need another mouth to feed."

"I'm going to bed, be sure you come over to my room and wake me up when you get up, and we'll go and have breakfast," I said getting up and starting to my room.

"Wolf," she said, jumping up.

"What is it?" I asked, turning toward her.

She laid her hand on my arm. "Wolf, you are a good man," she paused, "you are from good stock, I can tell. Good night."

She turned to go back to the couch and I caught her arm and turning her toward me, giving her a hug.

"Let's both be of good stock, as you call it. And this will be as far as it will go."

The next day Ruth and I purchased two tickets for Middletown, Ohio - the town where my Aunt Becky Joiner lived. We also received my reward money and I gave Ruth her five hundred dollars.

"You know you don't owe me this money," she said, and began to cry. I pulled her up close and she laid her head on my shoulder. "I love you, Wolf," she said through her tears, "no one has ever been this good to me before, not even my granny.

"Now, now, think what you're saying, you and I... we have a close relationship, but we are not in love."

She nodded and backed up. We both stood holding our luggage waiting on the train.

Here she came, blowing black smoke, huffing and a puffing. The brakes began squealing and she came to a stop, right in front of the depot. Some folks stepped on board the train while others made their way off. As I glanced up and down the platform, I didn't see the old ladies. They must have decided to stay for a couple of days to recuperate from the stage ride.

Ruth and I found a seat and settled in for the long ride. We would have to cross Missouri, the tip of Indiana, and Illinois before we would reach Aunt Becky's house in Middletown, Ohio. We were lucky in a way, which we had not known at the time we bought tickets. This was a passenger train and didn't stop at every crossroad and little cattle town. We also found out that this was one of the newest Pullman cars on this line.

"Wolf, how long do you think we'll be visiting with your aunt in Middletown?"

"You know, Ruth...I haven't even give it any thought, but one thing I have thought on...are you going back to Silver Springs when I make up my mind to go back?"

She didn't hesitate. "Do you want me to go back with you, Wolf?" she asked, leaning over on me.

All of a sudden, it was like a vision came to me; my pa did have a dream! Why couldn't I live it out for him? I was game!

"How would you like to live on a huge ranch... in that big house?"

Ruth spun around in the seat and looked me right in the eyes. "Wolf Man, are you proposing to me?"

"Now Ruth, get your branding iron out of the fire and cool it off. Let me explain what I got in mind and what is going to happen in Silver Springs in a year or so."

I explained how Huey Black had gunned down my pa...in cold blood, standing on his front porch - and how the railroad was coming right through my ranch; and I would end up with all the land in the valley south of Silver Springs.

"Wolf, if this was coming from anybody but you, I wouldn't even listen, but you have proved yourself."

"Well, I heard you say one time you had a gut full of the Wild West."

She looked a little sheepish, and smiled. "I've said a lot in my twenty years I've had to eat, but...I hope I'm on the right track now."

"Look! Don't carry all your eggs in one basket, I'm only going on fifteen, so what do I know? I've got it in my mind to kill old man Huey Black and his two bodyguards - if something or someone don't change my mind...and shortly."

"No more than I know, Wolf...you can't just shoot 'em down in cold blood."

"I know that! Ruth...I didn't fall off a turnip wagon going through Silver Springs - or hit my head on a rock."

"I know that, Wolf, I didn't mean that. But you will need a cause; it has to be self-defense."

"I have a plan when we get back...you are going back with me, ain'tcha?"

She looked at me as if to say 'I'm hanging with you like a tick on a hound dog's ear.'

For the next two days Ruth and I discussed our plans for the future, and what could go wrong.

"I'm looking forward to meeting your Aunt Becky when we get to Middletown, aren't you, Wolf?"

"I guess so. It's been a year since I saw Aunt Becky - and when she dies I reckon that will the last of the Mann family - as I know of. She was married to Bob Joiner who died last summer. You know, Pa and I didn't even go to his funeral."

"Didn't you say she married a much younger man?"

"Pa told me she had wrote and told him she was living with a younger man. I don't know if they are married or not."

There was a long silence; I was dozing in and out. I was hoping to soon get my feet on some solid ground.

"Wolf, have you noticed how we have been passing a lot of houses along the track lately? We must be getting close to town."

"Yes, I have - between naps. Aunt Becky lives right in town, so when we get off the train we'll not have far to walk to the house."

"I been thinking - I hope she'll have room for me."

"Oh, she will; she lives in a big house. As a matter of fact, she has a maid and a cleaning lady."

"Are you going to get me a maid and a cleaning lady when you and I move into our big house?"

Did I hear what I though I heard? Had she stuck that branding iron back in the fire?

"I can tell right now, Ruth, you have been on this train too long!" I think what I said had gone in one ear and out the other.

The train whistle began to blow to let the people know it was nearing the depot, warning them to get the horses, buggies, and wagons off the railroad tracks. After Ruth and I stepped off the train, we began to look all around. It was like being in another world... compared to Silver Springs.

# Chapter 8

We noticed a commotion and loud music coming from the south end of town. To settle our curiosity we began to stroll that way, although it was not in the direction of Aunt Becky's house. As we neared the goings-on, we discovered it was a carnival of some sort. It looked as if everyone was having fun. We ventured around so we could gander down the mid-way.

"We may need to go to your aunt's house first and settle in. We can come back later, don't you think?" Ruth yelled, above the noise of the barkers and pipe organs.

"That's a good notion, my fair lady," I agreed.

We started walking back in the opposite direction. It was a chilly night and beginning to get dark. As we walked along the sidewalk, I noticed there were lots of changes in the town since I was here last year. We came to Aunt Becky's big Victorian-style house that sat along others similar to it in the rich neighborhood.

"This is your aunt's house?" Ruth asked, admiring all the fancy woodwork around the second floor, and the high pointed roof. "I can understand why she needs help with this big house."

I rang the doorbell and we waited. Ruth turned to me and smiled as if she had found her place in life, and was loved and wanted by someone. We heard footsteps and were soon greeted by a colored, overweight lady wearing a long, white apron. Her hair was tied up with a blue bandana. She had a smile from ear to ear on her big protruded lips.

"You must be Wolf," she said, opening the door wider, "and who is this beautiful young lady? Don't tell me..."

I quickly spoke up, "No! We're not hitched. She is my secretary. We're traveling in the same direction." She rolled her big eyes as if to say 'whatever.'

"Well, you all come on in de house. Miz Becky was kinda expecting you after she received the telegram. Besides we's letting the warm air out." Ruth took my hand and walked close beside me. "Come this way, Miz Becky is in the living room keeping the fireplace warm."

Ruth squeezed my hand, and chuckled softly.

"Miz Becky, guess who we has here?"

"Come over and give your favorite aunt a big hug, Wolf, I'm so sorry to hear about your father."

I gave Aunt Becky a big hug. As always she and I laughed about being each other's 'favorites.'

"You are my only aunt and I'm your only nephew," I said.

"My, how you have grown in just a year. Let me look at you...my lord, Wolf darling, what have you got tied to your leg? Don't tell me it's a pistol. And who is this beautiful young lady standing behind you?"

I caught Ruth by the arm and pulled her around so Aunt Becky could look her over. "This is Ruth, my secretary; she takes care of all my books and money transactions."

Aunt Becky extended her arms toward Ruth to give her a hug.

"I'm so glad to meet you, Aunt Becky. I've heard so much about you since Wolf and I left Silver Springs."

"Well, I hope some of it was good. Listen... Susie was just fixin' to call us to dinner. I'll bet you two are starved near death after that long train ride. Susie, where are you at?" Aunt Becky called out.

"I be over here lis'nin to Mr. Wolf. I hear he be a fast gunslinger."

"Well... you need to be in the kitchen finishing dinner, you hear?"

"Yes, ma'am," she replied and left the room.

"By the way, where is Albert? Pa said you met a man after Uncle Bob passed on."

It was like I had let the wind out of Aunt Becky's sails. Her countenance fell and the smile disappeared from her face.

"I'm sorry Aunt Becky, did I say something wrong?"

She tightened her lips and a tear came to her eye. "No, you didn't say anything wrong, but you might as well know... I hate to hang my dirty laundry out in front of your friend."

Ruth knelt down by Aunt Becky's chair and took her by the hand. "It's alright, Aunt Becky, I'm just like family."

"Albert is downtown locked up in jail. I have lived in pure hell every since that sex maniac moved in this house. I never wrote your pa and let on that anything was wrong. I just kept a stiff upper lip and put up with it. I knew he and our young maid were sinning behind my back. But, thank God, he never got his grubby hands on my money. Well, to make a long story short, my maid married another man and they moved off down south. I hired Gloria Swift, the daughter of a lady I know at church. Gloria's a beautiful young lady, just out of high school, and sweet as she can be.

I still go to the meetings of the Garden Club on Wednesday. Gloria had been working for only two days when Arnold raped her. Well, it was 'she said, he said' in court. Arnold hobnobbed with the low life crowd and the crooked lawyers; and he is going to get off, scott free. I feel so sorry for Gloria; her life is ruined."

We sat and talked for the longest after dinner (which I call supper.) I gave Aunt Becky the letter Pa had written her the night he was shot - saying how she was to be my guardian until I turned twenty-one years of age.

Aunt Becky was right, the trial ended the day we arrived; and Albert walked away a free man while a young girl's life was ruined. All I can say is - he would later meet his match. We finished our business, about her being my guardian, with Aunt Becky's lawyer. It was all official and recorded in the courthouse. For what good it would ever do, time would tell.

When we arrived back at the house Albert was there, as if nothing had ever happened. I had told Aunt Becky that Ruth and I planned to walk down to the carnival south of town after supper. She and I got all dressed up and we were on our way. It was a chilly but beautiful night in Middletown, Ohio.

"You know, Wolf... now don't jump to any conclusions, and I don't have my branding iron in the fire; but these last several days I been really happy. I have a life to look forward to and I was looking forward to just being with you today. Look at us now, like two young lovers strolling together down the street. People pass us by and smile and I smile back. I have a clear vision now. No matter what happens, I have a life. I look forwards to going back to Silver Springs with you. I can tell, Wolf, you have a goal in life. You clearly have a vision... you have said you want to be the fastest gun in the world and avenge your pa's killers."

"Now, you are saying - you have this vision, and want to help me? In other words, you've found your life helping me find my life?"

"That's right, Wolf! You could say that. There is never a dull minute around you. You know what, Wolf? I think I'm falling in love with you, in spite of knowing I'm five years older than you."

"What does age have to do with falling in love with somebody?"

"Well, I can see where you wouldn't want to marry an old lady half dead, and someone you would need to wait on most of the time."

We were at the carnival entrance now. The smell of candy and the sound of music was in the crisp winter air. The barkers were standing at their tents, yelling, hoping to get our dimes and attention: 'See the fattest women, see the smallest horse, come in and see the alligator boy, see the fastest gun in the world.'

"Wait just a minute, Ruth, does that say 'the fastest gun in the world'?" I stood for a few seconds listening to the shots inside. "Let's go inside, Ruth, and see 'the fastest gun in the world.' I might learn something."

"Well, that's what it says, Wolf, 'fastest gun in the world,' but you know the old saying: 'believe nothing you hear, and half you see.'"

I have to be honest, I saw things that I thought were impossible, done with a 1873 Colt pistol just like the one I had hanging on my side. The man looked in a mirror and shot behind him. Then he shot with both hands, as good as with one.

"You think you will ever be able to do that, Wolf?" Ruth asked, sitting on the edge of her seat.

"I hope so; he sure makes it look easy."

The performer stepped out in the audience. "I need a volunteer," he said, twirling his six-gun around on his finger six or seven times.

Ruth quickly looked over at me, "Now's your chance."

I looked all around. There weren't many people under the tent and none of them looked interested in what was going on. I stood and walked up front where the artist was standing on a small stage.

"Thank you, young man, for your patience and generosity to come forward," he said in an actor type voice. "Now, if you will, stand sideways so the audience can see this fast gun experiment." I moved around as told, not knowing what in the cat-hair was a fixin' to take place. "Now, if you will, hold both of your hands out in front of you - that's it - as if you are going to clap your hands." I noticed everything the man said or did, as he stood very erect right in front of me. "By the way, what is your name?"

"My name is Wolf; I'm from Silver Springs, Oklahoma and just visiting the area." All the people gave me applause, including Ruth.

"Good, Mr. Wolf, I notice you are packing a pistol, as they would say out west. Now when I say 'Go' - clap your hands."

I noticed the man leaned forward a little, placing his left foot in front of his right, actually supporting himself on his right. Next, he put his right hand down by his holster, which was hanging low and tied to his leg. I watched as he cupped his hand and placed it very close to his pistol handle.

"Go!" he said plainly.

I quickly clapped my hands together only to slap both sides of a Colt sticking in my belly. The audience clapped and whistled with approval. "Again, again!" they shouted."

The man replaced his pistol in is holster and was ready. "Now, if you would, Wolf, be a little faster as you clap your hands."

I thought how can this be? I never saw his hand move.

"Go!" he said plainly.

I clapped my hands together even more quickly, I thought, only to slap the side of a colt sticking in my belly again. There was an uproar in the tent as he thanked me and I went and sat down next to Ruth. I sat and watched the rest of the performance. He bowed to the audience and thanked everyone. Then he started to close the heavy wine-colored curtain.

I quickly arose and moved to where he stood holding the rope closing the curtain. He recognized me coming up on stage and paused, probably thinking I would only take a minute of his time.

"I enjoyed your performance tonight and hope to be as good as you are one day."

"Wolf, if you and your wife would care to join me behind stage for a cup of coffee, I would be much a obliged. Since this is my last performance, we'll celebrate." I motioned for Ruth to follow us. He went ahead and closed the curtain and the three of us went into a huge wagon fitted with all the comforts of home.

"This is not my home. I use this when touring on the road, but I don't live far from here."

"In other words, you are giving up the show?" I queried, sitting down at a table where he was pouring the coffee.

"Yes, my wife is in bad health and I'm retiring. She and I have plenty of money, if we don't splurge. I have sugar, but my cow went dry."

"Black is fine. By the way, this is Ruth, my secretary."

"I'm pleased to meet you Mr. ?"

"Dobbs, Frank Dobbs, fastest gun in the world; and the wife and I have been all over the world. But today, I'm hanging up my pistols and my wife says amen to that."

"You say you don't live far from here, in which direction?"

"Up that way," Mr. Dobbs pointed.

"Well, that's where I'm staying with my Aunt Becky Joiner."

"Small world, isn't it? She lives four houses down the street from the wife and I."

He and I sat talking guns until Ruth began to fall asleep. "Could I ask a favor of you, since you are closing your business here at the carnival?"

Mr. Dobbs sat his coffee cup down and waited for what I had to say.

"Would you teach me to shoot like you do? I will pay you, and pay you well."

A big smile came to his face. "It has been a long time since anyone asked me that question. I tell you what, Wolf, be at my house at ten o'clock tomorrow and we will discuss it."

We left Mr. Dobbs and all I could think about was him teaching me; it was as if he was God sent to me, but I know God doesn't have anything to do with killing…or does he?

Ruth and I walked up and down the midway several times, seeing everything we wanted to see; then we started back to Aunt Becky's.

"Mr. Dobbs was a nice man, wasn't he, Wolf?" Ruth asked. She ran ahead spinning around in front of me.

Actually, it was still early but my mind was on tomorrow – I was hoping Mr. Dobbs would show me the secrets he had learned down through the years. Aunt Becky was still up when we came in.

"We thought you would be gone to bed when we came in," Ruth said.

"No, I thought I would stay up and wait on you children. It's been so long since I had kin to talk with."

"Aunt Becky, Wolf and I met one of your neighbors tonight. He lives just four houses up that way." Ruth pointed and sat down close to Aunt Becky.

"You are talking about Frank Dobbs and his lovely wife Lorain. I'm afraid, if the Lord don't intervene, she hasn't long to live. That's what the doctor says. She and I use the same doctor and we both belong to Middletown Flower Club. Course now, it's been a while since she's been with us."

"Wolf has an appointment with Mr. Dobbs tomorrow at ten o'clock. We're hoping he'll teach Wolf how to fast draw."

"Now, what in tar-nation does Wolf want to fast draw for? He'll fool right around and shoot someone."

"Shoot someone else...good lord! He's already killed four men, including three just getting here and he's planning to kill three more when he gets back to Silver Springs."

"Wolf! Get yourself over here and let me give you a good talking to. If I'm to be your guardian until you are eighteen, then I'm gonna give you some advice."

"Aunt Becky, I didn't know Uncle Bob was a gun collector."

"Don't change the subject, young man. Now, what is this I hear about killing all these folks up and down the country?"

"Well, yes'um, I did plug a few."

"Wolf, that is no way to talk about dead folks. But, we got a bunch around Middletown that needs to be plugged, that's for sure. One you could hit with a rock."

I guess she was talking about Albert.

"You were talking about your Uncle Bob. Yes, he did collect a few guns, but never seriously. If he has something you want over in the gun case you were looking at, you can sure have it - before Albert hocks it for a bottle of wine."

"There's a pair of engraved, single action Colts with pearl handles I sure would like to have - to remember Uncle Bob by."

"Well, my dear nephew, you have them for the asking - and a hug. I pray you don't shoot yourself in the foot, or some innocent bystander."

Now this made my day. Aunt Becky didn't know what she was giving away. Course, she didn't need the money or the special edition Colts, anyway. Her interests were a long life, her flowers, and hoping Albert would disappear out of her life. She said since the incident with the rape, Albert spent most of his time down at the billiard parlor guzzling beer.

"Can I have them now, Aunt Becky?" I was so excited I jumped up and ran back over to the beautiful oak gun case that sat by a large oil painting of Uncle Bob.

"Come here and get the key. It's in my pocketbook. Maybe you can find a key that will fit." Aunt Becky began probing through her pocketbook and came out with a ring of keys of all sizes. "I have to keep all the keys hidden from Albert; we are already missing things around the place."

As I rushed to the gun case with the keys, I noticed Ruth nodding and realized it was bed time. It was my good fortune when the fifth key I tested opened the gun case. What beauty, I thought. This was a sight to behold, for a young lad who had accomplished so much in so short of time. I could just imagine: Me in my all-black outfit - with two glittering pearl handled Colts hanging from my sides. I could see myself now, riding into a western town on my solid black horse - with silver conchas on my saddle, bridle, and hat band.

"Wolf, are you daydreaming over there? I'm going to bed." Ruth yawned, holding her hand to her mouth.

"I think that is a wonderful idea. The Flower club meets tomorrow and I need to be alert and in a sober spirit. Good night, all." And with those farewell words Aunt Becky left the room. I stood for the longest admiring the pistols.

"Mr. Wolf, if you are ready to go to bed, I'll start turning off some of these lights. Miz Becky wants to save on the gas bill. When Albert finally comes in, half drunk, he can fend for himself. I plum despise dat man."

I guess Susie was the butler and janitor, as well as chief cook and bottle washer, since Aunt Becky had lost her maid.

I reckon I had been in bed a few minutes or so when I heard something. I thought it might be Albert coming in half drunk, as Susie had implied. Well, there it was again - a pecking sound. I knew, in a strange house as big as this one, I would hear noises. I rolled over facing the door and the tapping became louder. It was coming from the door of my room. Then I heard a faint voice.

"Wolf."

I could tell it was Ruth. I eased out of bed and crept to the door. I unlocked and cracked it open, sticking my head out. "What is it, Ruth?" I asked in a whisper.

"Wolf, we forgot to hug good night."

"For crying out loud, Ruth, when did we start that?" I asked.

"I thought we'd start tonight, if it's okay with you."

"Well, we could have waited until tomorrow, but beings you are already here we can go ahead and start now."

I opened the door and Ruth threw both arms around my neck and pressed her warm body close to mine. "Wolf, I'm glad you and I started tonight, aren't you?"

"I'm glad too; I'll see you in the morning."

I closed the door and eased on back to my bed. I sat there just thinking: Was I getting involved in a situation I might need to 'head off at the pass,' as they say out west. I know I'm not all that old, but I know right from wrong, and Ruth is making it very difficult for me to keep my future mission clear in my mind - if you know what I'm talking about! Have I already let things get out of hand? Just like tonight with all that hugging business before she and I went to bed…just like the girls back at the Faye's Diner, all they think about is hugging and kissing. I'm not into all of that right now.

# Chapter 9

The rattling of pots and pans awakened me. My bedroom was closer to the kitchen than the rest of the other rooms. The aroma of coffee was prevalent. I heard the sound of popping eggs and bacon frying. I was nearly ready, all but putting on my gun rigging and tying the holster to my leg. I didn't know what time Aunt Becky usually got up. Then I heard a slight tap on the door. By now I was ready to go to the kitchen and sample the coffee.

"Are you awake, Wolf?" Ruth's voice was soft and low.

I was standing between the door and the bed and thought I'd have some fun with Ruth. "No! I'm still asleep."

"Now, Wolf...I didn't fall off that turnip wagon that came through Silver Springs, or have rocks in my head, either. Just open the dumb door, this is very important." I took two steps and opened the door. Ruth hastily eased inside and closed the door, leaning back against it. "Let's get our morning hug over first, and I will tell you."

I thought: Am I dreaming? Maybe I'm not up yet!

"Maybe you better kick me on the shin, or pinch me first."

"Why would I want to do a dumb thing like that?" she asked, putting her arms around my neck as she moved closer to me.

"I never knew we ever hugged in the morning, pray tell!"

"It's something new; we just started this morning."

"Now, Ruth, the man is supposed to make all the decisions, but since you are ready for a hug I'll make an exception this morning." I didn't have hugging on my mind. I was still wondering what was so dad-blame important. "Wasn't that hug a little longer than the one last night, Ruth?"

"It could have been...I can tell you know nothing about hugging; they have no time limit one way or the other."

"Well, how in the dickens do you know when you get through?"

"That's exactly what I mean, Wolf, hugging is like drinking a cup of black coffee. You can put cream in it, or you may want to add a little sugar in it."

"Speaking of coffee, would you tell me what's so important so we can go and get a cup?"

"Oh well, I weren't actually speaking about coffee, but never mind. Let me ask you a question...did you come to my room late last night and try to get in?"

"No! Why are you asking?"

"Well, I woke up to go use the....you know, and after I eased back in bed very quietly, I heard something or someone fumbling with the lock on my bedroom door."

"Well, it sure weren't me, but this needs to be dealt with. Do you think we need to confront Aunt Becky?" I asked, walking over to the bed and sitting down. "Now, let me ask you something, before we go eat breakfast."

Ruth came over and sat down on the bed also.

"Would you have shot a man, if he had broken into your room last night with ill intentions?"

"Wolf, it 'pears to me you do enough killing for the both of us."

Well, I didn't like the sound of that answer...if it was an answer at all.

"We're not talking about my killing... we're talking about - what are you going to do if you are attacked by some sex molester when I'm not around?"

Ruth twisted her mouth and shrugged her shoulders. I took the little Colt Derringer out of my pocket and tried to hand it to her. She jerked both hands back as if it had been a coiled rattlesnake or a fresh pile of cow dung.

"This little gun could save your life; it did mine. You remember the man that came storming out of the saloon and walked right up to me...both the stage driver and sheriff was standing there. If it hadn't been for this Derringer, I probably wouldn't be sitting here talking to a beautiful young lady right now."

"Wolf, that's so nice," Ruth said with a smile.

"What? Me disarranging the man's heart inside his body with a .38 slug?" Ruth was still smiling, not hearing a word I said.

"No! You called me beautiful; you do think I'm beautiful, Wolf."

"Ruth! For Pete's sake, we were talking about life or death. Will you touch the gun? It won't hurt you." Ruth carefully eased her hand over to touch the pistol like it was a crate of eggs.

"Wolf, darling...oh, I forgot to ask you...can I call you Darling, on special occasions?"

"I don't mind, Ruth. Just don't make a habit of it when we are around folks; it sound so personal. And what are the special occasions, anyway?"

Before Ruth could tell me the special occasions, we heard Susie screaming her head off in the kitchen, "Y'all come and get it; breakfast is getting cold!"

I'm one that doesn't have to be called twice. Eating is one of my favorite things I do - and do well.

"Come on, Ruth, we'll discuss the Derringer after we eat, before I go over to Mr. Dobbs' house at ten o'clock. "

Albert was sitting at the kitchen table when we entered the kitchen, smiling like a jackass eating briers. I spoke, he grunted, and the conversation at breakfast was somewhat diminished. Aunt Becky didn't say three words - and they were about the Flower Club meeting at ten this morning. I didn't make a comment at the time, but wondered if Aunt Becky or Ruth noticed how Albert never took his eyes off Ruth through the whole meal.

Susie, our chief cook and bottle washer as well as maid and butler, announced that as quick as dishes were washed up she was going to visit her sick mother across town, but would be back to cook supper.

"That's 'dinner' Susie, my dear," Aunt Becky corrected, "and I will be gone most of the day myself. The Flower Club meets at ten and I need to be there at nine."

"Wolf has a meeting with Mr. Dobbs at ten o'clock, and as for me, I have a good book I need to finish," Ruth added, getting up from the table.

Albert didn't say a word, but got up and walked out the back door of the kitchen.

"He is probably going down to the billiard parlor to guzzle rot gut all day," Aunt Becky commented, as she got up to leave.

Before leaving the house, I motioned with my head for Ruth to follow me to my bedroom. "Come on in and close the door. Now, Ruth, I don't have time to argue with you, but you said yourself - I make the important decisions." She nodded and sat down on the edge of the bed.

"First of all, did you notice how Albert eyed you all through breakfast a while ago?"

"No! I never made eye contact with that pervert. I didn't say anything, either. I was afraid you would get up and give him another hole in his ugly head. You know what he kept doing all through breakfast? Tried to play feet with me under the table. At one time I started to get up and walk out."

"Now, Ruth, I may be making a mountain out of a molehill, but I want you to take this Colt Derringer and put it in your pocket so you can get to it, just in case it's needed. Now, it is a three step procedure to it; and it just might keep you from being maimed, raped, or even killed. Now watch closely. You use your thumb to pull the hammer back; this is called cocking the gun. Then point to what you want to shoot and pull the trigger. Cock, point, and pull - you got that?"

Ruth took the little gun and gave it the once over, getting a good feel of the Derringer in her hand.

"Well, I'm going to run on over to Mr. Dobbs' and get started." I headed down the hall of the big house on my way to the front door.

"Wolf Mann! Aren't you forgetting something very important?"

I looked all around. I had my hat on, and my pistol strapped to my leg. "I believe I have everything I need. Is there something else I'm forgetting?" I asked, looking back at Ruth.

"Yes! You're forgetting to kiss me goodbye." And here she came.

"Now, just a minute, Ruth... we have never done this before."

"I know it...we have never been apart since we met on the stage coach; this is the first time we've had to say goodbye."

"You wanna go over to Mr. Dobbs' with me this morning?"

"No, Wolf, darling, I'm going to finish that book. Beings every one is gone, I'll have peace and quiet."

Now I'll let Ruth tell the story for a while...

Oh well, I thought, we pecked each other on the cheek. It certainly wasn't what I thought it was going to be. I done found out, when Wolf has his mind on something else I might as well leave him alone. I shut the front door and started down the long hall to my room. I was hoping I could finish the book with everyone gone.

As I pulled the curtain back to let the sun shine in, I could see it was a beautiful day - a little chilly, but one could tell spring was in the air and on its way by how the daffodils were popping up. I gathered up several pillows to prop on and made myself comfortable. I removed my boots. stripped down to my petticoat, and lay down, holding the book to my bosom.

I began to think - I do this a right smart now. I'm not even the same person I was when I came through Silver Springs and met Wolf. How could a life change just by meeting someone, just a boy, a fourteen year old boy at that? And here I am twenty, well I just turned twenty. Boy or not, I have fallen in love with Wolf Mann. I really don't know what lies in store for his future; he has already killed four grown men. And four houses up the street Wolf is

82

meeting with Mr. Dobbs, the fastest gun in the world, who is training him how to kill a bunch more. Oh well, time will tell. I have a life now.

I had a few more pages to read and was dozing in and out, when I thought I heard someone come in the front door. I wasn't familiar with this big house and had already heard several strange noises this morning. So, I went on reading. Now it might just have been my imagination, but I swear I heard footsteps in the hall. I listened... it was quiet as a church mouse, except for the sound of the squeaking floor as the footsteps got closer. I knew Aunt Becky said it would be late before she returned; and it surely wasn't time for Susie to get back.

"Is that you, Wolf?" I called out, quickly getting into my dress. There was no answer. I remembered I hadn't locked my door. I dashed to the door. It opened right in my face; and there stood Albert. His eyes were staring like a wild animal and his breathing was like the panting of a dog. The stench of liquor filled the room.

"No, Albert, leave now!" I begged, backing up.

He smiled and took a step toward me. I had backed up until the bed was touching the back of my legs. He was actually drooling at the mouth as he began to unbuckle his belt.

"We gonna have some fun, baby. You better get that pretty dress off if you don't want it torn!"

His pants fell to the tops of his shoes as he shuffled his feet toward me. He shoved me backward; I fell across the bed and began fight and kick at him.

"Go ahead, baby, and fight, it makes it even better."

I could tell I was over-powered. He was between my legs, leaning over me trying to kiss me now. I was slapping at him, and he kept putting my hands down at my side. He did this several times - until my hand touched the little Derringer in my pocket. I had forgotten all about it. The words of Wolf cane to my mind loud and clear: "cock, point, and pull."

By now, Albert had become as a rabid dog, licking my face and breasts and trying to rip my clothes.

"Cock, point, and pull," I kept saying to myself, "cock, point, and pull."

I managed to get the Derringer out of my pocket and across my stomach, up to his chest. With my thumb I cocked it and made sure it was pointed in the vicinity of his heart. Not really knowing what to expect, I pulled the trigger. The shot was somewhat muffled, but as Wolf would say: Albert knew he hadn't been mosquito bit.

Evidently, he had enough life and power left to stand up. Holding both hands against his chest, with blood running out between his fingers, his lips were moving but nothing was coming out. I watched as his eyes rolled back in his head. Then his knees buckled and he wilted to the floor.

I slid my boots on, straightened my clothes, and ran out the front door, heading up the street. As I neared Mr. Dobbs' home I could hear shots being fired. I could tell the shots were coming from the back yard. I didn't stop until I saw Wolf.

"Wolf! Wolf! Come quickly, I have shot Albert!"

"Shot Albert!?"

"Yes, he came into my bedroom and I had to shoot him."

"Would you excuse us, Mr. Dobbs, I'm afraid there has been an accident at Aunt Becky's house."

"Here, here now, Wolf, you and Ruth get in my carriage and we'll journey by the sheriff's office and report the accident on our way to your Aunt Becky's house."

I'll take the story back over now...Let me say - the undertaker had come and gone, and the blood was all cleaned up, before Aunt Becky and Susie arrived home.

Ruth and I were sitting at the breakfast table drinking coffee when Aunt Becky came in. The front door was in sight of the kitchen table and she came straight to us.

"How was your day, Aunt Becky" I asked, wondering how I was going to break the news and how she was going to take it.

"It was just great, and our guest speaker was fabulous. I learned so much about pruning my roses, especially with spring coming on," Aunt Becky said, pouring herself a cup of coffee.

"I'm afraid Ruth has been doing some pruning around here while you've been gone today." Aunt Becky looked surprised and Ruth hung her head.

"Ruth shot Albert today," I explained.

"Did you kill 'im. I hope? That's not what a good Methodist should say, I know, but God does answer prayers."

"I didn't know when I shot Albert it was an answer to a prayer, but he came into my room like the devil he was. And you can thank your beloved nephew for making me take this little Derringer and keeping it in my pocket," Ruth said, smiling at me.

"Aunt Becky," I said, "since Ruth has plucked the thorn out of your flesh and you have my guardian papers in order, would you come to Silver Springs and go to bat for me if my property goes to court?" I was hoping Aunt Becky would say yes.

"You know, Wolf, darling, I have always wanted to come west, and if I get to feeling better, and I think now I will, you can depend on your favorite aunt."

"By the time this case comes up in court, you will be able to ride a passenger train all the way from here in Middle Town to Silver Springs. And keep this in mind - you will have a beautiful house with your own room to stay in while you're visiting."

We three were still sitting around the table when Susie came in. Ruth saw her coming and poured another cup of coffee. Evidently word had already gotten out about Albert getting shot.

"Now Miss Ruth...what's dat I hear about you exterminating buzzards dis morning?" Susie asked, while putting on her long, white apron.

"Well, you pretty much hit the nail right on the head," Ruth replied.

"Why don't you tell me all about it whilst I rustle up some grub?"

Aunt Becky had retired to her room and I was going out in the back yard to practice my fast draw. I could do this without firing a shot. This was the first thing that Mr. Dobbs taught me. I needed to practice. 'Practice makes perfect,' he said, 'and you need hours and hours of practice.'

I knew it might look a bit silly so I tried not to practice where others might be looking on. I'm sure it looked childish; and since I was only going on fifteen, some might think I was playing cowboy and Indians. It was getting dark and a wee-bit chilly, so I made my way into the house and went straight to my bedroom. I did a double take; there was Ruth - sitting on my bed with her face in her hands and her elbows on her knees - looking like a dying calf in a thunderstorm.

"What's wrong?" I asked, sitting down beside her. I waited for her answer as I pulled off my boots.

"Wolf...I can't bring myself to sleep in that room where I killed Albert."

"What's the matter? Do you think Albert's ghost will come back and haunt you?"

"Okay! That did it...I know I'm not sleeping in that room now."

"Well... what do you plan to do? Don't tell me," I said, as if I didn't already know.

"That's right...I'll sleep in your room."

"But what will folks say, Ruth?...You know how rumors and talk gets started...us sleeping together."

"You can sleep on the floor, Wolf; or we could trade rooms."

"Not me! Did you see all that blood on the floor in there? I'd rather sleep out in the back yard."

"Suit yourself," Ruth argued, "I'm going to bed." She started taking off her boots.

"You gonna take your dress off, too?" I asked. I was getting nervous about this whole idea.

"Are you going to take your pants off?" Ruth questioned.

"Not if you gonna take your dress off, I ain't. Besides, we haven't even hugged goodnight, yet."

"I thought we could do that when you and I lay down in bed," Ruth said. She had a smile on her face as wide as Texas.

"I'm sleeping on the floor, Ruth! Somebody in this room has got to keep a civil head. So, let us do our hugging with clothes on."

# Chapter 10

The next morning I was over at Mr. Dobbs' house at ten o'clock. I found him waiting for me in the back yard, drinking a cup of coffee. He and I said our 'good mornings' and got right down to brass tacks.

"Now, Wolf, not only is there lots of practice going in to fast draw, but a lot of learning and remembering what to do. I would say most of your targets will be about waist high, unless you are shooting at a snake or a hawk - and neither of those will shoot back at you. I see where someone did an excellent job on extending the hammer on your Colt."

"Yes, it was a friend of mind, Kermit Travick. He owns the livery and blacksmith shop in Silver Springs, Oklahoma. And he is keeping Blackie; that's my horse. You ought to see my saddle and bridle! They are also black with silver conchas, just like my hat and gun rigging."

"Now, Wolf, don't be offended by what I'm going to say to you, but your beautiful black horse, saddle, bridle, and all your black clothes will not help you one bit when you stand on Main Street - facing a challenger with a .45 tied to his leg. Now, it helps to look the part, don't get me wrong, but always keep this in mind - your slug must reach him before his slug touches your body."

I was taking in everything Mr. Dobbs was telling me, hoping I wouldn't forget.

"So, being fast sometimes means being dead. Let me explain; being accurate would rank most important." I nodded that I knew what he was referring to. "One shot in the right place is better than three fast shots and three misses." Mr. Dobbs coached me, watching me like a hawk, showing me the mistakes I was making.

"Now, remember, my lad, as you take your stance to draw, start thinking about getting your finger on the trigger. As you bring your pistol up you must hold the trigger back, and fan with your left hand. Do you have any questions?"

"Yes, I have one. Do you think I wear my pistol too low?"

"I have been noticing that. This is strictly your preference. Do what feels comfortable to you. As I said one time...if it works, use it. First, master the fast draw without using up ammunition. Also, I noticed you don't carry your pistol on an empty cylinder. This is for your protection. You still have five shots left."

"What about using my left hand to fast draw?" I asked.

"I don't think it's a good idea, Wolf. Master shooting with the right hand first and it will make using the left-hand much easier."

I trained with Mr. Dobbs for two more days: he said he had shownme all he knew. It was up to me to practice every leisure minute I had.

I announced my plans to Ruth and Aunt Becky when I returned to the house. Ruth was so happy; while Aunt Becky was saddened to see us going back to Silver Springs so soon. I told her to get well and that I would send her a telegram when it was time to come out to Silver Springs.

The next day Ruth and I took the first train heading west, carrying a heap more back than we brought with us. I believe Ruth was more excited to get back to Silver Springs than I was. Course, she didn't know what I planned on doing. I intended to bring Huey Black to his knees; and ruin him financially. I would be his worst nightmare before it was over.

Every minute I had alone I spent practicing my fast draw.

"Wolf, you are going to wear the holster out before you get to shoot someone," Ruth said, watching every move I made.

"Do you think I'm getting any faster?" I asked, twirling my pistol.

"Lord, yes, Wolf, I can hardly see your hand move. But how do you know that you can hit anything? I never hear the gun go off."

I thought: 'That's a fair question and that is the next step in my learning.' We'd be home in two days and I could practice in the back yard with live ammunition.

One might call it backtracking, or a rerun backwards. When Ruth and I finally shed the train, we caught the stage to Silver Springs - another dusty, bumpy, two-day journey.

I hadn't said much about Faye's Diner in Silver Springs since I had known Ruth. I was hoping we'd be there soon.

"Have I told you about Faye's Diner?" I asked.

"Only in passing," Ruth answered.

"I think you are in for a surprise."

"Why do you say that?" she asked.

"I didn't tell you about Elie Mae and Margie, did I?" I said with a smile. I wondered what was gonna happen, hoping no jealousy would raise its ugly head with the girls.

"What about Elie Mae and Margie?" Ruth asked, spinning around in the seat giving me the barbarous eye. Sad to say, I could already detect a spark of jealousy and we hadn't even arrived yet. "Are you sweet on them?" she asked with a sour look.

"Oh, no - they may be sweet on me. Like all girls, I've found out, they like to hug and kiss every chance they get." I could tell that went over like a fly in the punch bowl. "Then there is Miss Faye...she was Pa's bride-to-be before he got killed by old man Huey Black. You know what Miss Faye told me?" Ruby shook her head. "She told me she's gonna have Pa's baby. Now ain't that something?"

"I hope to have a baby some day," Ruth marveled, with the smile on her face.

I let that statement go in one ear and out the other.

"You know my mother died having a baby. They said it was a girl...I never got to see it, with Mother dying and all."

Ruth just shook her head and started looking out the window.

I let our arrival be a secret. I hadn't let anyone in Silver Springs know I was coming. I can say one thing; it was a surprise when Ruth and I walked into the diner. It was almost embarrassing the way Ruth kept hanging on to me. It seemed that Elie Mae and Margie kept their distance; and I don't think Miss Faye was all that fond of me showing up with a girl six years older than me. I knew I had some explaining to do to resolve this matter.

I told Ruth to stay at the diner while I walked over to Miss Faye's house to speak to her mother, Mrs. Pittman. She gave me a look like 'who do you think you're bossing around,' and started following me. I stopped and waited for Ruth to catch up.

"Now, Ruth, I told you to wait at the diner...I wanted to explain to Mrs. Pittman the relationship between you and I. This lady don't stand for any hanky-panky. Besides, we will be staying in her house."

"I don't think we have any explaining to do." She said dryly.

"That's right! But I think I do. Now you can go back in the diner, or walk up to the hotel and wait; suit yourself."

Ruth gave me the dirtiest look and started toward the hotel. I stood for a minute trying to put two and two together. WasI being unfair?

Just then I felt a hand take my arm, I quickly turned to see who it was...Miss Faye had stepped out on the porch where I was standing. We were both watching Ruth when she suddenly stopped and turned toward me and Miss Faye.

"You all can go straight to hell; I got my own damn money."

And that was the last time I saw Ruth for over a week.

"Seems you got a problem," Miss Faye said, as she and I walked on to her house to see Mrs. Pittman.

"No! I just found out who's got the problem. Pa always said 'if you will give a monkey enough grape-vine he will hang himself,' and I guess that is true."

"I like the old Chinese proverb best... 'One can't make a silk purse out of a pig's ear," Miss Faye shared, as she started up the doorsteps of the big house.

"You was referring to Ruth, I gather?"

"Yes, I was. Girls like her are a dime a dozen. They have ruined their lives and now want to ruin yours. Haven't you ever heard? Misery loves company," Miss Faye volunteered.

"Is that something like - birds of a feather flock together?" I asked while holding the door open.

"I guess one could say that. You are not her type and she wants to pull you down on her level," Miss Faye added, as we graced the living room.

"Well, well, now if it isn't my favorite person," Mrs. Pittman said excitedly. "Come over here, young man, and let me give you a good flogging...What are you trying to do...break Billy the Kid's record? I've been reading about you, here lately."

"Oh, no, Mrs. Pittman, it wasn't like that at all. I was just target practicing and the gol'darn fools walked in front of my bullets."

"Faye, baby, would you go and get me a bar of that lye-soap and help me wash Wolf's mouth out?"

We three had a good laugh and caught up on the week that had passed while I was in Ohio.

"I guess you know the railroad coming through Silver Springs is public knowledge now. One can hear the workers blasting the right-of-way coming through the mountains north of town," said Miss Faye.

"Mrs. Pittman, you might as well know about Ruth before she causes a stink. Ruth is a girl I met on the stage as I was going to visit my Aunt Becky in Ohio. She had a sad-sopping story and like petting a lost hungry puppy, she has been following me ever since."

"Where did she say her home was, Wolf?" Mrs. Pittman asked, getting quite concerned.

"Well, that's just it, if she said, I didn't catch it. According to her she grew up in an orphans' home, lived with her aunt, and then her granny took her in until she died. She met this older man that was going to come west to get rich managing a saloon. All I know is I bought her food at a stage stop, a suitcase full of clothes, and a warm coat and boots." Mrs. Pittman and Faye listened as I went on. "I also gave her half the reward money I received from killing the outlaw who was trying to steal the strong box off the stage."

"Are you looking for some advice?" Mrs. Pittman asked. I nodded and waited. "Well, Wolf, a bad situation is like a bucket of cow guts - the more you stir them, the worse they stink. But nature has a way of crusting stinking things over, and making it tolerable."

"Is that something like letting a sleeping dog lie?"

"Wolf, I believe you got the idea."

And that I did. A week passed and I didn't see hair or hide of Ruth. I was back having fun with Elie May and Margie at the diner. I think Miss Faye told the girls what had happened and to not stir the bucket of cow guts.

I set up shooting targets behind Mrs. Pittman's house - far enough away so the gun fire would not be a nuisance to anyone. Other than making sure that the diner and big house had wood for heat and cooking, to earn my keep and buy bullets, I spent all my time at my shooting range - slinging lead and slapping leather.

After several weeks the scuttlebutt had infiltrated the grapevine around Silver Springs...that I was the fastest gun in the whole West. You should know that would bring in trouble, along with every gun happy galoot this side of the Mississippi River, to challenge me.

One morning, I guess about nine o'clock, I had emptied five shots at a target, with a tight group that I was proud of.

"Not bad shooting, if I do say so myself." I glanced quickly, and there was Calvin...one of Huey Black's hit men/bodyguards standing in the brush.

"You been standing there long?" I asked, blowing the smoke out of the barrel of my Colt.

"Long enough. I would be hesitant to tangle with the likes of you."

He didn't know, but his day was coming soon.

"You wouldn't be offended if I gave you negative criticism, would you?" Calvin asked, coming out of the bushes into the clear where I was standing.

"Oh, no, I'm always open for a good tip or suggestion that would improve my fast draw," I answered.

He might not have known at the time but if he helped me one iota, he was driving nails into his own coffin.

Calvin came a little closer. "It's not your shooting or your speed, it's your stance. I been watching the last several times you drew and shot. You let your opponent know when you are going to draw on him. You see, in a fast draw every split second counts."

I listened and thought this is making good sense even if it was coming from the man that shot my pa.

"Now, Wolf, if you move any part of your body, or change your expression on your face, your challenger will know you are ready to pull down on him." This said, Calvin stepped up beside me facing the target. "Now, watch this!" he uttered and drew and shot. "Did you know I was going to shoot?" he asked.

"I had no idea you was going to shoot."

"This is my point, Wolf neither does the man, with a .45 strapped to his leg, facing you ."

I knew what he was saying.

"Let us take, for instance, you call a man out of his house or a saloon. When he comes facing you, you need to be standing in the position you will shoot. I have been watching you, Wolf. You always get your feet ready first. You are giving your opponent time to let his brain know to go for his gun. I notice you lean a little forward, that's good, but do this as your pistol is coming out of your leather."

I had a couple of wooden dynamite boxes stacked up for a makeshift shooting table. There lay several boxes of .45 cartridges. I took a cartridge out, threw it to Calvin, and started loading my Colt. I watched as he poked his casing out on the ground and filled the empty cylinder.

I walked about twenty yards in front the shooting table, set up five tomato cans about a foot apart on a waist high rail, and came back.

"Now, watch, as if I was going to face five men, each with a .45 hanging on their hip." I stood for a minute not moving. Seemed the birds quit chirping, the crickets hushed and Mr. Calvin said not a word. All of a sudden I fanned my Colt as if it was on fire, and five cans hit the ground rolling. "Well!" I said blowing the smoke out of my pistol.

"Well, I'm glad I wasn't one of those tomato cans."

We both had a good laugh, but I didn't think it would be that funny when I soon rolled him down Main Street, full of lead.

"Wolf, that was perfect, it even surprised me; and I'm hard to be fooled."

"I would like to thank you for the good tip, and again, for these spurs. They are different and do attract attention."

"Glad I could help. I better get back to the saloon. Mr. Black might be screaming his head off. Oh, by the way, this means nothing to me but it may to you. You know that young girl that rode in on the stage with you several weeks ago? I believe she goes by Ruth. I didn't know where you knew or even cared... but she has a room upstairs at the saloon and the men are beating a path to her door. Now, you didn't hear that from me. I just felt like I owed you one, Wolf." Calvin turned and started back through the woods to the saloon.

I thought, that's the second time he said he owed me one. He is almost telling me he shot my pa.

I was getting a feeling for Ruth at one time, but I never led her on or did anything I was ashamed of. I eased over to Blackie where I had him tied in the shade.

"You about ready to ride up to where they are building the railroad?" he nodded with his head. "Blackie, did you really understand what I said? He nodded again, "I thought you did."

I guess about six miles north of town I began to see activity and hear a blast now and then. It was 'for shore' there was something coming toward Silver Springs. Way before I approached the workers I saw a small building which, to me, looked like a line-shack. The only difference was a sign on the side of the building which read: 'DANGER DYNAMITE.' Now ain't that something! I dismounted beside a beautiful, clear stream flowing down out of the mountains. As always, the cogs and gears in my finite brain began to turn. Dynamite. I thought I remembered Pa buying some dynamite to blow some stumps when he and I were clearing some fallow ground at our spread. Blackie had drunk his fill and I dropped down on my hands and knees to do the same thing.

I stood, patting Blackie on the neck, looking at the small building. I thought about a story Pa told about an old farmer back in Ohio. I don't remember the whole story; but the farmer grew corn. Now, as the story went, the rats completely infested his barn and began to eat up all his corn. Well, I guess he wasn't thinking, because the old farmer set fire to the barn and burned it down to get rid of the rats.

That's a good idea even if I did think of it myself; I'll blow the barn up. I was referring to the Silver Slipper Saloon, of course. I eased up to the building; it was as open as a lot gate. I chocked my saddle bags slam full of dynamite. Well, to make a long story short...I filled both of my saddle bags, full as a tick, and started back to town.

I pretty much had free range around the diner and the big house, as long as I kept it nice and tidy, made sure there was ample firewood to burn, and disposed of the garbage.

"Now, Blackie, old pal, if you will carry me by the Silver Slipper Saloon before you and I go to dinner, I will appreciate it. If you don't mind, let's check out the back of the damnable place."

The saloon sat at the end of town, basically by itself. If you had seen one, you had seen them all... a big two story wood frame building, built high enough for a person to crawl under. Windows in the rooms upstairs, but none downstairs, except on each side of the batwings at the entrance.

"Well, Blackie, I've seen all I need to see, and you better take a good look, because what you are seeing won't be here long. Let's go over to the diner."

While I was having lunch Miss Faye came over and sat down at our usual table, close to the kitchen.

"You know what I heard?" she asked, leaning over toward me.

"Let me guess...Ruth is back at her old trade."

"Yes! How did you find out?" Miss Faye asked, somewhat surprised.

"You know where I go to practice several times a day, behind the big house in the woods?" Miss Faye nodded, and I went on. "Well, this morning, same as yesterday and the day before, I rode off down there to practice. I tied Blackie in the shade, went over to my make-shift shooting bench and started to work...

# Chapter 11

...I guess I might have shot up a half of a box of cartridges when I heard this man's voice in the brush behind me. 'Not bad shooting if I do say so myself.' I took a quick glance, and there stood Calvin...one of Huey Black's hit man/bodyguards standing in the brush. 'Have you been standing there long?' I asked, blowing the smoke out of my barrel of my Colt. 'Long enough,' he answered and with that introduction, he and I had a good discussion. Calvin being a gunslinger himself, and still alive, I took his advice to heart. When Calvin started to leave, he enlightened me on the Ruth saga. This is when I thought about all the feathers."

"You mean birds of a feather flock together," Miss Faye added.

"Yeah, that's it. As my pa would say, 'an apple don't fall too far from its tree.' At times I remember Ma would say, 'a fruit picked from a tree is much better than one that falls at your feet.' I was getting a feeling for Ruth at one time but I never led her on or did anything I'm ashamed of. Good lord, Miss Faye, I'm fifteen years old and have killed four men! I know the difference between man and woman. And this hugging and kissing thing between Elie May and Margie, and even Ruth, is becoming a welcome gesture."

Miss Faye reached across the small table and took my hands. "What about me?" she asked in a loving voice.

"Especially you, but it's a special kind of feeling. I can understand why my pa fell in love with you."

"Is it kinda like a mother and son's love?" Big tears came to Miss Faye's eyes. She turned loose of my hands and began to dab her eyes with a napkin that was lying on the table. "Don't you get me to squalling in here in front of Elie Mae and Margie!"

Miss Faye nearly had her composure under control before I spoke up, "You know, according to the Bible, you are my mom."

Miss Faye looked somewhat surprised. "Where did you find that out?"

"Oh, it was my Aunt Becky. In our discussion one evening I told her I was going to have a little sister very soon. She said when you and Pa had sex you consummated a marriage in the sight of God."

Miss Faye jumped up and ran out the back door. Both Elie May and Margie saw her hasty departure and came over to the table where I was sitting.

"Is anything wrong?" Elie Mae asked.

"Oh, no, nothing time won't take care of," I answered.

"We sure love Miss Faye and wouldn't want anything to happen to her," said Margie.

I finished my dinner and carried Blackie over to the barn where I unsaddled him for the night. As I was rubbing him down, I began to think: Just how much dynamite was I gonna to need to blow the saloon all to hell and back?

I began to make some plan on how I was gonna carry out this covert operation, without getting blown up myself. First, I would work at night. Secondly, I would need to blow up the saloon when it was empty, as not to injure anyone.

I thought: If everything goes as planned - when Silver Springs puts on the New Year's Eve party south of town - there will be a string of tables that they've used for other occasions. The main attraction will be the bar-b-q and free beer. Of course, a few musicians will show up and there will be a barn dance. Huey Black will close the saloon down for two or three hours during the main festivities. Naturally, everyone will come for the free beer and food.

Mr. Grimes always furnishes the fireworks and most every lady brings a covered dish.

As I finished using the curry-comb on Blackie, I almost laughed out loud. That is when I will blow my big fire-cracker. Naturally, I will be at the party along with everyone else, so how can I be blamed? Oh well, I have less than a week to place the sticks of dynamite under the saloon.

Every evening after the railroad workers knocked off, Blackie and I would ride up to the dynamite shack and get two saddle bags full of dynamite. I thought I would just wait until the last evening before New Year's Eve to get the caps and a roll of fuse. I could tell the railroad was progressing right along.

Each night, dressed in all black, I would ease through the woods with a load of dynamite and, unseen, would crawl under the back of the saloon and place the sticks of dynamite up on the house blocks that held up the sills. If need be I had a roll of twine to tie them to the floor joists. Pa always said if you placed the sticks of dynamite close enough together the concussion of one would set the other off. Well, keeping that in mind, I did a fine job, I thought. Not knowing how far apart to place the sticks of dynamite, I might have overdone it…only time would tell.

It was easy to tell the year was ending and the big day was nearing. It was the talk of the town. Some of the bosses and foremen of the railroad were riding into town, having meals at the diner. Some were even taking rooms at the hotel. Two other establishments were breaking ground for buildings. Mr. Grimes said that progress seems to move right along with the railroad.

The old year, 1878, was ending and 1879 was coming on, and so was the big day. Fun, food, fellowship in Silver Springs. People would come from miles around. Some wouldn't even know the railroad was coming through town. Oh, well, it would come and go; but I had work to do.

I went to the barn to saddle Blackie to go practice. I would never forget the words of Frank Dobbs…the fastest gun in the world…'practice, practice, practice, this will make you perfect.' I had drawn and shot four rounds, started to reload and take a breather, when this man rode up.

"You got a minute?" he asked.

I recognized him as being one of Huey Black's hired killers. He was with Calvin and Huey Black the night Pa was shot.

"Lighten your saddle and come on over." I turned around and leaned back against my make-shift shooting bench.

"You know who I am?" The man dismounted and walked to where I was.

"Yes, you are one of Huey Black's personal bodyguards," I said, slipping my pistol back in my holster.

"I used to be, until this morning." He slightly turned his head looking away from me. "I was once a half-way decent person - until I hooked up with Huey Black and the likes of him. He killed that young girl, Ruth, Ruby, Rachel - you know who I'm talking about; you brought her here on the stage with you. Anyhow, Huey Black made it look like an accident after he broke her neck,"

"Could you tell me just how it happened?" I could tell he had more to tell than what he was saying, I don't know why but I believed him for some reason.

"First of all, I have never liked Huey Black, but he pays well. For an uneducated cowboy as myself, for no more than I know, it beats the heck out of sucking dust behind a bunch of beeves across Oklahoma. Anyhow, when we closed last night, all the customers had left the bar and there was no one at the tables. It was way after midnight and Huey Black, Calvin, and I was finishing up a nightcap when Calvin noticed that 'what's her name' went in Huey's office. Now neither I nor Huey seen her. It was upstairs and the lights were being turned out.

'You having company tonight, boss man?'" Calvin asked, tapping Huey on the arm and pointing up to the office.

"Come on, Jim, let's see what this bitch is up to,' Black instructed.

'I'll see you gentlemen tomorrow,' Calvin said. He and the bartender went out the front door, locking it behind them.

'Come on, Jim,' Huey snarled, and up the stairs he and I went. I was right behind him, having no idea what we would find. When we went in, she seemed not that surprised, but I could tell she had been looking through a file cabinet.

'What do you think you are doing, girl?' Huey Black screamed.

She just walked right between us, going out the door as if nothing had happened. Well, Huey grabbed a handful of her long hair and snatched her around so fast her neck snapped like a dry twig. She dropped to the carpet choking and gagging, and never drew another breath."

I could tell this got to Jim the way he told the story.

"'Go on to bed Jim,' he said, 'I can take care of this mess.' I just figured he would get some of the other girls to help him. So I went ahead and left. Now, Wolf, I didn't get any sleep last night, just thinking about the mire I let myself get into."

"You might as well finish the story - how Huey Black got rid of Ruth's body and why you are leaving Silver Springs," I stated.

"What happened next is the reason I'm leaving. As I said, I couldn't sleep. So I made up my mind to leave. I saddled my horse and headed south. I had to go right by the saloon, and as I approached the saloon I saw Jerd Coggins drive up in his black hearse and get down from the boot. The cleaning lady was holding one of the batwings open. Putting her hand to her mouth, she yelled, 'Hey Jim, come and give us a hand.' I wasn't curious, because I knew it had something to with Ruth. Wolf, when I walked in, the first thing I saw was Ruth hanging from the upstairs balcony, as if she had hanged herself. Now, the way I see it, Wolf... after I left, Huey Black drug the girl up to the railing and tied a rope around her neck, then dumped her over the side rail. Her feet lacked about eight inches from touching the floor."

"All I can say, she didn't deserve this and Huey Black will pay starting today."

Jim looked surprised. "Are you planning on calling him out for a gun fight?"

"Not if I don't have to."

"He wouldn't fight you fair anyway, Wolf. And I'll let you in on another secret... Ruth found out who killed your pa and was going to tell you when she got the chance," Jim said, getting a little fidgety, maybe thinking he had said too much already.

"All I can say, if Huey Black killed Ruth because she was going to tell me who shot my pa, she died for naught. I knew who shot my pa the night he fell to the floor. Huey called to my pa 'where's the boy?' Pa knew he was gonna get shot and he lied for me, 'he is over at a friend's house visiting.' Then my pa was shot three times in the heart. You remember what he said next? 'See if you all can find the boy.'

I moved away from the shooting bench with my feet in position to draw.

"No, no, Wolf, it wasn't me, honestly, it wasn't me. It was Calvin. I didn't know they were going to gun your pa down in cold blood. Why, he wasn't even wearing a gun."

"I know, Jim, but I am now... and it's my pa's Colt."

"No, no, Wolf, it wasn't me. Honestly, I'm no match for you."

"You said you were leaving town. Is that right?" I asked.

"That's right, Wolf. I was paid off last night for a month's work. Now I'm heading to south Texas."

"Somehow, Jim, I believe you. But could I see your peacemaker before you ride off?" Jim flipped the thong off the hammer and handed me his pistol. I took it and handed him my Colt with the high hammer. "What do you think Jim? Look at it good."

Jim twisted his mouth and slightly shook his head. "You got what it takes, Wolf, your pistol was empty. I could have killed you if I knew that."

I handed him his pistol back and politely said, "Well, you still can."

"No, Wolf, I'm through with killing and watching people being maimed and mutilated for no cause. For instance, your pa, I would give anything to right that wrong, although I was with the killer that did it."

"You say you will do anything to right that wrong. Just how far would you go to right that wrong?" I thought I would work Jim into my plan.

"That's right, except for killing; I'm through with that, Wolf."

"Okay, Jim, this is what I want you to do. As you know, today is the big New Year's Eve party at the south end of town. As a matter of fact, there are people already gathering right now. You also know that Huey Black don't open the saloon until all the festivities are over, usually about three o'clock or so.

Now what I want you to do - when all the girls, Huey Black, and Calvin have gone to the big celebration and the saloon is completely empty - you go around to the back of the saloon. On the left corner, where the building is settin' on a house block, kneel down and reach under the building. On top of the house block you will find a box of matches and the end of a dynamite fuse. Light the fuse and you will have over ten minutes to come on down to the bar-b-q or head south."

"Wolf, just what do you think will happen?" Jim asked, agreeing to help me out with this project.

"If everything goes to plan, it should turn the saloon into a tooth-pick factory."

About all we could do now was to wait. I went back to the diner. The girls were busy as bees, but stopped to give me the news they had heard this morning about Ruth.

"I just don't believe I could do what she did... hang myself!" Elie Mae exclaimed.

"Neither could I," said Margie.

I just shook my head and thought - I would let that sleeping dog lie for a while.

"Where is Miss Faye? Over at the house?" I asked, smiling at the girls.

"Oh, no. She's down to the New Year's celebration. We baked lots of bread and she carried it down for the big dinner. By the way, the diner will be closed for two hours."

"Are you going to dance with me, Wolf?" Margie asked, doing a little waltz with a broom.

"Are you kidding me? I don't know how to dance," I argued, as Elie Mae grabbed me, nearly embarrassing me to death.

"Come on, Wolf, I'll teach you how to dance."

"Good grief, Elie Mae, folks setting over there are looking at us!" I was standing there like an idiot and Elie Mae was jumping around like a clown.

"Move, Elie Mae! Wolf is more of a slow dancer," Margie explained. "Now, Wolf, just give me this hand...and get a wee bit closer, and put the other hand right back here."

"For crying out loud, Margie, that's your rump!"

Margie quickly looked all around - I guess to see if any one was listening. "I know it, Wolf! It has been hooked on to me for fifteen years. The first thing you need to learn when dancing... don't start naming body parts. We'll finish up this dancing lesson at the festivities, won't we, Elie Mae?"

"That's right, Margie, we sure will, but Miss Faye told us to close about twelve o'clock and come on down to the bar-b-q; and it's bout that time."

It seemed that everybody that was anybody was there. Someone had appointed Mr. Grimes the great privilege of saying grace over the food. As I saw it, most folks had done started and were going back for seconds. I can say one thing, the food was a plenty and the bar-b-q was delicious, and I'm sure the draft beer wasn't gonna run out no time soon.

I saw that Huey Black and his buggy full of whores had arrived. And there was Calvin, and Vinny, the piano player. You might say the crowd was wall to wall and they were still coming. The band had set up and began to entertain while the folks were enjoying themselves.

I knew Huey Black and his women weren't going to stick around long after dinner, and the big explosion hadn't yet occurred. Was there something wrong? Had the fuse gone out? Had Jim chickened out? Well, I kept waiting... and no sign of Jim or the big bang. Finally,

I couldn't stand the suspense any longer; I made my way through the crowd like a nesting turkey and found Blackie. I don't even think I was noticed. The saloon was quite a ways from the shindig going on. I kept a low profile and headed to the saloon. When I rode up, I noticed two horses tied to the hitching rail in front. I recognized one of the horses to be Jim's. The other one might be causing the delay. The front doors of the saloon were wide open.

I busted right on in like I owned the place and yelled out, "Where are you at Jim? It's Wolf!"

"Come on up here and give me a hand. I need some help!" Jim yelled back.

I ran up the stairs and dashed into the room where Jim was. It didn't take a Philadelphia lawyer to assess the problem. There lay some woman - half clothed, and either dead or passed out drunk, right in the middle of the bed.

"What are we going to do, Wolf?...I can't wake her up, and I'm darn shore I ain't gonna blow her up!"

"Roll her up in these blankets and we'll carry her outside. What about the other horse outside?" I asked, as Jim and I started out of the room with the woman.

"Wolf, there is no one else in this saloon. It was probably some drunk got in the wagon of a buddy and rode off to the blowout."

He and I carried the woman far enough out in the woods behind the saloon. We took along with the extra horse, which we tied to a bush. Jim and I lit the fuse and ran to the front to mount our horses. In a flash we were back at the New Year's party, and I don't believe we were ever missed.

As fate, or the devil, would have it, Elie Mae and Margie spied me in the crowd and here they came. I noticed Jim getting a plate to go. From that day on I never saw him again.

Huey Black was trying to round up his load of whores when the blast was heard. I can tell you one thing, I used enough dynamite; we could feel the concussion even down at the celebration. Over half of the crowd stampeded toward where the saloon once stood. There was praying, crying, and cursing. It was even noised in the crowd, by the religious bunch, that the girl who hanged herself last night had put a curse on the saloon. But I heard that Huey Black and Calvin blamed it all on Jim, since he couldn't be found.

# Chapter 12

The next day over at the diner, one of the dance hall girls told Miss Faye that she was standing out in front of the pile of sticks when a woman came walking out of the woods with a blanket wrapped around her. She said her eyes got big as saucers; and she swore she would never take another drink. I heard later that she was down at Billy Ridge teaching Sunday school every Sunday morning.

The explosion changed several lives in Silver Springs. I hear the town council now has a jail and a church on the drawing board. It changed Huey Black's life for the worse, as for as I could tell. I understood that two businessmen from back East had their eyes on Silver Springs for a business venture. A saloon and dance hall was their first choice, according to Mr. Grimes over at the grocery store.

It had been a month since the big explosion; and it was still the topic of discussion with anyone you might happen to be talking to. I always made sure I said goodnight to Mrs. Pittman before I would go to bed; she had accepted me as her grandson.

"Now, Wolf, I was thinking, just before you came in here, about the saloon getting wiped off the map."

"What was you thinking, Granny?" I asked as I pulled up a chair near her rocker.

"Well, now, some folk here in Silver Springs thinks that old girl, when she hung herself, she put some kind of a curse on the saloon.

Now, Wolf, I never did believe in that sorter thing. Just what do you think?"

"If I told you, Granny, you probably wouldn't believe it."

"Now, Wolf, if you told it, I would believe it."

"Okay, this is straight from the horse's mouth, so they say. Ruth didn't hang herself. Old man Huey Black grabbed her by her long hair and snatched her quickly around, and her neck popped like a dry twig. This is what Jim told me himself - in person. Then, according to him, old man Huey Black tied a rope around her neck and threw her over the upstairs rail, making it look like she hanged herself when the cleaning lady found her the next morning. Now, it was Jim that was telling me all of this, in person. He was there the night it happened. He also was with Huey Black the night Calvin put three slugs in my pa."

"Well, he ought to know, if he was there."

"He was there that night all right. I was under the house and didn't see who did the actual shooting."

"What about the saloon, Wolf? I haven't seen it, but Faye went up there with Elie Mae and Margie. She said it's just a pile of splinters with a piano setting right up on top."

"Now, Granny, this might be the part you won't believe. Oh, by the way... is it all right to call you Granny?"

"I guess so, it's sounds a little awkward, since I've never been called Granny before. You see, Faye was my only child and never had any children until now. So, go ahead and tell me about the saloon if you know anything about it at all."

"Now, Granny, that is the understatement of the year...I was the one that blew it all to smithereens."

"You was?"

"Yes ma'am, I sure did, I used a little too much dynamite, but it's hard to tell about something like that. I never have blown up a saloon before."

"Now, Wolf, darling, as young as you are, that is hard for me to believe." Granny put both arms on the chair and leaned back.

"See, Granny, I told you that you probably wouldn't believe it, but it was easier than shoeing that horse I tried to shoe last year by myself."

"I know, Wolf, but it seems like a big deal to me," Granny said.

"You can rest assured, it was easy. The hardest part was crawling around under the saloon at night. I never knew if I was gonna meet up with a sidewinder or a scorpion when I was laying all them sticks of dynamite on top of the house blocks." I could tell Granny believed the saloon story now.

"I tell you what, Wolf, let us leave off the sidewinder and scorpion. I'll probably dream about them tonight, but I do want to mention this, Faye is worried to death about you. She tells me she has customers that come in the diner and tell her you are the fastest gun in the whole West. Do you have any idea what this means?...I'll answer my own question; you will be in danger, not most of the time, but all the time, day or night. No matter where you are, someone may step out from around a bush or the corner of a building with an ax to grind or an itch to scratch."

"I have give this lots of thought, believe me, I really have. But until I get the men that killed my pa in cold blood, I just can't get my head on straight. I hope you halfway understand."

"I do, Wolf, and sad to say, it's the law's job, but Silver Springs has no law. It's Huey Black's law - or you will wind up dead; your pa proved that."

"I'm here to change all of that, Granny, if it kills me trying. I have made up my mind to get Huey Black back for murdering my pa. I know, you don't believe in ghosts and curses, but before old man Huey Black dies I'm gonna drive him insane. Killing is too good for him; that would be too quick and easy."

"All I got to say, Wolf, you better watch your back. That old buzzard don't have what he has got by being stupid, you know.

One could tell that spring was in the air. And for one, I was thanking the Lord for some warm weather. The railroad was on the move, also. It was inching right on along north of town. Old man Huey Black was on the move, too. His crew had burned and moved all the rubble from the old establishment and was ready to build

110

back. He had let it be known his new saloon would be the biggest and best this side of the Mississippi River. All I knew, it was costing him a fortune because he was having all his material shipped in from New York and Chicago. Most of the timber and lumber was cut and dried locally. I could say one thing, from the pile of lumber, and all the windows and doors covered up under all that tarp, it was gonna be a monster of a building.

Even Miss Faye was thinking about adding on to the diner, and I couldn't blame her. All the new buildings and businesses coming to Silver Springs with the railroad, not to mention the stockyard that was already under way, would bring her more customers.

Yes-sir-ree-bob! Silver Springs was on the move! The city council appointed Mr. Grimes as mayor until one could be voted on in the summer. And, according to Miss Faye, who was present at the town meeting, they were looking for a sheriff; and the job was now open. She also said that the only one that opposed the idea was Huey Black. I was keeping my eye on that big pile of lumber and material for the new saloon they'd start building any day. It would be a shame if it got struck by lightning and burned up.

Even Miss Faye had caught the spring fever. She decided the diner needed a new coat of paint. I got an early start, and I will admit, it did look better. I cleaned my brush and washed up for dinner.

"Wolf, I want you to say hello to that man, dressed in the gray suit sitting over by the window, before he leaves. He is Charlie Cole. He is in town to build a big saloon," said Miss Faye.

A light came on in my head and I stood there plumb dumbfounded.

"Is anything wrong?" Miss Faye asked.

"Oh, no. I've just been out in the sun too long. Just give me today's special." I strolled on over to where Mr. Cole was sitting. "Pardon me, Mr. Cole...Miss Faye asked me to say hello to you. My name is Wolf Mann."

He picked up a napkin from the table and wiped his mouth. "Won't you sit down, Wolf?" he asked.

"Well, I normally sit over there next to the kitchen, but if you insist." I pulled out a chair and sat down.

"I do insist. I wanted to meet the fastest man with a pistol, in the West. That is what the young ladies told me as I was being served."

"You can't believe half what Margie or Elie Mae says. Those two girls are love struck. All they got their minds on is hugging and kissing, and I'm right in the midst of the whole thing."

"Are you sweet on either one of them?" Mr. Cole asked.

"You might say that, but I can't make up my mind which one I got my druthers on."

"Well, that isn't what I wanted to talk about. They tell me you were right in the midst when the saloon in town blew up. They tell me you knew the man that blew the saloon up."

"That's right, about as good as I know myself. Why do you ask?"

"Well, I wouldn't want someone to blow up my saloon when I get it finished, would you?" Mr. Cole asked.

"Definitely not. And I didn't want somebody to shoot my pa down in cold blood either; but they did and I know who done it!"

"Wait! Wait! Now, Wolf, you need proof to make a statement like that. This man or woman - whoever you said killed your pa - can carry you to court if you don't have proof. I know, Wolf. I'm a retired Chicago lawyer."

"I got proof, I got lots of proof...I seen them shoot my pa."

"You saw them shoot your pa?"

"Well, I didn't see the man that pulled the trigger; at the time I was under our porch and the three men were on horses... I could have touched the horses' legs... and one of them men put three slugs in Pa's chest and he fell to the floor. Mr. Cole, blood from my own pa dripped to the ground through the cracks of the porch, right in front of my eyes."

"You should have told someone and let justice be served. Where was the law, and what about the sheriff?"

"I can tell you didn't run much research on Silver Springs before you made a commitment to put a saloon here," I said.

"Oh, no, Wolf, I'm under no obligation as of yet. I'm just trying to find out if my establishment will pay off in the near future. I'm retired, with money in the bank, and can go to another town."

"I'm only fifteen years old, Mr. Cole, but if I was you, I would break ground as soon as possible and start building your saloon. Read my lips, I haven't said a word, Mr. Cole. The other saloon that is in progress will never be built; and the man that owns it is going bankrupt very soon."

"Wolf, I'm taking you at your word; and being a lawyer for thirty years, I can tell when a man is telling the truth. I specialize in reading between the lines."

"Well, I pray you don't take this retirement too serious. I will need to hire you before the year is out; and you need to get rid of that derby hat before Saturday night. That is between the lines."

Two weeks had passed. I had finished painting the diner and Mr. Cole had broken ground for his saloon. It was practically right across the street from the Huey Black's Silver Slipper. I thought to myself, that's gonna go over like a lead balloon. The one reason Huey Black hadn't started building his saloon – spring round-up had started, and he was selling off some of his cows. I had gotten wind that he wasn't doing all that well financially, and that was playing right into my hands.

Hired help around Silver Springs had become as scarce as hen's teeth. With the spring round-up, the planting of the crops, and all of the new structures going up, it was difficult to find an able body willing to work. I understood that the railroad engineers were purchasing right-of-way property through the valley, which took in our old home place. I had one more chore to do, then I was gonna drop the bomb and let lightning strike.

I rose early this late spring morning and made my way to the stable. I saddled Blackie and rode up to the diner, which was just opening for the day. I thought I would ride out to the Turner ranch and check on his brood cows, which he had never paid me for. I tied up and went inside.

"You reckon someone could find a girlfriend in this place on this beautiful morning?" I called out.

I guess that opened the hen house door. Here came Elie Mae and Margie.

"Could I take your order, sir?" Elie Mae asked. "What would you like to drink this morning, and what type of girl friend are you looking for, sir?"

"Very tall with bright red hair - and my usual with coffee," I said, knowing that Elie Mae was a brunette and Margie had black hair.

The two girls looked at each other then twisted their mouths. "Let 'im get his own coffee," Elie Mae said to Margie, and they started back to the kitchen.

"Wait! Wait, ladies, I was only kidding!" They stopped and came back to see if I'd changed my mind. "No, really what I'm looking for is a cute, little, rich blonde who loves pistols."

"You see what I mean, Margie...there is no hope for Wolf!" Elie Mae stated, "he is hung up on this hair color."

"Wolf! Have you got something against black or brunette headed women?" Margie blurted out.

I started laughing and this riled the girls. So, just before blows broke out I thought I would humble myself.

"Wait! Wait, ladies...this is the honest truth; you see I have my hand on my heart."

The two girls looked at each other and shrugged their shoulders. They did this cross over thing with their arms and waited.

"Really, what it is, you're both so beautiful and so lovely, I can't make up my mind without hurting the other. I couldn't bear to live if I hurt either one of you." I hung my head and closed my eyes, then sniffed a time or two like I was crying.

They both leaned over me and started hugging and kissing my neck, patting me softly, and rubbing my back so gently.

"Wolf, darling, I didn't know you loved me so much."

"That's right, Wolf, baby, we do love you and we are making it so difficult for you to choose between us," Margie said, almost in a crying mode. "Let me move to New York, Wolf darling, and then you won't need to choose between Elie Mae and me."

"No! No, Margie you have a sick mother. Let me move away to California. I love you so much, Wolf."

"Please, no! Elie Mae, if either of you move off I would kill myself. Could you darlings give me a little more time to make up my mind, and help me every chance you get?"

"What are you three doing over at that table?" Miss Faye yelled out, "having a love-in or a séance?...I need some help in the kitchen!" Miss Faye knew how to use a damper, that's for sure.

"I'll get our baby's breakfast. You can get his coffee, Elie Mae," Margie said, raising my head and kissing me right in the mouth.

Don't say it. I know I might have done the wrong thing, but I was loving it, especially the last part. I finished my meal and went by the kitchen before I left. I didn't turn over a can of worms as they say...I had turned over a barrel of snakes. The cheek kissing had evolved into lip kissing.

Miss Faye was at the check-out counter when I started to leave.

"Do you know if anyone has applied for the sheriff's job yet?" I asked.

"Not as I know of, but the town council meets tonight. How about you taking the job?"

"Me! Are you kidding? I'd be done shot somebody, sure as the world."

"Well, you do anyway; you might as well get paid for it."

"Besides, I might be too young, don't you think?" I asked.

"Not if the city council votes you in," explained Miss Faye.

"I know right from wrong, but not enough about the law to be sheriff of a town. Look, my mom-to-be, I'm going over to the general store. Mr. Grimes said I could look at some catalogs on gun rigging. I think I'm gonna start wearing my two pearl handled pistols Aunt Becky Joiner gave me."

"Well, you be careful. I worry for you now more than ever."

It was a slow day, not many folks stirring in the street. Even Mr. Grimes looked laid back.

"Good morning, Mr. Grimes...wonder if you have time to look with me through that catalog you was talking about?"

"I guess so, Wolf. I haven't had a customer this whole morning. Whatcha got in the box?" he asked, coming over to the main check-out counter.

"It's the engraved Colts with pearl handles."

"Well, by gum, Wolf, if that ain't something. You said your aunt just gave 'em to you?"

"Yes, she sure did. They belonged to my Uncle Bob Joiner. As far as I know, they have never been shot."

"I can tell you one thing; you got something to be proud of. Do you want a gun belt for these pistols?"

While Mr. Grimes was admiring the pearl handle grips, some cowboy walked in and began to browse around the store.

"Just one moment, cowboy, I'll be right with you," Mr. Grimes spoke out, as he put the fancy Colt back in the velvet lined case.

I couldn't help but look out the window and see an older man sitting on a well ridden horse, glancing up and down the street. I didn't say anything at the time, but he struck me as a look-out. The fellow in the store was pushing thirty, raw-bony with high cheeks.

I just stood in my space leaning on the counter, while Mr. Grimes eased over to where the cowboy was looking at some tin cups and plates.

"Can I help you, young fellow?...Wait! Wait! Now young fellow you don't need that!"

I wasn't paying that much attention to the two, but what I heard didn't sound like normal dialogue to me. I turned to face Mr. Grimes and the cowboy.

"Don't anybody do anything stupid and you will stay alive!" the cowboy exclaimed, holding a .45 in Mr. Grimes' gut.

"Look, young fellow, if this is robbery I don't have any money in the store right now; I just opened up an hour ago."

"We don't need your money, mister. Me and Dodger robbed a bank over in Gully Town and we need a few Henrys with plenty of ammunition."

I could have already drawn and shot him four or five times, but I didn't want him to shoot Mr. Grimes.

"If you will step over this way, you can help yourself."

"Give me them two leaning right there," the cowboy pointed with his pistol.

Two Henrys were standing together on the end of the gun rack. Mr. Grimes laid them on the counter next to my fancy engraved Colts.

"Now, give me the ammunition!" The cowboy blurted out, at the same time spying my fancy Colts.

"These six boxes are all the cartridges I have in the store for the rifles." Mr. Grimes laid them on the counter next to the rifles.

"That will be fine. I'll just take these fancy six-guns, too."

"I wouldn't do that if I were you, young fellow!"

"And could I ask why? I'm the one holding the pistol."

"Okay, but you are going to make Wolf mad."

"Did you say I'm gonna make the boy mad? Make the boy mad!" the cowboy sneered, "and look, he's wearing a Colt and dressed up in his gunslinger costume, or is that your Halloween trick-or-treating outfit?"

I thought - this will be the first time I have ever drawn on a man holding a gun on me. Mr. Grimes stepped back.

"Why don't you holster your pistol, mister, and draw on me, you yellow belly asshole. You just stay out of this, Mr. Grimes."

"If your mama don't mind, sonny, I would be glad to."

"And, if you don't mind, could we step outside in the street? It's no use getting the floor all bloody. You might want to get your buddy on the horse out there to help you."

"Don't go outside, Wolf, a few guns ain't worth getting killed over," Mr. Grimes begged.

"As for you, old man, you stay right where you are. If you stick your head out the door, I will blow it off."

I made my way out into the street and took my stance to make my play. The cowboy stepped off the boardwalk, stopped about twenty feet in front of me, and eased his pistol slightly back in his holster. I had already taken the thong off my hammer and loosened my Colt in my holster as I was coming outside. I watched him like a hawk. When he moved his right front boot, I fanned three chunks of lead in that direction. The cowboy barely touched the handle of his pistol.

I wheeled quickly and dropped to my knees as the man on the horse went for his six-gun. Too little, too late. I emptied my gun into his heart. He hit the ground with a thud and never moved. I was reloading my Colt when several men, including Rooty Picket and Mr. Grimes, walked up to the scene.

It wasn't long until Archie Dykes from the newspaper showed up, along with Doctor Fletcher, although there was nothing he could do now. Curtis Flynn, from the bank, made his appearance. Of course, word reached the diner, and here came Miss Faye, wringing her hands. Even Kermit Travick from the blacksmith shop was in the midst of onlookers. I think Jerd Coggins was the last of the townspeople to arrive. He drove up in his black hearse to get the bodies.

"Could I have everyone's attention? Please! Could I have everyone's attention?"

Everyone stopped their talking and turned their attention to Mr. Grimes, who had stepped back up on the boardwalk.

"Ladies and Gentlemen, a few minutes ago I was being robbed at the point of a gun, and the robbery was stopped by this gentleman right here!" He pointed to me. I was standing over by the hearse, talking to Kermit Travick about my horse. "Come here a minute, Wolf!" I eased over to where Mr. Grimes was standing. "At our last city council meeting we voted to elect a sheriff; the vote was six to one to do so. But, as far as I know now, no one has applied for the job. I make a motion, that we, as a town, elect Wolf Mann as sheriff of Silver Springs!"

Most everyone yelled out 'yes, yes.'

"What have you got to say, Wolf?"

"You all can believe this or not, but this has already been discussed this morning. I'll give everyone here the answer I gave Miss Faye...I personally think I'm too young."

You could hear murmuring in the crowd as the people discussed the decision.

"Could I say one thing?" Miss Faye asked, stepping up on the boardwalk beside Mr. Grimes, "I am a member on the board. I told Wolf it didn't make any difference the age, it was who the city council voted on, and if he could do the job."

"Does anyone have any other comment one way or the other?"

"There's no doubt that Wolf can do the job. From what I've seen and read, he's the man for the job."

# Chapter 13

On that day, March 19, 1876, I was elected sheriff of Silver Springs. The next two weeks the town rounded up enough money and laborers to construct a jail. Kermit Travick did all the metal work and guaranteed us that nobody could break out of the bars he had built. I had my own office up front and a stable for Blackie around back. The small wood stove and cot in a small room behind my office, was nice...all the comforts of home.

Most of the framework was up for Charlie Cole's new saloon. And I had even seen some workers poking around in Hugh Black's gigantic pile of saloon material. I guess everyone was so busy they didn't have time to get in trouble. Course, I had lots of complaints, mostly from the women: drunken husbands, wife beating, and adultery. My words to them were, "I have no control over these things, ladies. I have only two solutions to your problems...leave 'em or shoot 'em." No one ever took my advice.

The stockyard was built and the train track had come right to the edge of town. Curtis Flynn had remodeled and enlarged the Silver Springs Bank. I thought things were going just too good.

This particular morning when I arrived at my office Josh Turner was sitting on the porch of the jail. I hadn't seen Josh in a few weeks.

"What's going on my man?" I asked as I opened the door. "Bring yourself on in here and give me some good news about our cows."

"Wolf! It's all bad news. Pa sent me over to tell you all our cows are gone!"

"Our cows are gone!!!! For Pete's sake, Josh, what did you and your pa do, sit on your lazy asses whittling and spitting and let them wander off?"

"I told Pa you was gonna be mad," Josh muttered, hanging his head.

I had an idea where they were; but someone would have to go through old man Huey Black's herd to find them. That would be hard to do without getting shot by his men on the range. Sad to say, they had orders to shoot first and ask questions later.

"Have you and your pa tried looking for them?"

"Yes, we have, Wolf. They are not on any of our land, and we won't go on Huey Black's property!"

"Now, Josh, the way I see it, you and your pa was a little slack on watching over your herd. I know that is difficult at best, since it was only you and your pa. But, without much prodding from Huey Black's drovers, the cows are back on their old stomping ground. We had plenty of grass and water, and the brood cows are dropping their calves; and they're as happy as a duck in a dough pile."

"Well, how are me and Pa gonna get them back now?" Josh asked.

"You ain't! And that's out of my jurisdiction. The city council has made it very plain to me: I'm the sheriff of Silver Springs, not the whole Territory of Oklahoma. I'm not to be gallivanting all over the place hunting outlaws."

"I thought you were my friend!" Josh said, getting up to leave.

"Not anymore! I'm your sheriff."

Josh Turner walked out of my office, straddled his mount and rode away. As I sat back down, I began to think about what I had said to Josh Turner: Just how serious am I gonna take this sheriff job? After all, I was getting paid to uphold the law. Who is entitled to the law? Was I breaking the law when I blew up the saloon? Would I be breaking the law when I set fire to old man Huey Black's pile of lumber? Different thoughts were running through my mind.

Was I a hypocrite - defending the law on one hand and breaking it on the other? I knew somewhere in the Bible it said: 'Vengeance is mine sayeth the Lord, I will repay.' I'd heard my pa say that many times. Sometimes, I thought we needed to help Him out.

It was right after dinner when the weather turned for the worse. The sky was dark and in those conditions in Oklahoma, one never knew what to expect: lightning, tornadoes, hail, or a downpour. This is the evening I'd been waiting for. I already had me a gallon of coal-oil and a box of matches. Blackie was saddled. There was no one on the street; most shop owners had closed for the day. Mr. Grimes had brought inside everything usually on display in front of his store.

At times the whole sky would light up. The lightning was as bad as I have ever seen it in Silver Springs. I thought - only a fool would get out in a mess like this. The lightning was popping all over town. I wanted bad weather, but not like this. I had just about built up my nerve to go up the street and set fire to the pile of lumber.

All of a sudden the front door to my office burst wide open. In staggered Jake Nimes, along with a fifty mile an hour wind that blew paper all over the office, and the hat off my head. I thought for a minute the devil had done got me. Now Jake Nimes was practicing to be the town drunk way before I blew the saloon up. Each night he would bum drinks off the customers and, the next morning, drain empty whiskey bottles behind the saloon.

"Wolf! Wolf! Come quick and look up the street, the saloon is burning up!"

I instantly regained my composure, ran out on the boardwalk and looked up the street. It wasn't Charlie Cole's saloon. It was the building material...all of the lumber...belonging to Huey Black.

"Thank you, Lord, thank you very much!"

The flames were leaping to the high heavens. Poor old Jake Nimes was nearly crying. This was where he had gotten addicted to alcohol as a young man. I had heard his story about his family, and even felt sorry for him.

"Cheer up, Jake, you can't cry over spilled milk," I said, still thanking God for this miracle. "Listen, Jake, you hear that?"

"I don't hear nothing, Wolf, but the wind whistling," Jake answered, nearly falling off the boardwalk.

"There it is again, Jake, they are calling my name."

"Wolf, Wolf!" The voice became louder and louder.

"Jake, you can't hear that? I believe the angels are coming after me."

"Wolf, Wolf!" The voice became louder and louder, and closer and closer. The hair on my arms began to stand up .

"I can hear the angel now, Wolf. Do you think they will take me with them to heaven?"

"I don't know, Jake. I don't believe you're ready, but who am I to judge?"

Our angel turned out to be Elie Mae. She was  about to blow away as she came running across the street. She was nearly out of breath and all covered up when she approached me.  As always, she threw her arms around my neck, and I pulled her close.

"Is this you, Elie Mae? What's wrong, darling? Catch your breath and tell me what's going on. Are you scared of the lightning?"

"No, no, Wolf...it is Miss Faye. I think she is a fixing to have that young'un, and she wants you to ride quickly over an' fetch the doctor."

"Wait right here, Elie Mae, darling, I'll be right back. Let me run and get Blackie. Jake, you go inside and close the door and wait until I get back."

I dashed around back, mounted Blackie and came galloping around front.

"Give me your hand, Elie Mae, and swing up behind me; and you'd better hold on tight."

As my pa would always say: 'we lit a shuck' up the street to Doctor Fletcher's office. Elie Mae and I had no trouble seeing, because the fire had the whole north end of town lit up.

I slid off Blackie, handing Elie Mae the reins. "Stay right here, baby, I'll be right back." And with those few words I was knocking on the doctor's door. I heard footsteps coming toward the door; it was Mrs. Mildred. "I need to see Doctor Fletcher!"

"Well, Wolf...I've been expecting him any minute; the weather is so bad I'm beginning to worry."

"Where has he gone?"

"It was about two or three hours ago, that oldest boy of Mrs. Kelley came to get him. Said he thinks his ma fell and broke her hip."

"Thank you very much, Mrs. Mildred." I dashed back to Blackie and mounted up.

"He's over at Mrs. Kelley's house. I know a short cut. You hold on tight, Elie Mae, baby."

Oh well, we were blessed again. He was just leaving.

"Doctor, you are needed over at Miss Faye's house. Elie May says she is in labor."

That's all it took and the doctor was on his way. I prayed he would not be too late.

Elie Mae and I arrived at the house ten or twenty minutes before the Doctor did. She and I rushed inside to check on Miss Faye, who was in plenty of pain. The baby hadn't arrived yet, thank God. Elie Mae and I stepped out of the room while Doctor Fletcher did his examining.

"Can we sit in the swing on the front porch?" I asked Elie Mae.

"Oh that's great, Wolf!" I could tell she was a happy young lady and full of herself tonight. She let me sit down first, and then she sat down as close to me as she could, without sitting in my lap.

"I have great news for you, Wolf...but it might not be great for you at all."

"Now, Elie Mae, I don't understand that kind of talk. You have good news but it's not good news. Maybe you could explain?"

"Well, you said you were having trouble making up your mind between me and Margie."

"Yes, I remember uttering that comment several weeks ago."

"Well, Wolf...the dilemma is over for you. Margie and her folks are moving to California on Thursday. Her pa has a good job out there."

I jumped to my feet pulling Elie Mae up with me. "Let me tell you somethin' girl...you was my choice two weeks ago, before I ever knew Margie was moving. I don't take seconds; so never think Margie was for me. I was just waiting to tell you."

"Wolf, you have made me the happiest girl in the whole world. Can we kiss with passion now?"

"Yes, darling, but let's let it be as far as it goes, you understand?" She nodded and our lips met.

Ever how long it was, Elie Mae broke our kiss. "Darling, is that a baby crying?" she asked softly.

"I'll bet that's my little sister Mama just had."

"Now, Wolf, darling, you don't know that." Elie Mae was pulling me toward the front door.

"I do, too. You wait and see," I held the screen open for Elie Mae as we rushed toward the bedroom.

There stood Doctor Fletcher holding a baby. "It's a little girl, y'all," he announced, with the biggest smile on his face.

Elie Mae looked at me as if to say, how did you know?

"Y'all need to thank Grandma sitting over there. She did all the work - got me the hot water and held the lamp," Doctor Fletcher said.

You could tell Granny was proud she now had a grandchild by her own blood. "Aw, you old fossil, you are just going on," she referred her comment toward Doctor Fletcher.

"Can I call you Mom, now, instead of Miss Faye?"

We all started laughing. Doctor gave the baby back to Mom to nurse, then he and I stepped back into the living room.

"Wolf, how is the sheriffin' job? I haven't seen much of you here lately. Been staying busy?"

"I been staying busy all right, mostly complaints. But I do have two major problems on the horizon. I sold about three dozen brood cows and a handful of plug horses to Mr. Turner and his son Josh, before I went to Ohio. They have set over there on their front porch whittling and spitting and let some of Huey Black's boys run off all their cows. Now, if that isn't enough, when Huey Black finds out that all his material has burned up...you know who he will blame? That's right, Mr. Charlie Cole."

My prediction was right. The first thing the next morning, Charlie Cole showed up with a complaint and wanted to know what I was going to do about it. His men were being threatened on the job - by you know who. Word was out that Huey Black was accusing Charlie Cole's men of setting fire to his pile of lumber.

"So what are you going to do, Wolf? You are the sheriff," Charlie Cole pointed out.

"Mr. Cole, you being a big time lawyer, you've probably forgot more law than this poor boy will ever learn. When is accusing somebody of somethin' agin the law?" I asked.

"Well, there is going to be a killing if this keeps on."

"Now, Mr. Cole, I can do somethin' about a killing," I said dryly.

"This isn't the way it's done in Chicago," Mr. Cole commented.

"This ain't Chicago...this is the rugged Oklahoma Territory - a land of gunslingers, cutthroats, bushwhackers, and renegades. Just get you a Henry and clean house with that mob of polecats."

"Sheriff Wolf, I never heard the like." Mr. Cole got up to leave.

"Well, Mr. Cole, that's what you asking me to do, ain't it?"

Another week passed and Mr. Cole's prediction was right. Two of the men hired to work on the new saloon were bushwhacked - one shot dead right on the job, and the other died at the doctor's office that night.

Needless to say, Mr. Cole was the first one in my office when I opened up the next morning,

"Well, Wolf! You've had your killing, now what are you going to do?" Mr. Cole asked firmly.

I took a warrant document and handed to him. He looked puzzled.

"What is this?" he asked, his face turning red.

"You should know...swear out a warrant for the man or men, and I will go and serve it."

"But I don't know who shot my workers."

"And neither do I!"

"But you are going to do something, aren't you?"

"Yes! I'm gonna serve the warrant just as soon as you get it filled out. And in the meantime, I'm going to scout the area where the shots may have come from. If any of the other workers happened to have seen anything... have them come by the office."

"Sheriff Wolf, I don't think you will be talking with workers from my saloon. They have all quit."

"Well! Can you blame 'em?"

Mr. Cole slightly turned his head. "You know, Wolf...I got a hell-of-a lot to learn about the Oklahoma Territory, haven't I?"

"I guess so...Mr. Cole. Without some law out here, it is two steps forward and three backward. If I did arrest someone and stuck 'em in a cell back there, old man Huey Black's men would have em' out before you could boil a chicken egg," I agreed.

"This is going to be hard for me to admit, Wolf. I'm old enough to be your grandpa and I have never had anyone shoot at me. I understand you have already killed five or six men, and you have just reached your sixteenth birthday."

"Mr. Cole, don't you every consider me to be a hard nosed killer. I have done what I had to do to stay alive. And one day, and it won't be long, I'll call Huey Black and several of his hired guns out for killing my pa. And when the smoke and dust settles, I pray I can avenge my pa's death. There will be bodies lying in the street out there. Nothing says one of 'em won't be my body, shot full of holes and turning the sand red where I lie."

I could tell by Mr. Cole's expression, this wasn't back East talk. As our conversation was coming to close, Mr. Grimes, the store owner, eased in and headed for the coffee pot.

"Good morning, Mayor! Are you here on business or for coffee?" I asked, looking around for my cup,

"Well, it shore ain't for this coffee...Wolf, you need to learn how to cook, or at least make coffee."

We three had a good laugh. Mr. Grimes set his coffee down, and started unfolding a newspaper. "Have either of you read a newspaper from back East, lately?" Both Mr. Cole and I shook our heads "no" and the mayor continued. "Well, it appears the sovereign states has elected themselves a new president while we been out west trying to survive in this rugged territory," Mr. Grimes said, opening up the paper.

"I knew Rutherford B. Hayes was running for president, and Colorado was taken into the union last year," Mr. Cole explained.

"Well, according to the newspaper, we out here in the Indian Territory will be getting some law and order, although we have not became a state of the union, yet. It also says: 'The Territory will now have a governor who will be appointed by the President of the United States. The President will also appoint the Secretary of the Territory and the three members of the Territorial Supreme Court, each of whom will also serve as a judge of the district court. The legislative body is to consist of a Council of thirteen members and a House of Representatives of twenty-six members, all of whom are to be chosen by popular vote, to serve for a term of two years. The statute laws of Nebraska were adopted as the laws of Oklahoma Territory until the same should be modified, amended or superseded by act of the Territorial Legislative Assembly. It was under these laws of Nebraska that the various county, city and township organizations were affected."

"So, what you are saying, Mr. Grimes, is that we have a telegraph, a railroad, and a federal judge, at our asking, is that right?" I asked.

"Yes, and I highly recommend the city council get behind Mr. Cole and have the Territorial Legislative Assembly appoint him as circuit judge of the township of Silver Springs," Mr. Grimes said, looking at Mr. Cole.

"Wait, wait now! I don't know if I'm qualified to be a judge."

"You're more qualified than anyone in this town. You said yourself that you were a lawyer for over thirty years," I said, "and if the city council voted you in, would you take the job?"

"You do plan on making Silver Springs your home, don't you? I see a great future for you here," said Mr. Grimes.

"I guess so, if the people don't mind the judge owning a saloon."

"We'll be voting on a judge, not a preacher!" Mr. Grimes said boldly.

"Well, you know we will be needing one of them soon enough, don't you think?" Mr. Cole acknowledged.

"Okay, I'll be getting a telegram off to Washington right now," said Mr. Grimes as he left my office.

The next two weeks passed with no word from Washington. But things were going well in Silver Springs. By now we were all getting used to smoke from the steam engines and the noise of the railroad The stockyard was in full swing, doing a world of business. Oh yes, the town was growing by leaps and bounds... everything but Mr. Cole's saloon. But neither was Huey Black doing anything about restarting his saloon. One could say it was a Mexican stand-off; but if you asked me, I saw a killing brewing.

There was one more issue that was pressing; that was the thirty five head of brood cows that belonged to old man Turner - cows that he never paid me for. Something had to be done, but to do something without some bloodshed was near impossible. What was that old saying Pa would use? 'Where there's a will, there's a way.' I had the will, but just hadn't found a way yet.

With nothing more to do but sit around the sheriff's office and think, I picked up the newspaper Mr. Grimes had left a few weeks ago and began to read through the few pages, mostly looking at the pictures. I didn't read all that well. After nearly dozing off several times, this monstrosity of a thing that favored a rifle caught my eye. 'Shoots accurately - more than a mile', the paper read. Now I wouldn't mind having me one of these toys. 'Comes complete with the rifle, a telescope and carrying case', for ninety-eight dollars. Just between you and me, I thought the Sheriff's Department needed one of these babies. So, without too much fanfare, I ordered the rifle from New York.

Now, being sheriff of Silver Springs came with lots of advantages as well as disadvantages, such as hearing rumors on folks, both good and bad. The latest rumor, and it could be the truth - Huey Black was broke, out of money. According to my source this is why he hadn't started to build his saloon back. First of all, Huey Black had built a very lavish house on his ranch that cost thousands. Then he bought my pa's ranch and paid twice what it was worth. Last, but not least, all that material and fine lumber for the saloon went up in smoke - not to mention the payroll for his hired help each week.

This was what Mr. Grimes told me that Curtis Flynn told him; each time Huey Black went east he would draw large sums of money out of the bank and carry with him. Now this was just hearsay, but Huey Black had supposedly lost a fortune gambling.

As my pa would say: 'if something doesn't happen soon then something is gonna happen', and that it did. I had finished up a good breakfast at the diner and had some fun with Mom and Elie Mae. I could tell it was gonna be a hot day as I moseyed on my way to the office. I was expecting my gun in on the train today, and I was hoping to ride out to see Josh Turner and his pa.

# Chapter 14

I was about rock-throwing distance from the bank when Curtis Flynn, the president of the bank, came running out into Main Street screaming his head off.

"The bank has been robbed! The bank has been robbed!"

It being Saturday morning, Main Street was filling up. I dashed to the bank to see what all the noise was about. It didn't take me long to see that somebody had robbed the bank. The vault door was blown might near off the hinges, a trace of black powder was still evident, but the bank safe was cleaner than a hound's tooth. Evidence showed that whoever did it had come through the back door. It had probably happened during some bad weather about three o'clock that morning. The robbers had used two mattresses, from a bed in a small back room, to silence the noise of the blast.

Curtis Flynn, the bank president, asked the onlookers to leave the bank. He announced that it would open soon. Someone had drug the mattresses back to the small room in the back. As far as I could see, there was not a clue in or around the vault. I went to the back door and I could tell it had been half rotten before it was broken into. I went into the back room where the two mattresses were put back. I was examining the top mattress when I snorted the scent of Rum-Maple tobacco. Now ain't that something - Huey Black had been here. I made my way back up front where Curtis Flynn and Mr. Grimes were standing together talking.

"Pardon me. How long has it been since Huey Black has been in this bank?"

Curtis Flynn and Mr. Grimes looked at each other. I'm sure his name had been brought up.

"Sheriff, I haven't seen Huey Black in the bank in over a week, or longer."

"Well, sir! He is your man, without a doubt!" I said boldly.

"They are some strong words, Wolf. How can you be sure?" Curtis Flynn questioned, looking around to make sure no one was hearing me. "This town is scared to death of Huey Black and his murdering outlaws."

"Come to the back with me; you too, Mr. Grimes." I led the way and we went into the small room where the two mattresses were. Mr. Grimes was closer to the bed where the mattresses lay.

"Lean over, Mr. Grimes, and tell me what you smell."

He did as told and began to sniff like a good Red-Bone trying to pick up a deer trail. He then slowly straightened up and looked right at Curtis Flynn. "Wolf has got'em nailed, Curtis, that mattress is full of Rum-Maple tobacco smoke."

"Now, now, Grimes, let us not jump to conclusions. Other folks use that kind of tobacco."

"Not in this town they don't, Curtis. I stock Rum-Maple smoking tobacco only for Huey Black, because he asked me. No one else has ever asked for it since I've been in business," Mr. Grimes answered. With a trace of disbelief from Curtis Flynn, Grimes nodded at me.

"We could form a posse and go after him. Mr. Flynn, you could even ride along with us." I remarked, watching Curtis Flynn turn three shades of yellow, mostly down his back.

"Oh, I'm sorry, Sheriff, I don't ride well. Someone needs to stay in town to watch over the bank. I have men working on the door around back, you know."

"That is right and I'm not ready to lead a one man posse by myself." I looked around once more, and figured I had done all I could in the bank. I headed for the front door.

"Are you leaving?" Mr. Grimes asked.

"I guess so, there's nothing else I can do here."

"Let me walk with you," he said and we made an exit. On the way to the General Store, we talked as we walked along.

"Wolf, Silver Springs is a very nice town now but we got one sore spot!"

"You're saying it's like sticking a splinter in your finger, it stays festered up until you get it out."

"That a very good analogy, Wolf, and old man Huey Black is that splinter. We know he shot your pa, or had it done. You and I know he robbed the bank," Mr. Grimes stated.

"Yeah, and he shot two of Mr. Cole's men or had it done, not to mention killing Ruth Allen and throwing her body over the rail as if she had killed herself. We have all this knowledge, Mr. Grimes, but our hands are tied," I said.

"But, Wolf, there must be something that can be done."

"Yeah! Kill 'im."

"I know, Wolf! But that's against the law," Mr. Grimes pointed out.

"Killing my pa was against the law, too!"

"I know, and so is robbing the bank; but two wrongs don't make a right."

Just before Mr. Grimes went in the store I told him of my plan. "I've thought on this a lot, Mr. Grimes, and I've decided to break into Huey Black's house and find the money he stole from the Silver Springs Bank."

"Break into his house!"

"That's what I said. I'm going to climb up on top of his house and go down through the chimney."

"Surely you're not serious!" Mr. Grimes quickly snapped back.

"I darn shore ain't gonna walk up to the front door and knock." We both started to laugh. "Oh, by the way, I need to get about fifty foot of rope before I leave the store."

Mr. Grimes looked at me as to say...God have mercy on your soul. He got me the rope.

I eased on over to the new train depot and went in to survey the premises.

"Can I help you, sir?" A voice came from behind the counter but I didn't see anyone. I thought the clerk was lying down or maybe the railroad had hired a midget who couldn't be seen over the counter.

"I need to pick up a package." I made my way on over to the counter and strained to see what the problem was.

"Are you alright, Mister?" I asked.

The poor man was sitting down right in the middle of the floor. "I'm okay, sir, I just can't get these boots to go on," the clerk replied.

"Why didn't you try 'em on when you bought 'em?" I asked.

"They were a present from Mother, back East. She says everyone out West wears boots."

"Maybe they are too little, or your socks are too thick."

"Have you ever had this trouble?" the man asked, trying desperately to get the boot on.

"Only when I've stepped in some dog pee."

The depot attendant looked up at me as if I was putting him on. "What has dog pee got to do with putting on a pair of boots on?"

I stood there thinking to myself, how did this man get this important job with the railroad? "Dog pee makes your sock wet on the bottom, and your foot won't slide in your boot," I told him.

"We don't have any dogs around here, but I did walk through some spilled water. What did you do when you walked through the dog pee?"

I thought to myself this is ridiculous. "You need to turn your sock over."

134

"Turn my sock over...what will that do?"

"Well, for one thing, the sock will be dry on the bottom and your boot will slide right on." I stood there like a complete idiot watching the transaction.

"I'm sorry to keep you waiting, mister, but you're a pretty smart fellow."

"I know. That is why the Town Council hired me to be sheriff."

"Now what was that you wanted?" he asked, walking around in his new boots.

"A package! A package for Wolf Mann."

"Was it supposed to be here?" he asked, still prancing around behind the counter, "I don't see it anywhere, do you?"

"No I don't see it out front lying on the counter. Maybe it's in the back. Maybe, while you're breaking those new boots in your ma sent ya you could sashay around in the back. It's probably lying on a shelf back there."

Well, he disappeared behind a heavy brown curtain that led to the back and I leaned over the counter and waited and waited and waited.

"Everything okay back there?" I called out.

I didn't hear a word. I just figured he didn't hear me so I waited a few more minutes. Getting me an attitude to give this joker a piece of my mind, I walked around the counter that ran nearly all way across the front of the depot and peeped behind the heavy brown curtain. I didn't see or hear him but the back door was wide open. Of course, it was hard to hear anything because of the steam engine sitting just a few feet from the back of the depot.

I'd had enough of this foolishness, so I went into the back and started down the aisle between the shelves toward the back door. There lay the man with the new boots - bleeding from the head. I quickly checked him out. He was still breathing and just seemed to be knocked out by a pistol whipping.

I ran out the back door. There stood two men with rags in one hand and an oil can in the other.

"Did you fellows see anybody come out of this back door?"

"Two men just rode off on horses, going that way," one of the men stated.

"Is that all you seen?" I asked in a loud voice.

"I'm afraid so, sir," the other man spoke up.

"You two might want to knock off an' check on the railroad employee that is down on the floor just inside the depot. I'm going to see if I can chase the two men that hit him."

As soon as I turned to go get on Blackie, I smelled a whiff of Run-Maple tobacco scent lingering in the air. Was it one of the two men with the oil cans?...That would be easy enough to find out.

I quickly mounted Blackie and rode around to the back door of the train depot. By this time, the two men had the clerk on his feet.

"Do either one of you gentlemen smoke?" I asked.

"We don't smoke, mister, but you are welcome to my plug," one of the men said, reaching toward me with a plug of chewing tobacco.

"Thank you anyway, sir." I pulled the reins around, kicking Blackie in the ribs and commenced to follow the trace of Rum-Maple scent in a hurried fashion. It wasn't long until I caught up with the two riders; but I kept my distance. I supposed it to be Huey Black and Calvin, his bodyguard, the man who had given me the spurs. The two riders turned off the main trail and headed for the H B Ranch. I knew then it was Huey Black and his hired killer. It wasn't any use to go farther. I'd just get my head blown off by some of his look-outs.

I turned Blackie around and headed back to the railroad depot to see if "new boots" had found the package with my new rifle and scope. I did lots of soul-searching on my back to the depot. How long could this go on? How long could Huey Black do what he wanted to in Silver Springs? Could I outdraw Calvin when it came to a show down? Could I outdraw both of them? Calvin sticks to old man Huey Black like a tick on a dog's ear. I can tell you one thing; I ain't scared to call them out. That's what I ought to do, right on Main Street, one Saturday morning, before a crowd of people.

I guess I was only a half-mile from Silver Springs when I saw a rider coming. I flipped the thong off the hammer of my Colt and pulled it up and down in my holster several times. I just might have to draw on someone. Whoever it was, they were in more of a hurry than I was. I pulled up and turned sideways to see who it was. Of all people, it was Jake Nimes, the town drunk.

"Mr. Wolf! Mr. Wolf! Kermit Travick loaned me this horse and told me to come and find you."

"Just slow down now, Jake, and tell me what Kermit sent you out here to tell me."

"Mr. Wolf, he said there is two men waiting at the sheriff's office to kill you!"

"How did Kermit Travick know I was out here on the Old South Road?" I asked, as he and I started on back to town.

"He said he saw you following two men out this way. He said he didn't recognize the two men, but he couldn't mistake your horse."

"I sure thank you, Jake, you might have saved my life. I think that calls for a fifth of hard liquor, don't you, Jake?"

"Oh, yes, Mr. Wolf. Bless you in that gun fight. I'll be praying for you."

He and I passed by the livery before I rode on up to the jail. Kermit Travick saw us coming and was waiting out front of the blacksmith shop.

"Wolf, I don't know who the two men are, I've never seen them before. They asked if I knew you, and I told them I did and that you were the sheriff here in town. I also told then that you had ridden out of town, and no telling when you would be back. I had hopes that they would get discouraged and leave before you come back. Well, they didn't leave - but rode straight to your office and dismounted.

"Is that their two horses tied up in front of the jail house?" I asked, riding further out into Main Street.

"That's their two horses, alright; but I don't see hide or hair of them, do you?"

"I just imagine they are standing around to the side out of the sun. What did they look like, Mr. Kermit?"

"Now, let me see, I kinda specialize in judging character. They were both in their late twenties; one was wearing his gun rigging low, while the other didn't have his holster tied to his leg. Their mounts were run-of-the-mill, nothing fancy, just a couple of plow boys if you ask me. But you never can tell; sometimes a barking dog will bite."

"Well, Mr. Kermit, I'm sure much-obliged to ya for sending Jake to warn me. Sorry I messed up your work. Now, let me get to mine. Jake, you might as well go on over and tell Jerd Coggins he will be needed up at the jail house."

I rode slowly right up Main Street toward the jail. I have never been in a hurry to kill someone or get killed myself. It's times like this I wished I was in some other profession. As Pa would say: 'You made this bed, old boy, now you sleep in it.'

I was across the street from the jail house when I stopped, slowly dismounted, and looked all around. I tied Blackie to a hitching rail and rubbed my face on his long jaw, "You be praying for me, old buddy." He nodded his head as if he knew what I was up against.. I left Blackie across the street from the jail and walked across the street to where the men were. I sure didn't want him to catch a stray bullet, if I could help it.

It was a beautiful day, not a cloud in the sky. It was high noon and the sun wasn't favoring either one of us. I flipped the thong off the hammer of both pistols and screwed my hat tight on my head.

Every killing is different, I thought, as I started across the street toward the jail. Would they both come out and stand together - or one hide and bushwhack me from behind a building? One thing for shore, I was a gonna find out. I stopped in the middle of the street and took my stance just like Calvin had taught me. I reckon the young man was standing in the shade watching me when I rode up. I stood my ground as he came out in the edge of the street and began to shift his boots in the loose sand.

"I hear tell you came to kill me, is that right?"

"That's right..." and that's the last he ever said on this earth.

I drew and fanned three bullets right through his heart – leaving a hole one could stick a fist through. I kept my stance, looking for the other fellow to run out shooting. He ran out alright, but he wasn't shooting. He had his hands in the air waving. When he reached the man I had just shot, he fell across his body and began to scream.

"I told you, Curtis! I told you not to come over here, Curtis! Mama even told you not come over here." The man looked up at me with the saddest eyes. "You've killed two of my brothers, mister. This was my youngest brother, Floyd, he was twenty-six. You killed my older brother, Donald, robbing a stage coach several months back."

It's times like this you are lost for words and don't know what to say.

"My brother, lying here, has already killed two men in Texas; and one of them was a lawman."

He reached in his pocket and took out a piece of paper and slowly unfolded it, then handed the paper to me. At first glance I could tell it was a reward poster for a thousand dollars, dead or alive.

"You killed him, mister. I thank you, and Mama thanks you. Have you got a place to bury him around here, Sheriff? I'll pay for his burial," the man said, as he got up.

By this time, many folks had gathered around, including the undertaker, Jerd Coggins.

"I don't believe I caught your name, sir, but I'll be more than happy to give your brother a proper burial. I'm sure Kermit Travick up at the livery stable will buy your brother's horse and saddle. That is, if you don't plan on taking them back with you."

"My name is Robert Corby. Everyone just calls me Rob back home in Paris, Texas. My pa was an outlaw and my two brothers grew up following right in his footsteps."

"Is your pa still living?" I asked, nearly feeling sorry for the man.

"Oh no, a Texas Ranger shot and killed him several years ago while he was robbing a bank in central Texas.

"Well, Rob, I hate to hear about all the tragedy you've had in your life. I apologize for being part of it. Tell you what, while the undertaker takes care of your brother's body and Kermit Travick takes care of your horse, I'd like to take you over to Faye's Diner. She is my mom and the dinner won't cost you a cent."

"That's right neighborly of ya, Sheriff. I don't know the last time I had a square meal."

Word of the shooting had done made it over to the diner by the time Rob and I walked in. The girls were wringing their hands and biting their fingernails. I introduced Mom and Elie Mae to Rob, then took my favorite table by the kitchen.

# Chapter 15

Elie May served our food, with pep in her step.

"Mr. Rob! The Sheriff and I are getting married one of these days. He's done and asked me, well, near about. Ain't that right, Sheriff Wolf Mann?" She smiled and stood there waiting for my answer.

"I guess so, Sugar Plum, if I'm not killed by then."

Mom made her way over to our table before Rob and I finished eating. She came up behind me and put her arms around my neck. "Did Mr. Grimes tell you the Town Council received a letter from Washington this morning?"

"No! I haven't seen'em. I have been chasing crooks and getting almost killed."

"Oh well, the Town Council is having a special meeting tonight at seven o'clock."

"I'll be there, if my rifle didn't come in on the train." I could tell she didn't know what I was talking about. She twisted her lips and started back to the kitchen.

Rob and I ate and drank our fill, said good-bye to the ladies, and headed back over to the jail house. By the time we returned things were back to normal. I took down some information from Rob and sent him on his way with a pocketful of money. I went around back in the shade, mounted Blackie, and started over to the railroad depot.

I began to look around for Jake Nimes, because I owed him a bottle of rot-gut. I forgot Jake Nimes was on Jerd Coggins payroll - digging graves for our illustrious undertaker. I tied Blackie to the rail and eased on in the depot. The counter clerk looked like he had been in a hatchet fight - and every one had had a hatchet but him. He was reading a book when I walked in but quickly caught my gaze.

"I found your package after you left, Sheriff." He laid his book down, walked to the end of the counter and slid the box my way. "If you will, just sign here and you can be on your way."

"Could I ask you a question before I go? I know who the two men were that pistol whipped you. If you want to swear out a warrant for their arrest I'd be more than glad to arrest them."

"I know who they were too, Sheriff, and I want to stay alive; if it's alright, let's just drop the subject. Besides, it was a personal matter anyway."

I picked up my package and walked out, wondering what Huey Black and the depot clerk had going on between them. I rode back around to the jail house and tied Blackie in the shade, so he could nibble on the bale of hay and drink from the tub of water that waited on him there.

As I started in the back door, I heard a train whistle blow. The connection between "new boots" - the railroad clerk, and Huey Black began to make sense. The train that was robbed last Thursday was supposed to have been carrying the payroll for the workers; but it wasn't on board. The clerk fed Huey Black some bad information about the strong box that was coming in by freight; it was on a different train. And "new boots" paid the consequences with a .45 barrel up side his head. The way I had it figured, Huey Black was blackmailing "new boots." I might as well have been barking at the moon, since I had no proof.

I put the package on my desk and began to open the well-packed box. Naturally the gun came unassembled; and I needed some tools to do the job of putting the rifle and scope together. As I read the instruction book that came with the rifle, I found I had all the tools I would need in my desk drawer.

I can say one thing, according to the size and weight of this monstrosity - I believed it would do what the instructions said, and more: 'Will shoot with accuracy, up to one mile, do compensate for the wind.' I couldn't wait to zero my scope in. I knew I would go where one could see for a mile or more. The instructions made mention of a higher powder load that would make the rifle more deadly. The rifle came with two boxes of ammunition. I would have to make sure to buy the same brand and bullet weight or the sights would need to be readjusted again.

As I sat there admiring my gun I said to myself, "The scope on this rifle is worth the price of the rifle. You know, I'll bet I could get close enough to see if our cows are on Huey Black's ranch without being seen. I have my work cut out for me tomorrow. I will also run by and see Josh Turner and his lazy pa."

I put my gun under the mattress in the back room, locked the jail house and started over to the diner to get a meal before tonight's meeting.

When I entered the diner, here came Elie Mae. "Are you ready for your supper, now?" she asked, and followed me over to my favorite table next to the kitchen. "I didn't embarrass you today when I mentioned us getting married to that stranger, did I?

"Oh no, that was Rob, nice fellow. I had just killed his younger brother, or did you know that?" I asked, sitting down.

Elie May also sat down and took both of my hands and nearly started crying. "Wolf, can I say that I love you, sometimes? I know how you are; you don't want a girl hanging on to you or embarrassing you in front of your friends. But, Wolf... can I call you Darling, when there is no one around? I'm sorry, I'll get your supper. I'm making a fool of myself.

While Elie Mae was rustling me up some grub, Mom came over to my table. "Son, I'm going over to the house to feed your baby sister and get ready to go to the meeting tonight."

"I'll see you over there after a while. I'm gonna eat and help Elie May close up."

Mom closed the front door to the dinner and turned the OPEN and CLOSED sign around. There was no one in the diner now but Elie Mae and me. I could hear plates and cups rattling and clinking together. I couldn't see Elie Mae from where I was sitting. I eased up and made my way into the kitchen. She was washing up a few dishes in a big sink and didn't notice me when I walked in behind her. I put both arms around her waist and drew her very close to me, laying my chin on her shoulder.

"Wolf, I hope that this is you! What do you want?"

"I came in here to make a fool out of myself."

She struggled to turn around to face me. She dried her hands, discarded the towel, and put both arms around my neck.

"Can I help you make a fool out of yourself, Darling?" she asked. Then our lips met.

This was the first time she and I ever made what she called "passionate love making." I knew one thing, when Elie Mae whispered, "I love you, Darling," in my ear it became real habit forming, even better than sopping syrup.

The meeting had already started by the time I got there, thanks to Elie Mae. Mr. Grimes had the floor and was explaining the letter from Washington. I was having a hard time getting my mind on this meeting. If they knew what I had given up to come to this dumb, dry meeting, they would give me a raise - to buy me a gallon of syrup. I wonder if Elie Mae loves sopping syrup as much as I do?

"Sheriff! Sheriff! Are you listening to the meeting going on? We're voting, and you were talking about sopping syrup."

"I vote yes, order two cases of Blue Ribbon cane syrup."

"Sheriff! The committee isn't voting on buying syrup. Are you all right? We all understand the trauma of two men coming to town trying to kill you this morning, Sheriff, and how it affects an individual."

"It ain't killing that messed up my head, Mr. Grimes, it's all that syrup sopping I did a while ago."

Oh well, I came to myself, and found out if I locked someone up in the hoosegow we could get a judge over in a short time. Mr. Charlie Cole was concerned about bringing law and order to the Oklahoma Territory.

"I make a move to vote Huey Black off the board of directors in town," Curtis Flynn offered. "We have proof he was instrumental in robbing the bank."

"I'll second that motion," said Kermit Travick, "he killed Fred Mann in cold blood, and we have a witness to the killing."

"Okay, you heard the motion - all in favor say aye, all that opposed say nay - the aye's have it."

Huey Black was voted off the board by one hundred per cent. I couldn't help thinking, instead of opening up a can of worms, this bunch here tonight turned over a barrel of snakes. The meeting was dismissed and Mom and I headed for the big house.

"What do you think is going to happen when Huey Black finds out he has been voted off the board?" she questioned.

"Mom, your guess is good as mine. I would prefer to put him in jail, rather than kill him."

"Son, which ever way it goes, don't you take any chances. I couldn't stand to lose you," Mom said, taking my hand.

"Mom, do you care if me and Elie Mae get married one day? I'm going on seventeen."

"I don't mind, Son. I know one thing…that little girl loves you. That's all she talks about. Why, if something happened to you, it would kill her."

"I think I fell in love with her tonight, Mom."

"She will make you a good wife, Son. I have no doubt."

"I don't know what will happen from one day to the next as long as Huey Black is alive. He thinks he owns this town; and he will get rid of anybody that gets in his way."

"We will see what tomorrow brings. As you said one time, as long as you don't lock up any of Huey Black's hired killers you aren't in any danger."

"I hope you are right, Mom, but one day if someone breaks the law I will lock him up or kill'em."

"And that's what is worrying me, Son."

"Mom, don't you worry about me as long as I got two Colts hanging on my hips. You don't know just how good I am with a six-gun. I have got to stay alive to prove I am the youngest gunslinger."

"Well, if you don't mind, Son, I'll be praying for you all the while."

Mom and I went on into the house and I made my way over to where Granny was sitting in her rocker. I gave her a big hug, then sat down beside her in a wing back chair.

"Did you have a good day, Wolf?" Granny asked, laying her embroidery over to one side.

"Don't let me stop you, Granny; what you are doing is sure looking pretty."

"I'm getting tired and my eyes are hurting anyway. You never did answer my question."

"Well, let me put it this way...I have had better days; but I plan to have a better day tomorrow."

"Could I ask what is so special about tomorrow, Wolf?" Granny asked, as she leaned back in her rocker and closed her eyes.

"Granny, I ordered me a long rifle that will shoot a cotton picking mile, according to the instructions. It has a scope I can put on the rifle - as long as my leg. According to the papers that came with it, I'll be able to read the label on a Mason jar a mile off. Now, don't you let on to anybody I have this contraption. I don't mind telling you I am gonna use it. I also ordered a silencer with the scope and rifle. That was optional." I could tell I had lost Granny with all these newfangled mechanical devices.

"My lord, Wolf, it won't be long they will be putting engines on wagons."

"I don't think so, Granny. How would you steer it without a horse?"

Granny shrugged her shoulders and twisted her mouth. "Wolf, darling, that may be the hold up."

I was up the next morning over at the diner when Mom got there. I was talking to Elie Mae and helping her fire up the wood stoves. I ate a good breakfast and asked Elie Mae to fix me some vittles to go. I hugged and kissed the girls goodbye and told them to pray for me today. They never knew what to expect when I walked out of the diner anymore.

I headed for the foothills just south of Huey Black's ranch, still trying to conjure up a plan to bring his numbers of hired hands and sharp shooters to a bare minimum. I tied my horse in the bushes at the foot of the mountain that overlooked old Huey Black's ranch house. I made my way up to the top of the mountain with my new toy. Out of sight, I made myself comfortable, and began to install the scope on the barrel of the long gun, according to the instructions. Piece of cake, I thought. I shoved the silencer up on the barrel of the rifle and tightened all four screws, just as instructed. Of course, I knew how to load the rifle, for it was a bolt action that just held one shell.

I looked down through the scope. My, my, what a view! I noticed the windmill in the barnyard, first. The water tank took up the entire scope, so this was a perfect target to sight with my new rifle. I put in a cartridge, put the cross hairs right in the middle of the water tank, and pulled the trigger. I didn't hit the water tank, but I scared the devil out of a dozen or more chickens feeding under it.

I quickly put in another cartridge and raised the back sights, placing the cross hairs in the middle of the water tank, and pulled the trigger. I didn't hit where I was aiming; but I struck water - low and to the right. I made a modification to the rear sights and put in another cartridge. I placed the cross hairs in the middle of the water tank and pulled the trigger. Bull's-eye! Water was squirting out twenty feet in the barnyard. The ducks and geese were having a ball. I tweaked the rear sights and brought the pattern to the size of a water bucket hanging on the barn.

I went ahead and put six more holes in the water tank, close to the bottom. I shot holes in all the cow and horse troughs. I also shot holes in the coal-oil tank that sat in the back yard of the house. That would put a stop to the lights. I shot the transmission to the wind blades and watched the black oil drain to the ground.

Oh well, I guess when I hit the transmission, fifty feet up in the air, it made a noise that was heard in the house. Two cowboys came running, watching the water pour to the ground. I just figured I had worn out my welcome so I packed up and moved out. On my way back to the sheriff's office, it dawned on me what might be the consequences of this rampage I just endeavored in. I heard Mr. Cole using those big words.

Now speaking of Mr. Charlie Cole...just as shore as a hog will wallow, old man Huey Black would blame Charlie Cole for doing the damage to his place. And, to make matters even worse, when I came riding back into town, Charlie Cole had hired five or six men to work on his unfinished saloon. I pulled up and looked the situation over, thinking to myself: as sure as a momma cat will lick her kitten, there's gonna be a killing right here this morning - just as soon as old man Huey Black can assess all the damage he has incurred at his ranch.

I just figured Huey Black's men would pull the same stunt as last time, and ambush the men working on the saloon from the woods across from the unfinished building. I remembered there were three or four sticks of dynamite still in my saddle bags. I kicked Blackie gently in the ribs and rode out in the brush - about where I thought the shooting would be. I rid my saddle bags of the four full sticks of dynamite and with a small, wild, green grapevine, I made a bundle. Then I pulled it up in a skinny pine so it could be seen from the porch of the jail house.

Me and Blackie rode out of the thicket without even being noticed. Blackie was happy to have fresh cool water and peanut hay to munch on until the shooting started.

I went through the back door and put on a pot of coffee. I just had an idea I would be having some visitors soon. While my coffee was brewing, I put a round in my long gun and stood it just behind the front door. Christmas is slow coming but I don't think we have ever missed one yet. I poured me a cup of java, went out on the porch, and took the load off my boots. I leaned back against the wall in a straw bottomed, straight chair - and waited.

I could barely hear the hammers up the street, but I knew the workers were still busy on the saloon. I carried my cup back inside the small kitchen and brought my long gun back with me. Using a porch post for a prop, I leaned the rifle up against it and sighted the scope until I found the bundle of dynamite. It was a clear as crystal perfect shot.

Just before I took the rifle down, I had to do a double take. I thought I saw something in the background. On the second scan, I could faintly see four or five horsemen dismounting. They all had rifles.

I carefully placed the cross hairs back on the bundle of dynamite and waited until I heard the first shot. I slowly pulled the trigger and did myself some land clearing up the street. I ran back through the jail, hiding my rifle. I mounted Blackie, and with a fast gallop I was on the scene before the leaves stopped falling. By this time, most of the workers from the saloon were over in the midst of the cowboys — who all now had bad hair dos and were hard of hearing.

"Gather up all the rifles and hand guns, these men are going to jail," I said to a young men standing by. "The rest of you catch up their horses. Do you have a wagon over at the saloon?" I asked the older man who had been shot in the shoulder.

"Yes, sir, Sheriff, it's still hitched up."

"Get one of the younger men to run over to the building and get it. I don't believe two of these scum bags can walk."

The five men were gentle as lambs, still wondering what went wrong. I noticed two of the men that were closest to the blast were bleeding from the mouth. By the time I got the bunch loaded in the wagon and on the way to jail, we had a pretty good audience - because the blast did create some curiosity in Silver Springs.

"I see we're going to christen the new jail today." I quickly turned around, and there stood Mr. Grimes and Doc Fletcher.

"Am I glad to see you two, especially you, Doctor! You need to check these men over and give your bill to the mayor, there."

"I might as well telegraph the circuit judge and have him come to town so we can have a trial for these men as soon as possible."

"That's right, and I hope to have Huey Black and his hired guns behind bars, too, if I haven't killed them first."

It seemed that everybody that was anybody was milling around the jail house, wondering what had happened to Huey Black's men we had just locked up.

# Chapter 16

No one was saying anything, but there was a feeling in the wind that the town had gone against Huey Black and finally locked up some of his men. Everyone knew what he would do to get this town back under his thumb. This town was full of cowards, including all of the City Council, even Mr. Grimes. "Don't rock the boat and everything will be fine," he would say. Everything was not fine. He had killed my pa.

I know what the whole town was thinking right now. Apologize to the five men you've just locked up and turn them loose. Don't make Mr. Huey Black mad, or he will ride in here and shoot up the town.

"Sheriff, I need to talk to you; and I believe I have the consent of all the townspeople and the Town Council. What are we all going to do when Huey Black rides in here tomorrow, kills you, and breaks all his men out of jail?"

"Then, I suppose you order some yellow paint and start with your store. Paint Doctor Fletcher's house next – and then take orders from Huey Black the rest of your life."

Mr. Grimes hung his head and walked out the back door of my office. I waited for the doctor, locked up all the cells, then the front and back doors, taking the keys with me. Blackie was still saddled, so I mounted and rode over to the diner. As always, Elie Mae met me at the front door, threw her arms around my neck and gave me a juicy kiss.

"Look, I want you to do something for me." I handed her the ring of keys. "Keep these keys. If I'm not back by dark, when you leave for home, hang the key ring over the knob on the front door of the jail and walk off."

"Okay, I will. By the way, how was the dinner I packed for you?"

"I will find out soon, I'm gonna eat it for supper."

"Wolf, Darling, I heard you arrested five men and locked them up in your jail," she said, all excited.

If Elie Mae only knew.

"I don't know about it being my jail. I'm gonna ride over to see Josh Turner and his pa. I'll see you in the morning and we'll do more kissing." I knew this made her day. I blew a kiss to Mom in the kitchen and left the diner.

On the way over to Josh's house, I thought I would see what Elie Mae had fixed me for dinner. I untied the syrup bucket hanging on my saddle bag and opened it up. Well, bless her little pea-picking heart; there was a cat head biscuit the size of a saucer, with a pork chop, as big as a horse collar, stuck right in the middle. I pulled up by a clear stream and Blackie began to drink while I filled my canteen with cool water. I was riding and eating my fill.

"Blackie, you don't know what you are missing, you should have been a man." I quickly thought about what Huey Black was going to say and do when his five cowboys didn't come back from town. "No Blackie, I'm sorry, you're better off as a horse."

I looked back in the bucket and there was another biscuit, just drenched with cow butter and blackberry jelly. I took one bite and knew it was a sin to eat the whole thing in front of Blackie, so I tore off a chunk and reached way around and gave it to him. I could tell that put some pep in his step. I continued to eat. Then Blackie stopped right in the middle of the road and stretched his neck way around, looking up at me, licking his lips.

"You want another bite, don't you?"

Now if I told you he nodded his head up and down, you would think I was lying. I tore off another big bite, gave it to him and we went on to my destination. Josh was whittling on a stick, and his pa was seeing how far he could spit tobacco juice into the front yard without hitting a chicken.

"How are you fellows doing this fine evening?" I asked, dismounting to let my saddle cool.

"Just tolerable, Sheriff; I've been under the weather and Pa's gout has about got'em down. None of the chickens are laying and both cows are dried up," Josh Turner answered, laying his whittling stick down by his side.

"Well, you two, cheer up. I've got a job for the both of you and you will get paid. If we're lucky, you can get your cows and horses back."

That seemed to encourage the duo. At least, I got their attention.

"Is that right, Sheriff? You know that me nor Pa gets around very pert anymore."

"Well, Josh, this job is right down your alley. All you need to do is use one finger." Josh quickly looked over at his pa, who was just fix'in to squirt a stream of tobacco juice out in the yard.

"You reckon we can find time to tackle this job, Pa? You heard what the sheriff said... we may get our cattle back."

"Do you two still own a rifle, or something that will make a noise?" Josh jumped up and started into the house.

The old man finally said something. "We ain't got any shells fer'em."

"That's all right; I'll buy y'all two boxes of cartridges."

Josh came out of the house toting two rifles relics from the Civil War.

"For crying out loud, Josh, will they even shoot?" I asked.

"They did, before the rust got'em," he said, smiling like a Billy goat eating briers through a web fence.

"Never mind, I have plenty of hardware for you and your pa. If y'all will, carry what you need for a day or so, hitch up your wagon and follow me to the jail. We'll eat supper when we get there...Don't forget your stick."

It wasn't long till we were heading for Silver Springs. I was hoping Elie May was still at the diner. It was getting dust dark by the time we pulled up at the jail house.

"Josh, you can unhitch the wagon and park it around back. Go ahead and corral your mare in the pen. There's oats and fresh peanut hay. I'll be right back with us some supper. Just make yourself at home."

Elie Mae was just finishing up when I walked in the dinner.

"I surprised you, didn't I, Darling?"

Elie Mae spun around and ran to me. I could tell she was crying, her eyes were red and wet.

"What's wrong baby?" I asked.

She grabbed me so tight and shook nervously. "Oh, Darling, I just couldn't hang these keys on the jail house door...I knew if I did, I would never see you alive anymore."

"Is this why you're still here waiting on me?"

She nodded, and broke down crying bitterly. "I know what is going to happen in the morning, that's all I've heard all day...how old man Huey Black is going to ride into Silver Springs, shoot you down like a dog - and everybody else in sight."

"Now. Baby Doll, the Wolf Mann has got something to say about that. Don't you believe what all the cowards in this town are saying; you just wait and see."

"Wolf, Darling, I'll wait for you forever."

"Elie May, did you have any leftovers from dinner and supper? Josh and his pa are over at the jail, and I promised them something to eat...They are going to help me in the morning."

"Yes, we've got plenty, it was a slow day. I reckon everyone was scared to come into town...I guess you know why."

"We know better, don't we, Baby? Can you lock up and bring the grub on over to the jail?"

"Wolf, Darling, for you I will do anything you want me to."

"Anything for me?"

"Yes, anything, Darling." She put her arms back around my neck.

"I'll be seventeen Saturday, will you marry me?"

"Wolf, don't say that if you don't mean it. I am already crazy to sleep with you. Please forgive me, Darling, I shouldn't have said that. But I'm just a little girl that needs a daddy. You do understand, don't you?"

I was explaining to Mr. Turner and Josh what to expect in the morning when old man Huey Black and his paid cutthroats would ride up in front of the jail.

"Let me help you with that basket, Elie Mae."

"Did you tell'em, Wolf, Darling?" Elie May asked as she unpacked our lunch.

"Tell' em what?"

"You and I are getting married after Wednesday, and we are going to have a birthday party, too."

Well I didn't quite know what to say.

"That's right, we gonna get hitched after Wednesday, an move back on the old home place, we plan to raise children and white-face Hereford cattle."

I thought Elie Mae was gonna have a fit. I guess she finally believed me now. We finished our meal and got back to the business at hand.

"Now, Josh and Mr. Turner, if you will, listen, this is very important - what I'm telling you - and what I want you to do." I handed both of them a loaded rifle to inspect.

"Check these rifles. Do you two know how to shoot these rifles?"

They both nodded their heads that they knew.

"In the early morning, before old man Huey Black gets here, I want you both to plant yourselves on each side of the jail house so as not to be seen. Like I said, get hid - with a cocked rifle trained on the man nearest to you. Now, listen, it will be Huey Black riding between at least four men, two on each side of him. I'm assuming his bodyguards, other than Calvin, his right-hand bodyguard, are the five men back there in cells. I suspect the ones that ride with him tomorrow will be just ranch hands. Now, this doesn't mean they *can't* shoot a six gun. This means they *can* shoot from a horse. Now remember this, when the first shot is fired every horse will be spooked - and it's hard to be accurate with a six gun. Do you have any questions?"

Both Josh and his pa were giving the rifles close examination. "One question, Sheriff, you ain't been too clear as to what you want us to do in the morning."

"You are right. Now listen...on each side of the jail is a building. You and your pa get hid - but make sure you can see the rider closest to you. Make sure you have a cartridge in the chamber, then go ahead and cock the rifle and put the sights on the man sitting nearest you. At the sound of the first shot, you pull the trigger and shoot to kill. Keep shooting until there is not a man sitting in a saddle. Do you think you can do that? It means my life."

"I can," Josh replied.

"What about your pa?"

I believe it was the first time I had seen Mr. Turner smile. "Boy, I don't believe I have ever told you, but this ain't my first rodeo. I rode with the best of'em at Vicksburg."

I reached into my desk drawer and retrieved two silver stars. I offered each man a badge.

"Raise your right hand!"

They both raised their hands.

"Now, repeat after me, I promise to uphold the law of Silver Springs in the Indian territory of Oklahoma."

I watched as they pinned the stars on their shirts proudly.

"You fellers can look over there in that box by my desk and pick you a six gun rigging. Make sure they are loaded; and you can have them. They are guns and belts I've taken off the men I have killed. I hope they do you men more good than they did them laying up there in boot hill."

Josh and his pa didn't say much as they dressed themselves with Colts.

"I'm gonna check on the men in the back before I turn in. You and your pa can sleep here at the jail; there is a bed in the back."

I eased on in the back where there were three cells. I had the men split up, two in the cell on the end, two more in the center cell, and the mouthy polecat closer to my office. I had left a lantern burning, just out of reach of the prisoners.

"You fellers enjoy your supper?" They all turned their gaze toward me but never said a word. "How about you two that were spitting blood, how are you doing? You know I can get the doctor back if need be."

"I guess we can make out until morning. Do you know what Huey Black is going to do in the morning when he rides into this town?"

"Oh great! You are able to talk. That's good. Which one of you helped your boss rob the bank up the street, kill those two men that was working on the saloon last week, then run off all of Mr. Turner's cows? And how in the dickens did you men get blown up this morning? Did you check your water tank at the ranch? What about the saloon that blew to smithereens a few months ago? Has the cat got your tongue? Huey Black will meet his waterloo when he rides in here and faces me tomorrow. I have killed seven men and I ain't but sixteen. Calvin is the one that put three slugs in my pa's heart, and I will empty my revolver in him. You men will stand trial, so make up your stories. Don't forget to call on the Lord, the One that made you. Think about that precious mother that carried your sorry ass for nine miserable months and had you. Well, have a good night's sleep. Breakfast will be served about six o'clock."

Elie Mae had gone on home. She lived with her grandparents not far from the jail. I walked on over to the house, hoping to get a good night's sleep. Mom was holding my little sister in the living room and talking to Granny, who had heard all about what was going to happen tomorrow. Huey Black and his gang of desperadoes were going to ride into Silver Springs and shoot every living soul, me being first.

I had never seen such a room full of 'down and outers' in my life.

"I see you all ain't heard or realized that Huey Black is going to face the most difficult obstacle of his entire life."

"Son, darling, how can you say a thing like that and keep a straight face?" Mom asked, looking at me with the saddest eyes.

"Have you and Granny forgot I am the world's fastest gunslinger on earth?"

"You are just trying to cheer us up. We all know Huey Black and his ways. Wolf, baby, why did you lock his men up in jail? You know he owns this town…he practically built it by himself."

"Granny, I can't believe you said that! It's as if you are condoning sin and killing."

I believe Granny realized she had stepped in her mess-kit. "But, Wolf, darling, we must let God do His will and His work and not get in His way."

I believe if I had been outside on the grass, I would have thrown up. I walked around in front of the fireplace, about half way between Mom and Granny, and quickly drew my beautiful engraved pearl handled Colts, twirled each of them several times, and dropped them back in my holsters. Granny and Mom were watching me like a hawk. I hung my thumbs in my belt with legs spraddled and took my hat off.

"Now, I don't claim to be a preacher and I don't reckon to be a religious sort... but I'm God's man for the hour and I know it. They nailed my Jesus to the cruel, rugged cross two thousand years ago on Golgotha's Hill and as He drew His last breath, He said, 'It is Finished.' Wolf Mann will be working for God now."

I looked at Mom and Granny and big tears were running down their face.

"My glass is not half empty, my glass is half full. I am on the winning side of the law. I am the law."

The next morning was the big day. Mom and I got up early and went on over to the diner. She began to prepare breakfast for the men over at the jail, including Josh and his pa.

"Did Wolf tell you the good news, Miss Faye?" Elie Mae asked, as we all worked together.

"He said so much last night, and it was all good."

"Can I tell her, Wolf Darling?" Elie Mae asked excitedly.

I nodded. "You go right ahead, I just forgot last night."

"Me and your son is getting married after Wednesday! Can you believe it?"

Mom took a step back and opened up her arms to me and Elie Mae. We three hugged and kissed each other.

"Can I call you Mom, too?" Elie Mae asked. She was still so excited as she packed the lunches.

"You better call me Mom, or me and Wolf will get you."

Elie Mae helped me carry the food over to the jail to feed the men. Mr. Turner had the coffee brewing already and Elie Mae brought a big pot from the diner. She sat down inside and waited for the men in the back to finish. She had planned to carry the tin plates and cups back to be washed.

Josh and his pa had finished and were outside with me.

"Now, Josh, this looks like a good place to hide. You are safe and you can see the whole thing from here. Remember... go ahead and put a round in the chamber and take bead on the rider closest to you. At the sound of gunfire, blow him out of the saddle."

Me and Mr. Turner walked around to the other side of the jail and found him a good place to hide so he would not be seen by the riders.

"I'll tell you same as the boy - go ahead and put a round in the chamber and take bead on the rider closest to you. At the first sound of gunfire, blow the man nearest to you out of the saddle."

As I started back inside the jail, my eye caught sight of four men coming out of the hotel up the street, walking toward me. I didn't recognize any of them; they were too far away.

"So, this is the way it's going down."

I flipped the thongs off the hammers of both colts, eased out into the middle of the street and set my feet. I caught a glimpse of Elie Mae coming out the front door of the jail with a load of dishes. About that time she looked up the street, and saw four men strapped with Colts and toting Winchesters, coming my way  Needless to say, the dishes hit the ground and Elie Mae began to scream.

"Get back inside, girl!  Don't get me and you killed!"

All of a sudden a warm feeling came all over me, just like the times Mom would lift me out of the wash-tub behind the wood stove. I remembered them cold winter nights back in Ohio.  She would surround me with a warm quilt and hug me so tight. "I love you, Son" she would say.

# Chapter 17

"Sheriff, Sheriff, are you all right?" A voice touched my ear.

"What?"

"Sheriff, are you okay?"

I opened my eyes and there right in front of me stood four men, toting enough hardware they could have defeated Santa Ana at the Alamo Mission.

"Sheriff, we sent a telegram to our boss, Charlie Cole. He's in Chicago finishing up business. We told him that you single-handedly saved our lives yesterday... and his reply...'arm yourself and give the young sheriff a hand.' So here we are."

I bit my bottom lip to keep from breaking down and glanced up into the clouds to see if I could see Jesus. I knew He had been here a minute ago and given me a hug.

"Well, I suggest you go into the jail and get yourselves a cup o'coffee. Just walk around the dishes and step over the girl lying in the door way, I'll take care of her."

I started picking up the dishes and putting them back into the two baskets while Elie Mae was coming to.

"What happened, Wolf, darling?" she asked, looking all around. "Where did all the men come from?"

"God sent them while you were asleep. Now, you get back to the diner and start dinner. Tell Mom we are going to have at least ten extras, not counting the ones in jail."

"Can I have a kiss, just a little one, please? I know all these men are watching."

I helped Elie Mae up from the floor and led her around the corner of the jail out of sight of the others. "Put your arms around my neck, you beautiful lady, and give your lover a good juicy kiss." I put my arms around her waist and let them slide below her apron sash, pulling her as close as I could. She stood on her tip-toes and buried her breasts up into my chest, squeezing my neck so hard it cracked.

All of a sudden, she turned loose and pushed back," I must go and help with Miss Faye with dinner. You just better not get killed over here this morning - or I will sure nuff kill you." She ran around the corner of the jail and picked up her baskets then tore out like bees were after her.

I walked out to where Josh was standing watch, "You okay?" I asked.

"Fine, Wolf, I mean, Sheriff."

"I know what you mean. How would you like to be my deputy when this is all over?"

"Are you talking about a full-time job?"

"That's right, a full-time job. You know Silver Springs is growing by leaps and bounds. Well, think about it anyway!"

"I don't have to think about it, Sheriff, I'll gladly take the job."

I kept a sharp eye on the street for Huey Black's men to come riding into town; I figured it was about time. I walked out to where Mr. Turner was hiding.

"Are you doing alright in there, Mr. Turner? You see we got us some help."

"Yes, I see that. We may get this job done without firing a shot."

I thought I would put the same question to Mr. Turner. "Now, sir, just keep this under your hat until this is all over, but I asked your son to be my deputy when this is finished and Huey Black is behind bars. Do you have any objections?"

"No, I don't have any objections; I believe it will do him good. At least he'll have a paying job."

"Now that I have part of the family working, how about you taking my job as sheriff of Silver Springs? You and Josh can move into town. Think about it, I think I see some riders coming."

I quickly made my way back into the jail and told the others to step out the back door and stay hid until they were needed. "Two of you walk around the left side of the jail and two around the right side. Make sure you have a cartridge in the chamber - and shoot to kill."

"Now, Sheriff, you can tell we are not cowboys - but folks from Chicago can shoot."

By the time Huey Black and his men rode up in front of the jail house everything looked as normal as usual. He knew none of the townspeople were going to help; they were all cowards. And as soon as he bluffed or killed me - like he did my pa - the town of Silver Springs would be under his thumb again.

I watched as they passed the side window; Huey Black was leading the pack. The jail house door was closed.

"Sheriff!" came the same rough voice I had heard the night my pa was killed.

I flipped the thong off the hammers of both my colts and made sure they were loose in my holsters. I walked out onto the porch and stopped in shooting position. I knew Calvin noticed. After all, if the truth were known, he had no dog in this fight. He was looking for a paycheck and didn't care where it came from. There they sat, Huey Black, Calvin, and two polecats spaced out on either side. There was no doubt in my mind I could draw and kill both Calvin and ole man Huey Black, and probably one or two of the others, but I wanted Huey Black to stand trial for his crimes.

"Can I help you gentlemen this beautiful morning?" I asked.

"Yes, you may. I understand you must have five of my men locked up in your jail - since they didn't come to the bunk house last night."

"So, what is it that you want? They are wanted for attempted murder. I stopped them after one of your men shot an older man in the shoulder, and before they killed the other four men working on Charlie Cole's saloon. Now, I know Mr. Huey Black don't want to break any law this morning. The circuit judge will be here Friday to pass sentence on these men for their mischief."

"Now, you listen here, boy, I'm here to get these men."

That did it!

"Huey Black, this boy is arresting you for the robbery of the bank up the street and having my pa killed. I suggest you dismount and come on inside the jail. You other men can ride on out of here without being killed."

I could tell Calvin wasn't to going to draw on me while he was seated on his horse.

"What kind of fool do think I am, boy?" Huey Black asked with a smile. He turned and looked around at Calvin.

"I have no idea; I haven't studied up on fools lately. But you will be the biggest dead fool in Silver Springs if you don't slide out of that saddle...There's twenty cocked rifles pointed at your heart right now."

"You can't bluff me, boy!" Huey Black looked back at Calvin about the same time the four men came walking out from behind the jail.

"He ain't bluffing, Mr. Black, and there's men in both of the buildings on each side of the jail. I'm damn shore I ain't gonna pull down on Wolf - and me setting on a horse."

The two cowboys sitting beside old man Huey Black, and the one sitting beside Calvin whipped their horses around and high-tailed it back the way they had come. Just then Calvin slid out of the saddle and started walking slowly across the street, not looking back.

I stepped off the porch and took several steps. "Stop, Calvin, or I'll kill'ya!"

"You ain't never shot a man in the back, Wolf." He stopped and turned to face me. "Wolf, old buddy, I see you are wearing the spurs I gave you. My ma gave them to me, they are clean. I crossed the line the night I shot your pa. I'm so sorry... but that doesn't bring him back, he was a good man." Then he did exactly what he told me not to ever do; he positioned his feet and leaned over to draw. He never touched the handle of his Colt. I fanned five shots off before he hit the ground. When I turned around old man Huey Black was going into the jail with his head hanging down.

The four city boys made it around front and saw that everything was under control.

I eased over to the two closest to the door and asked, "Would you two mind escorting Mr. Black to a cell in the back? The keys are hanging on the wall. Put everything he has on him in the top desk drawer. I'll be back dreckly."

I walked over where Mr. Taylor was still hidden behind the door of the storage building. He had managed to rustle a bale of last year's hay to make a pretty good couch for his weary behind. He was now focusing on a chaw of tobacco, when I called out.

"You okay in there? You ain't asleep, are ya?"

"No, but I shore have done my self some day-dreaming."

"Okay, listen up... give me the rifle, you won't need it, now. I want you to go over to the general store and get you some new clothes - pants, shirts, and underclothes - if you need them. I want you to throw them brogans in the trash can and get yourself a pair of walking boots, a belt, and a hat. Tell Mr. Grimes to put it on my running account and tell him I'll catch'em sometime tomorrow...Wait now, don't go running off. When you get outfitted, drag your carcass right on over to the barbershop next door and tell Rooty Joiner you want a bath, a shave, and a haircut...tell him I said... to make you look like a sheriff when you walk out of his shop. Also, tell him to put it on my running account and tell him I'll catch 'em when I can. Wait a minute, now, don't run off, yet. When you get all dolled up come on over to Faye's Diner, and the town will buy you a beefsteak big as that horse collar hanging up there on the back wall."

I made my way back around to the jail house and watched Jerd Coggins and Josh load Calvin's body into the black hearse.

The four men from Chicago were sitting on the edge of the jail-house porch, so I eased over to where they were.

"I want to personally thank you fellers for the help a while ago."

"It was the least we could do, Sheriff. After all, the men would have cut us down like dogs and we know it. We already heard about two workers that had been killed working on that saloon."

"Sheriff, my name is Bill Malone," he extended his hand to me and we shook. "It's my pleasure to meet you, Sheriff. Back East we read about the fast guns out West and I just figured it was only a fiction story."

"Sheriff, my name is Terry Turk." He also shook my hand. "I'm married and the wife and I have two boys ages two and five. I heard the man you killed say he killed your father, is that right?"

"That's right, Terry. I was there when it happened. I didn't see the actual shooting because I was under the porch of the house where we lived at the time. The man you locked up had my pa shot and beat us out of our ranch."

"Sheriff, I'm Jerry Campbell. I own a business in lower Chicago. We fellows have been talking about moving out here."

"That's fine. As you can see, there is plenty of room out here in the territory. By the way, gentlemen, the town of Silver Springs is feeding you dinner over at Faye's Diner today. Where is the older man that managed to get himself shot in the shoulder? "

"He's back at the hotel nursing that shoulder. It's giving him some pain this morning."

"Well, I hope he is able to go with us for dinner," I stated.

"If there is anything that will get Arthur out of bed, it is a free lunch," Terry chuckled.

"Who's your young deputy, Sheriff?" asked Jerry.

I looked around and there stood Josh Turner. "This is my dear friend, Josh Turner. He and I came out West with our folks a little more than a year ago. By the way, Josh, you might as well introduce yourself to Calvin's horse. He won't need it where he's going."

"You're giving that horse to me?" Josh turned and pointed. "I don't know much about horseflesh, but that's a fine animal."

"Not with out a proper vote, I ain't. Do you four men agree for me to give Josh Turner that stray horse, without an owner, standing over there tied to that hitching rail?"

Every man agreed with a yes.

"Well, Josh, you own that horse. The vote was unanimous - five to none. Now that you have a horse to ride, how about you taking old man Huey Black's horse down to the livery stable. Tell Kermit Travick to take care of him until the Circuit Judge decides what he's going to do with Black. Then stop by the hotel and tell Arthur to bring his Yankee frame over to Faye's Diner and I will buy him a cow steak big as a nail keg bottom. You can also tell Kermit Travick to wash up and come on over."

I saw Elie Mae coming with the prisoners' food, so I ran to help her.

"Wolf, the good news is all over town how a sixteen year old boy rid this town of the killing and corruption Huey Black has caused for the last twenty years. But Wolf you are my man and I can't wait until Wednesday. Maybe you could take me around behind the jail again after awhile."

I went with Elie Mae to serve the men in the cells. Wasn't anything said. It was like feeding humble sheep.

"You two men that were bleeding from the mouth yesterday - bring your plates and come with me." They followed me out on the porch. "Go ahead and sit down, Elie Mae will bring your drink...which one of you men fired the first shot yesterday?"

The men looked at each other.

"It was Cable, the loud mouth in the cell by himself."

"Is that right?" I asked the other man.

"That's right," he answered.

"I never caught your names, though it makes no difference. I'm gonna let you men go when you finish eating,"

"My name is Conway and this is my cousin, Travis, we are up from south Texas. We haven't known old man Huey Black all that long - but if you wiped out Calvin, you know how to fan a Colt."

166

"How about the other two men in the center cell, who are they?"

"Just a couple of drifters - good old boys just trying to find a place to light," said Conway.

"I'll be right back." I eased on into the back of the jail. "You two men come with me, bring your plates and cups."

We went on out on the porch with the others.

"I'm letting you fellers go. Tell you what, if you can make out until after Wednesday, when I get married, then you've got a job with me, full or part-time."

"What are going to do, Sheriff? My name is Jeff Coleman. I met Huey Black before the saloon blew all to hell. I never did figure that out."

I near about started laughing. "You would have blown all to hell, too, if you had four cases of dynamite setting under'ya."

"Now, Sheriff... you didn't have nothing to do with that, did you? And what about yesterday, how did we nearly get blown up - with no one around?"

"What I want to know is, how in the devil did that water tank get full of holes and no one at the ranch heard a shot?" one of the gentlemen asked.

"Oh, well, men, you might as well find out now. I have magical powers that no one knows about. Y'all think about what I said; after Wednesday I'll be hiring. You can stay over at the bunk house on the ranch. Huey Black won't be over there bothering you."

I locked up the jail and the rest of us walked on over to the diner for lunch. Mom let us pull a couple of tables together, and our seating arrangements were settled. I was to sit at the head, or else. I knew when I had been out-voted and I didn't care to find out what the deal was. The ladies were serving when Mr. Turner came walking in. Now he was a sight for sore eyes. Josh didn't even recognize his own pa.

We were well into our lunch, when Elie May came over to see if we needed anything.

"Have you told the workers about Saturday, Wolf, darling?" I had to think real quickly.

"You want me to tell them about my surprise birthday party?"

"Yes! And there is something else that's going to happen, or has it slipped your mind?"

"Elie Mae, it must have already slipped my mind. You know how forgetful I'm getting here lately."

Elie Mae eased around me without a word and picked up a big serving fork. "Wolf Mann! I know you have been thrown from a horse, beat up, and shot at; but have you ever been gouged with a fork?"

"Now, now, Sweetheart, keep your cool! My memory is gradually coming back to me, little by little."

I was already through eating. I shoved my plate back on the table and stood up. I put my arm around Elie Mae's waist and pulled her close to me.

"She and I want to invite you all to our wedding at ten o'clock, that's on a Saturday morning, and then my birthday party afterwards. While I'm standing let me say, I'm giving up the sheriff job, and me - and my darling standing next to me - is going back to my old home place where my pa was shot and killed. This is where her and I plan to build a ranch of which the Oklahoma Territory has never seen the likes. My love and I are gonna raise miles and miles of white-faced Hereford cattle, and a house full of babies."

Mom came over and put her arms around my neck and hugged both me and Elie Mae. I could tell Mom had something to say when she turned loose of us and moved to one side.

"I was going to announce this at the wedding, but now is as good a time as any. As we all know, Silver Springs is growing in size every day - with the stockyard and the railroad and all the new businesses going up on Main Street. Just to think, my son is taking my only good hired help from me. I'm selling the café."

For a second, you could have heard a pin drop. By this time, the diner was full of workers from the stockyard and even some of the store owners.

"Now don't look so grim and long faced or you will make our new owner feel bad. He's sitting right here at this table."

Everyone began to look around at each other.

"Go ahead, Mr. Campbell, stand up and give us a speech."

Again, we were all surprised when Mr. Campbell shoved his chair back from the table and stood up. "First of all, I make better beef stew than I do a speech. As I was telling the sheriff only a short time ago, I own a small café on the south side of Chicago - which is becoming a hustle an bustle from daylight until dark. I'm Jerry Campbell and my wife is Stella. She plans to be here by train tomorrow. We have two daughters. Becky is twelve and Mona is ten. They are extremely well-trained waitresses. I am a very good friend of Mr. Charlie Cole. He told us about this establishment and thought it would be a good investment for Stella and me.

I know beyond a shadow of doubt there is a lot about the West and the western cooking I have to learn. But I learn fast, and I plan to enlarge the same as Miss Faye planned to do. I'm hoping she will stay on for a spell and guide me in the right direction."

Mr. Campbell received a round of applause and sat back down.

# Chapter 18

"Now, now, wait just one minute!" I boldly shouted. "Before you scatter like quail, there are several members of the Town Council here. I hope you will consider Mr. Turner for my replacement and let his son, Josh, be his deputy. They both did a superb job helping me apprehend Huey Black and his nest of polecats."

Another applause, went up. The girls were now busy waiting on tables of the latecomers. I made my way over to where Mr. Turner was finishing up his bread pudding.

"Keep an eye on our prisoner and watch over the jail while Josh and I ride out to the Huey Black's ranch. We will be back as soon as possible."

He nodded and I motioned for Josh to follow me. He and I struck a trot over to the jail and were soon mounted and on our way to Huey Black's ranch.

"What are we up to, Wolf? This is just like old times."

"Yes, I remember when we first met, Josh. We were down by the creek fishing in that big, black hole."

"You remember, we both caught enough bream for dinner? I still got that old fishing pole - and when me and Elie Mae get moved in I'm gonna take her down to that creek bank and catch us a mess of bream for our supper."

Josh didn't say much more until we stopped at the ranch. I could tell in his voice there was a quiver of sadness, for he had lost his best friend to a sissy girl. But what did I need with a hairy legged boy? We tied our horses, and started toward the house.

"Wonder what's wrong with that windmill? It's sure making a racket!"

"It probably needs some oil, I would think."

"How are we going to get in if the door in locked?" Josh asked about the time we stepped upon the porch.

"I brought a key," I said, looking at Josh.

"There is one thing I can say about you, Wolf, old buddy, you think of everything."

I reached for the knob and twisted; it was locked. As I took a step back I took the thong off the hammer of my Colt. I drew the .45, twirled it several times, and fanned three or four slugs through doorknob and lock. The big hardwood door began to squeak as it cracked and slowly eased open.

"That key will open most locks," I said, blowing the smoke out of my barrel and reloading my pistol.

"But ain't that against the law?" Josh asked as we walked in the living room.

"We are the law. Help me find Huey Black's safe."

"It's probably in his office or den."

"Well, lead the way."

And sure enough when he and I walked through the double glass doors with white lace curtains, there it sat, a black vault, head high.

"I'll bet you fifty cents to a ten dollar poker chip it's locked." Josh pulled the handle several times and fiddled with the big brass knob. Then he turned around and looked at me like a dying calf in a thunder storm: "I guess you've got the combination?"

"Yeah, but I left it in my saddle bag. I'll be right back,"

I had found out the combination to most safes was a half stick of dynamite and about a six inch fuse - with a good fresh Du Pont cap.

171

I had an idea this safe was gonna be contrary and hard to persuade to open, so in my spare time I had concocted me a never fail combination.

When I returned to the safe Josh was sitting behind Huey Black's big mahogany desk sampling a bottle of muscatel wine. I slid the stick of dynamite under the handle, close to the big brass knob, and lit the short fuse. I hurriedly started back to the living room to get behind the couch. I stopped and looked back at Josh, warning, "I wouldn't sit there if I was you!"

I guess Josh heard the hissing and smelled the smoke about the same time he saw my combination. He jumped the desk and passed me before I got to the living room.

About the same time he and I jumped behind the big couch in the next room. We had no trouble hearing the blast. We sat up looking into the smoke-filled office.

"Wolf, old buddy, next time, if there is ever a next time, use a longer fuse. You liked to have killed both of us."

The smoke began to clear out so we could see.

"You reckon it opened?" I asked, not knowing what we would find when we went into the office.

Well, the huge safe was open and there was the money from the Silver Spring Bank, still in the sacks. The bills were banded in stacks - not to mention the silver and gold coins.

"Wolf, there in no way our two horses can carry all this weight back to town."

"Don't either of you move, I'll kill you where you stand; this money is not going back to town."

It was one of Huey Black's men I had turned loose from the jail. I caught the voice.

"Now, both of you slowly turn around, face me and keep your hands where I can see'em!"

I remembered I had not tied my hammer down when I reloaded my Colt after shooting the lock off the door. I also remembered what

Calvin had taught me… watch for mistakes. It didn't look like me and Josh were gonna live long enough for this buzzard to make one.

"Which one of you boys want it first?"

He smiled, then took the barrel of his pistol - literally covering part of his face - and shoved his hat back on his head. A light went on in my brain. That was his mistake and this would be my fastest draw ever. He was still touching the rim of his Stetson when I weighted him down with lead.

"You reckon they have a wagon in the barn?" I asked Josh as I reloaded my pistol.

"A-a-a-a what?" Josh uttered, white as a sheet.

"Josh! Did you pee in your pants?"

He looked down at himself. "No, sir, that's wine I spilled when I jumped the desk before the safe blew up."

"Oh well, I'll take your word. Was you scared?" I asked as I started through the house for the back door.

"You darn tooting, I thought we were goners! Wasn't you?"

"No, man, the fat lady hadn't sung yet. Let's see if there is a wagon in the barn."

We soon found a wagon and a horse that would stand still long enough to get a collar over his head. By hook and crook, Josh and I completely cleaned the vault out - except for important papers and rare books. We had two corn sacks half full of coins. And a dead cowboy.

"What are we gonna do with all this paper money and this ton of coins?" Josh asked.

"We'll think of something by the time we carry this body over to the morgue. I just hope Jerd Coggins is there," I said, as Josh pulled around to the back of the funeral home.

It was mite near dark when we arrived at the jail. Mr. Turner was there waiting for us when we drove up.

"Have you made up your mind?"

"Well it is one thing for shore, Josh; we can't leave it laying out here in this wagon all night."

"We may stack it in that small bedroom in the jail, and we can put a bunch of it under the bed," Josh concluded, getting out of the wagon. "Wolf, old buddy, I seen four or five of them gold coins I sure would like to have!"

"Some of the coins was like brand new," I acknowledged, as I eased on around behind the wagon.

"Does that mean I can have them?"

"Course not! That's against the law, Josh!"

"But you said we were the law!"

"That's right, Josh, old buddy...but we are not thieves." I guess I got Josh's dander up.

"Look, Wolf, you and I rode up to this ranch house uninvited and dang near shot the door off the hinges. You practically ruined the man's fine safe. Then we loaded up everything that was worth anything and drove off. Now I ask you... what does that make us?"

"Heroes, my man, heroes; you and I are heroes cause we got Silver Springs' money back.

With the help of Mr. Turner, Josh and I managed to get all the money and coins into the little bedroom in the jail. Our plans were to be over at the bank when it opened the next morning and have Curtis Flynn, the president of the Silver Springs bank, to come over and get the money. That was simple enough - until Mr. Turner threw a monkey wrench into the whole idea. And he was right...how would Curtis Flynn know what money was the bank's money, from all the rest? Why, he could say the gold and silver coins came out of the bank!

"Mr. Turner, you sure muddied up the water, but you are absolutely right. How do we know that Curtis Flynn is honest?"

"We don't, but by now, the bank should have a written statement of every cent that was taken from that bank," said Mr. Turner.

"So, we get the list and look it over and carry him the exact amount of money that was stolen from the bank. Then we can worry about who all the coins belong to. Let me ask you another question, have you been keeping close tabs on our prisoners?"

"Oh, yes! Old man Huey Black wants me to send a telegram for him in the morning. From the way he talked, it was going to be to some hot shot lawyer in the East. He let on to the other man that when the trial was over he'd own this town and everything in it, again."

"All I can say is...Huey Black is a dreaming. Anyhow, I'm going on home and get me a good night's sleep. I will see you and Josh over at Faye's Diner about six o'clock in the morning."

I made sure the horses were properly put up in the stalls and walked over to the big house.

"I imagine you are tired out, after the day you have had," Mom said, bringing little sister over to give me a goodnight kiss.

"You didn't know I got all the money back that was stolen from the Silver Springs bank?"

"No, you didn't!" Was Mom surprised!

"Oh, yes, I did! It is over at the jail locked up, as we speak."

"Well, I know you're happy. You retrieved all of your money - not to mention all that belongs to the other people of Silver Springs."

I looked all around. "Where is Granny, isn't it a little early for her to turn in?"

Mom was feeding the baby and rocking her to sleep. "Mother is not feeling well today. She took her medicine and went on to bed. Wolf, darling, I must warn you, the doctor tells me she is going down fast. Now I don't want to believe him, but sometimes we have to face reality. Mother is not able to change diapers and care for Freda. Here lately, I've been spending more time at home than at the diner. And with the crowds at dinner, I can't keep running back and forth between the house and the diner."

I could tell now why Mom was giving up the diner. "What do you plan on doing, Mom?"

"Oh well, I will have to do what I must, and carry the baby to work with me each day. Freda is big enough to sit up, with pillows around her... so I'll put her in a box in a corner of the kitchen. The girls will be more than glad to help me."

I could tell mom had made up her mind. "That's getting the baby up mighty early, isn't it?" I asked, getting up to go to bed.

"Are you kidding?" Mom said, "Freda is up wanting to be fed anyway. It's all going to work out, you will see. Good night."

"I'll walk over to the diner and carry Freda for you in the morning. I have a busy day. Good night, Mom."

After a peaceful night's sleep and a good breakfast at Faye's Diner, I made my way to the jail house with pep in my step and a song in my heart. What I found was - the money, along with my long-time friend and his father, the would-be sheriff, missing!

Now, the two deputy-turned-outlaws had a comfortable lead. No telling what time they had loaded the money into a buckboard and started south. They knew full well that I would be hot on their trail in short order. The worst thing happened...it began to rain cats and dogs and washed out any sign of tracks. Well, this did throw a wrench in the cogs and would slow me down. I started saddling Blackie and putting two and two together - and it equaled Mexico. They would take the shortest route to Mexico. They were driving a wagon, and I figured Mr. Turner knew that I was riding a good horse and would soon to catch up.

I rode the better part of four hours with my mind running ninety miles an hour. I had an idea Mr. Turner and Josh knew I was on their trail and it was time for me to catch up. They also knew they were no match for my shooting skill. The two would find a perfect spot for an ambush and hide the buckboard among the rocks. They would also hide themselves higher up in the rocks on each side of the road, knowing that my six gun would be no match for their rifles.

As my mom would say, reality set in. If my friends, who I had given a job to put food and clothes on their back, would rob me, they would kill me for a wagon load of money.

After several hours of hard riding, I decided to pull Blackie off the trail. I dismounted and carried my trusting friend up into the rocks. I knew both me and my horse, Blackie, needed a rest and it would be dark soon. I knew if I was to be ambushed it would be between the two high ledges where the pass was very narrow. I unsnapped the gun-case - and there my beauty lay. The long brass telescope glittered in the westward-sinking sun. This was my pride and joy. The rifle weighed a ton but would shoot a mile.

I began to search all up in the rocks with my rifle scope. Lo and behold, there was Josh, stirring around trying to find a good spot to ambush me. With close aim I placed the cross hairs on my one-time close friend. Josh and I were near the same age. I had plenty of time. I pondered the situation, knowing full well if a slug from the rifle hit him anywhere on his body at this distance it would blow his arm or leg off. And he would surely die before I could get medical help. I just couldn't pull the trigger. I began to search the rocks for Mr. Turner. Soon I spotted his grinning face among the boulders. He had a rifle trained up the road. The only shot I had was his head - and if I pulled the trigger there would be no head.

I began to think how someone had shot my pa, leaving me without a dad. Lord, what must I do? I started putting the mail order rifle back in the case, making sure everything was placed properly. Just before closing the rifle case I heard a blood-curdling screams from down the way. Quickly I began to focus the rifle scope in the direction of the ungodly screams. The focus was jumpy, but I could tell it was Josh running down from the rocks. The best I could tell, Josh had a snake in both hands.

With my rifle in hand, I ran to straddle Blackie. Then I heard three shots in the distance and was puzzled. What I thought I could see, in the distance, were two bodies lying in the middle of the narrow road. When I reached the gruesome scene I slid out of the saddle, thinking to myself this chapter was closed. The two rattlesnakes had bitten Josh numerous times on the face and neck. Mr. Turner had run to help his son by shooting the snakes, then turned the gun on himself, seeing Josh was dead. I stood still for a minute or two, then looked up into a clear blue sky. "Lord, You do work in mysterious ways at times." I brought the buckboard around and loaded the two bodies, noticing Josh had his pockets full of gold coins. "If you could have waited, old buddy, we could have walked on streets of gold."

The sun was high in the sky by the time I pulled up to the morgue with the two bodies the next morning. I explained to Jerd Coggins, the undertaker, what had happened. The next stop was the Silver Springs Bank, where Curtis Flynn, the president, was certainly surprised to get all the money back in the bank. The final stop would be breakfast, and a bed for my weary bones.

I thought I would mosey by the jail and check on the prisoners before I hibernated for the rest of the day. And to my surprise, I found the mayor, Mr. Grimes.

"I can tell you brought the money back," said Mr. Grimes.

"Now, how did you know about the money?"

"That loud mouth back in the cell next to Huey Black. By the way, his name is Rex Foster and he thinks old man Huey Black's fancy city lawyer is going to get him off."

"How are you getting off today?" I asked to Mr. Grimes.

"Oh well, it's a slow day and the wife is watching the store. She thinks we haven't been giving you any support, and I will be the first to admit she was right. How could a sixteen-year boy put Huey Black behind bars single-handedly?"

"Wait now, Mr. Grimes, don't be throwing too many roses my way, I thank God for sending those boys who were working on the saloon to my rescue, and Mr. Turner and his son, Josh."

I told Mr. Grimes the whole story, rattlesnakes and all. He just shook his head. "God looks after you, don't he?"

I unsaddled Blackie, gave him a quick rub down and promised him I would do better later. I think he had his mind on the double portion of oats and fresh peanut, hay not to mention a cool shade.

The girls at the diner, were dying to hear the news. I believe if I didn't hurry and give up this sheriff's job Elie Mae was going to have a nervous breakdown. I ate me a good breakfast, then went over to the house and took me a bath and slept for nearly three hours. I was dozing in and out when I heard a faint knock on my bedroom door. Not wanting to disturb Granny up the hall, I eased up and tip-toed to the door.

"Who is it?"

"It's Elie Mae."

I turned the knob and cracked the door. "Come on in, Darling."

I opened the door a smidgen more and Elie Mae threw both hands over her mouth to catch her breath. "I can't, Wolf, darling."

"Could I ask why?"

"You ain't got any clothes on."

I looked down and she was right. "Well, just keep your eyes closed and come on in. I will put on some, it's about time I get up anyway."

I led Elie Mae over to the bed where she sat down. I started putting on my clothes. After I was about buttoned up, I eased over to the bed and sat down beside her. Elie Mae quickly put both arms around my neck and we began to kiss.

"Oh, Wolf darling, stop, this is not what I come over for!"

"Don't you like it?"

"Oh, yes, yes! I love kissing you, Darling, but Miss Faye sent me over to see if you would mind going up to get Doctor Fletcher to look in on Mrs. Pittman."

"Is Granny worse?" I asked jumping up, grabbing for my boots.

"All I know is what Miss Faye has told me in the last few days, and she said it doesn't look good."

Elie Mae went back to the diner and I started up the street for Doctor Fletcher.

"The doctor is in the back room finishing up with a patient, Sheriff, he'll be right out. I guess you're looking forward to the big day?"

"I have three big days coming up, my wedding, my birthday, and the trial for Huey Black - and that big day is worrying me, Mrs. Mildred."

I could tell Mrs. Mildred was searching for a word of encouragement for me, the way her face had lit up. "You know Wolf, the word 'worry' is not in the Bible, so why should we use it?" she asked.

"Who's worried?" The doctor asked, coming out of his back office. "I couldn't help overhearing the conversation."

"The sheriff was telling me he was concerned about the court case coming up involving Huey Black.

"I would be, too, there's no telling what that old buzzard has up his sleeve, Mildred."

"If that doesn't just beat all. Doctor, that was no encouragement, to our young sheriff."

"Now, now, Mrs. Fletcher, don't reprimand your husband too harshly, I know where he is coming from. It ain't that old man Huey Black is guilty or innocent. It may be the results of the crooked judge or the bought off lawyers."

"Wolf! You are mighty young to be talking like that." The Doctor turned red faced and looked at his wife.

"Are you saying, don't make waves, leave well enough alone? Now, I don't want to cause friction standing in your living room in front of Mrs. Mildred...but if the judge lets old man Huey Black walk, I'll be on my way to Washing D.C. to talk to that bunch of liars."

The doctor knew that I knew he was a 'yes man.' I turned around when I reached the door to leave and looked at the doctor and his wife. "When they lay me upon boot hill beside my pa, they will be burying another man without a yellow streak down his back."

When I left the doctor's office I knew I hadn't gained many points, and may have lost a few. But I meant every word I said. I thought I would ease by the jail before I went to the diner for supper. When I walked in, there sat Rooty Picket, the town barber, talking to Mr. Grimes. They both looked surprised and quietly pointed to the back of the jail where the cells were.

"Huey Black's lawyer is with him," said Mr. Grimes

"How long has he been back there with that buzzard?" I asked, looking around the corner.

"He came in on the train this evening, and he wants to see you."

I thought, I'll bet he does and I hope he gets the impression I don't like him no better than the snake he is talking to. I poured me a cup of coffee and sat down. I guess the lawyer had finished talking to Huey Black and heard my voice. He came out to where I was sitting sipping on my coffee, as if he was in complete control. He was wearing a three-piece, black, pin-striped suit, carrying a brief case, and smiling like a jackass chewing on a cocklebur.

# Chapter 19

"Good day to you, Sheriff, I'm glad I caught you." The lawyer laid the briefcase on the end of the table and opened it up. He shuffled around in the top papers and laid a document on the table...shoving it my way. I noticed Rooty Picket looking over at Mr. Grimes, wondering what I was going to do.

"I guess you're wondering what the document is all about," the lawyer said.

"Not really, I'm not interested!"

"Now, Sheriff, you had better be interested, this is the law. I highly suggest you pick it up and read it...I'm putting up bond for Mr. Huey Black."

I could detect a glimmer of the lawyer losing control. I set my coffee cup down, reached for the sheet of paper and began to wad it up. After it was neatly crumpled up, I tossed it in a garbage can over by the desk. I could tell that went over like a big burr under a thin saddle blanket.

"That's against the law!" the lawyer shouted.

"I'm the only one wearing a star in this office and I say it's not against the law to throw paper in a trash can."

Rooty Picket looked over at Mr. Grimes with his half way smirk of a smile.

"What about it, gentlemen, do you think I broke the law?" I asked, pulling my coffee cup my way to see if I had left a drop.

"I could have you arrested and locked up for what you just did."

The ring of keys was lying on the table right in front of me. I picked them up and tossed them up on top of his briefcase.

"Why don't you just lock me up back there with all the other law breakers?"

I'm here to tell you, the lawyer's face turned as red as a fall sunset. He snatched up his briefcase, dumping the ring of keys back onto the end of the table. The fancy lawyer did an about face with his nose in the air, and proceeded to leave.

"Don't let the door hit you in the butt, city man!

"I'm glad you're sheriff - and not me," Rooty Picket said, getting up to make his exit.

"Don't forget we are having a Council meeting tonight," Mr. Gibbs remarked.

"You know I had slam forgot about that meeting," said Rooty Picket, looking back over his shoulder.

"Well, it is gonna be an important meeting, Mr. Rooty, make sure you tell everyone, and Mayor, I need to talk to you before the meeting tonight," I said, getting up to go back to the kitchen. "Come on back here in the kitchen, Mayor, I want to show you something." I poured me about a half cup of coffee and pulled one of the corn sacks of coins out from under the bed. About the time Mr. Grimes eased into the small room I dumped the sack of gold coins in the middle of the mattress. His eyes got big as saucers as I pulled the second bag of coins out from under the bed.

"What, in the name of the Lord, is all of this?" he asked, in an almost breathless voice.

"I thought maybe you could tell me," I said, taking a gulp of my coffee.

"How would I known Sheriff, did it come out of the bank?" The mayor sat down on the side of the bed and went to sifting through the gold coins, letting them fall through his fingers.

"No, there was only paper money took from the bank. That is according to Curtis Flynn, and he ought to know. And it is all put back into Silver Springs Bank."

" Now, Sheriff, what puzzles me is - how did you get hold of all the bank money in the first place?"

"Well, Mayor, sometimes a man has got to do what a man has got to do. As you well know, Huey Black robbed the bank. At times I'm a mite slow, but I began to put me a plan together knowing that bank money had to be somewhere. Since it wasn't in old man Huey Black's pocket back there in that cell, where would be the most likely place to put the money?.. At his house. Since there was no one in Silver Springs to issue a search warrant it was safer there than anywhere else. Now, Mayor, what I'm going to tell you - only five people will ever know this and three of them are dead...that only leaves me and you." I went ahead and told him what Josh Turner and I did to get the money.

"Now, the way I see it, Sheriff, you broke the law; but one could say you took the law into your own hands. That would be ludicrous to say the least, you are the law. Since Huey Black is the one that broke the law in the first place, it was your job to retrieve the bank money at all costs."

"I'm glad you feel that way, Mayor, but here is where the boot will pinch...when that city lawyer finds out Huey Black don't have a pot to pee in or a window to throw it out of. When Huey Black finds out his big home vault is as empty as last years bird's nest, there's gonna be a strange odor in that cell back there."

"Sheriff, suppose you and I carry all these coins to the bank. We can get someone there to roll and count this money and get Curtis Flynn to put in the bank, under Silver Springs' account until we find out who it belongs to."

"I personally think that's a good idea, Mayor. Let's carry it on over before the bank closes. At least we'll have it out of our hair," I said, starting to put the coins back into the sacks.

"Have you heard that Jake Nimes is back in town? I understand his sister persuaded him to quit drinking," said the mayor.

"I know she had her hands full. Wonder who the next town drunk is going to be?"

"Do we need one?" We both started laughing.

"We are the only western town west of the Mississippi River that don't have a saloon."

"We've had lots less trouble, too."

Our mayor and general store owner opened the Town Council meeting with prayer, and it seemed everything was in order. All the Council members were present. The old business was taken care of and the new business was at hand. The main topic of discussion was the trial of Huey Black and where it would be held.

Kermit Travick raised his hand and was acknowledged. "As I see it, the new saloon that belongs to Charlie Cole is not finished but well dried in, and would be plenty of space for a temporary court room."

"That's a good idea," said Rooty Picket, "we could pitch in and build some temporary benches."

"I'm sure if Mr. Charlie Cole knew our plans he would have the tables and chairs shipped in time for the trial," I suggested.

"Then this will be the place," the mayor agreed. "Every one in favor say aye, all opposed say nay. The ayes have it, so the trial will be held in Charlie Cole's saloon."

Curtis Flynn raised his hand and was acknowledged. "As I understand it, our sheriff plans to give up the job as soon as the trial is over. Is that still your plan?" I looked over at the mayor and he nodded.

"Yes sir, Mr. Flynn, you hit the nail right on the head, that is my plan. I killed the man that shot my pa and will see the man hanged that caused it to happen."

"Sheriff, I hope you would reconsider, we would have a hard time finding a man to replace you."

I looked over at the mayor who nodded again. Again I stood up, then looked over at Elie Mae who was sitting, with Mom.

"No, Mr. Flynn! The town won't have any trouble finding a man for a sheriff. I was only a child when I took this job, not dry behind the ears, I have heard many say. I was only fourteen when I shot my first man dead. He was taking the only thing I loved on the face of this earth. Old man Huey Black took my pa I loved. Before that the devil took my mom, when she was trying to give me a litter sister. Who do I run to at night when I wake up and see the faces of the eight men I've killed? Many stand for seconds staring me down, full of lead slugs, choking on their own blood. Who do I run to?

I know I have killed some mom's son. What would I say when I look her eye to eye? I have killed some dad's son - whom he taught to hunt and fish as a little boy. Maybe a husband - with a loving wife at home with a couple of nursing babies. How will I explain to them why I shot their pa? There is no reason these kids are growing up without a daddy.

No! No! Mr. Flynn... my killing days is through! It wouldn't be fair to the one I love. She's setting right over there by Mom - most of you know her as Miss Faye. And my wife-to-be is Elie Mae, the loveliest lil ole gal in Oklahoma Territory."

As I sat back down, Elie Mae was smiling all over herself and she threw me a kiss. Mr. Grimes, our mayor, stood back up to adjourn the meeting.

"Now, let's don't forget the wedding Saturday. I understand a birthday party is also in the making, and I believe the sheriff tells me his Aunt Becky will be coming all the way from Plainville, Ohio. Now, if there is no more business, I will see you all at the wedding Saturday."

I had deputized Jake Nimes earlier in the day so I could have help at the jail. He thought he was something when I hung the star on his shirt. He was more surprised when I told him he was gonna get paid for the job.

Elie Mae ran to me as soon as the meeting was over. "Oh Wolf, darling, those were the sweetest words you said about me. I can hardly wait until our wedding night to get here."

"Well, I meant every word I said. You want to walk with me over to the jail before you go home? I need to check on my hired help." I could tell Elie Mae loved the gesture. Actually, we had had very little time alone together. She and I both worked all the daylight hours.

It was a beautiful, clear night in Silver Springs as we walking along hugging each other up. There was a cool south breeze keeping the temperature at bay. Only a few of the street lights were burning but a full sky of stars overhead lit our way. Elie Mae and I was standing at the front steps of the jail getting our last bit of hugging and kissing done. She had turned to go inside when we both saw the fire flash... from what appeared to be a gun up the main street...then we heard the shot. I felt the pain in my left shoulder, the velocity of the slug spun me around and I fell on the steps. Elie Mae began to scream. When she grabbed me and got blood all over her hands, she screamed even louder.

After Doc and Jake Nimes put me in the bed in the back of the jail, Doctor Fletcher explained to me how he had but made it to his office after the town meeting when he heard the shot and Elie Mae screaming. He went on to say he thought he might be needed and headed back, to find me bleeding like a stuck pig."

"Where is Elie Mae?" I asked, looking at the hole in my new shirt.

"She ran to tell Miss Faye and lay still! I've just got the blood stopped."

"Doctor, I'm so glad you heard the shot and Elie Mae screaming and came running," I said.

"Wolf, old buddy, you better thank your lucky stars you are still alive. Four things happened to make that so: first of all, I was close by; second, the bullet went clean through; thirdly, the slug didn't hit a bone; and fourth, I see you are going to have two fine nurses," the doctor said getting up to leave.

"No, Doctor, I don't believe in lucky stars. If the stars were so lucky, I wouldn't have got shot in the first place. But I believe in God being the reason that I am still alive."

Elie Mae and Mom were taking on over me like high society would take on over a toy poodle a fix'in to have a litter of ten puppies.

"Wolf, darling, you sure gave me and your Mom a scare a while ago," Elie Mae let on, as she was holding my hand and running her fingers through my hair.

"Well, Elie Mae, darling! I wasn't exactly turning cart-wheels over the idea of getting shot, myself."

"Wolf, my baby, do you think we may need to postpone the wedding for a week or so?" Mom asked with such sincerity in her voice.

"Mom, darling, I was shot in the top...not the bottom."

"Sheriff, do you have any idea who shot you?" Jake Nimes asked.

"Yes! It was one of Huey Black's men on the outside still working for him. There were two of his men that visited him today in his cell. When they find out he doesn't have any money to pay them with, you can bet your bottom dollar they will be scarce as hen's teeth to find around Silver Springs."

The rot gut whiskey had all but ruined Jake Nimes brain but he had enough sense to know what I was talking about.

"In the morning, bright and early, I want you to go up the street... Elie Mae can show you where the gun shot came from last night... and see if you can find anything the shooter may have dropped, especially, the shell casing. Anything I may use for evidence."

Doctor Fletcher highly suggested I stay put for the night, and not be moved. I guess the bed in the back room was a good idea after all.

"Well, I'm not leaving him!" Elie Mae exclaimed, looking around at the doctor.

"Well, I'm not leaving, either!" Jake Nimes announced, "I can sleep in an empty cell up front until morning.

"I'll be praying for the lot of you," Mama said, "but I have a starving baby and a sick mother at home so I will see you early in the morning."

After everyone had left the jail for the night, it got quiet as a church mouse. Jake Nimes had locked up the place tighter than Dick's hat band. He had barred both front and back doors to the jail and turned the lamps down or off.

One could hear snoring up front but out of the three sleepers, I couldn't tell who the mortal was. I guess an hour or so had passed, but I had so much on my mind I couldn't sleep. The dim lamp sitting in the kitchen on the stove was giving off ample light. I could plainly see Elie Mae was not comfortable sitting in that straw-bottomed, straight-back chair. I motioned with my head for her to come closer. She leaned over and as her soft, silky hair fell in my face I could feel its warmth.

I whispered in her ear. "Do you want to lay with me, Darling?"

"Is there room?" she asked, in her soft, still trembling voice.

"We'll have to get close; is that alright?"

"Oh, Wolf, darling, I'll get very close, but I don't want to hurt your shoulder," she said, sliding her shoes off and easily getting into bed with me.

I rolled up on my good side so my hurt side would be on top, leaving my right arm to hold her. The doctor had pulled my shirt off; so I was nude from the waist up, but under the cover.

Elie Mae was snuggling and inching up to me as close as she could. "Is this alright, dear?"

"Elie Mae, honey, what are you doing with that long white apron on? Are we gonna cook up something tonight?"

"My lord, I wear the dumb thing all the time; I don't know when I got it on or off at times."

She pulled the apron off and hung it on the foot of the bed. She eased back up close to me and I hugged her up close.

"How can you be comfortable with that big, long dress on buttoned up under your chin?"

She sat up and put her feet on the floor. "You know, Wolf darling, it is uncomfortable, and besides, I'm getting it all rumpled up and I planned to wear it tomorrow."

She carefully unbuttoned her collar and slipped out of her dress, then laid it on the foot of the bed. She smiled real big and laid back down.

"Oh my, my, Wolf, this is much better now that we are really close." She and I began to kiss and snuggle, I had my hand on her hip. "You know, Darling, this is the first time I ever kissed laying down and I believe I like it much better than standing."

"Why is that, Elie Mae baby? I like it both ways."

"Well, it's pure and simple, if you get weak and fall out, we are already laying down. You know something, Wolf? This is so silly and it's terrible to even think such a thing; but I'm certainly enjoying your getting shot."

"You know something, Darling? I even forgot I was shot; I don't even hurt now."

"Wolf, have I told you lately how much I love you? I believe if I could slip out of this cotton petticoat we could get much closer, don't you?"

"No, no, Baby, we can't slip out of nothing else tonight. Let us go to sleep."

It must have been the medicine the doctor gave me or Elie Mae's loving, but I slept like a log. Everyone was up and stirring when I woke up. It took me a few minutes to come to myself.

"I see you're not dead, Sheriff. How about a cup of coffee?" Jake Nimes asked from the kitchen.

"Now, I don't mind if I do. Where is Elie Mae?"

"She ran over to the diner to get breakfast for all of us and, by the way, Sheriff, there is a young cowboy sitting out on the front porch. Says he is waiting on you."

"What did he look like, Jake?" I asked, reaching for my coffee.

"He was about your size and probably the same age. He looked like he had been rode hard and put away wet. I'll answer your next question before you ask...the young man is packing hardware hung low, tied to his leg," Jake answered, as if it was just another day at the office.

I reached for my boots and started putting them on. Old Doc had bandaged me up pretty good last night, I didn't feel any pain.

"Jake, my man, if it is all right with you, I'll take care of this little matter before breakfast." I began to look all around. "What did y'all do with my gun rigging last night while Doc was patching me up?"

"Doc took them off ya and handed them to me; I hung 'em there on that hat rack."

"I see the hat rack and I see my hat, Jake...but I don't see no guns," I explained.

"Miss Elie Mae hid 'em!" Jake exclaimed.

"Miss Elie Mae hid 'em?"

"That's what I said, Sheriff. Miss Elie Mae hid 'em, to keep you from shooting anybody else."

"Well, what about somebody shooting at me?" I quickly asked.

"I don't guess she thought about that when she hid your pistols. I just suppose she was going by what you said at the meeting the other night."

"And what was that?" I snarled.

"Your exact words, Sheriff? 'My killing days is through, it wouldn't be fair to the one I love.' Now, what do you say... do you deny your own words?"

"No! I don't deny my saying that, but that was before some gun happy galoot showed up wanting to make a name for himself by outdrawing the fastest gun slinger in the world!"

"I don't reckon Miss Elie Mae thought about that, either."

"Well, I'm going out and talk to the young man on the porch. Did Elie Mae say she was bringing me a clean shirt?"

"Yes, she did, and she told me to keep you in bed, too."

I made like I didn't even hear Jake, but went on out front where the young fellow was sitting on the edge of the porch.

"Good morning, sir," I said as I squatted down and leaned back against a porch post. "Can I help you in some way? My name is Wolf Mann, I'm the sheriff of this town of Silver Springs." I extended my hand.

"Well, Sheriff, I'm pleased to finally meet you. I have read much about you in the newspaper here lately, and they say you are the fastest gun in the whole world. Is that right?"

"Well, now, I just suppose the newspaper is right."

"Let me introduce myself. My name is Jeff Dunn and I have never been in the paper. I am the fastest gun in Texas... and Texas is a big place."

"Have you ever killed anybody?" I asked Jeff Dunn.

"No, not yet. That is why I am here - to kill you - and I sure nuff will be somebody. I'll get my name in the paper and maybe even my picture, too." The young man gloated with a smile on his face as wide as Texas.

"Well, I have good and bad news for you this morning, Jeff. My girlfriend and wife-to-be saved your life; that is the bad news. She has hid my pistols and that is the good news."

"You mean to tell me I have rode half-way across Texas to pull down on you and you don't have a shooting iron?"

I could tell the young man was greatly disappointed.

"You reckon if I talked to your girlfriend it would help?" Jeff pleaded.

"I don't know, Jeff, she is mighty head strong at times and we have never had an argument about anything."

"Elie Mae is here with the breakfast. Y'all come and get it while it's hot!" Jake shouted out the front door of the jail.

"Now, I didn't come here to eat, Sheriff," Jeff said, getting up."

"Come on and eat a good meal. I know you probably rode half the night to get here to have a shoot-out. Let's eat first - and we have got the rest of the day to discuss the shooting."

Elie Mae was serving the prisoners so we took a seat at the table in my office. We were loading up on steaming hot coffee when Elie Mae finished serving.

"Wolf, darling, you didn't introduce me to your friend!"

"I'm sorry, Elie Mae, this is Jeff Dunn and he has ridden half way across Texas to challenge me into a gun bout this morning."

"I hate to be the one to spoil your day, Jeff, but my husband is not feeling well today. He received an unwelcome bullet last night. That is why the shoulder is all bandaged up this morning."

"Does this mean you're not giving the sheriff's gun rigging back to him until he gets well?" Jeff Dunn spoke up.

"No! I'm not ever giving the pistols back... to get himself killed."

"But Miss Elie Mae, whoever heard of a sheriff with no guns?"

I guess Elie Mae had unpinned the sheriff's star off my bloody shirt to wash, and put the star in her pocket. Elie Mae nonchalantly walked around to where Jeff Dunn was sitting. She reached into her pocket and retrieved the star. In a sort of loving way she leaned over his shoulder and pinned the star on Jeff's shirt.

"You can be our new sheriff. Now, Jake, when you and Jeff get through eating breakfast, carry him over to the general store and tell Mr. Grimes to swear him in as the new sheriff of Silver Springs."

"Wait just a minute, Elie Mae! Don't I have something to say about the goings on?" I asked.

"No! Your ma said if you could gallivant around this morning I was to bring you over to the house and put you to bed. The doctor is coming by about twelve to look after her mother, and he can check on your shoulder, too."

When I got to the house, before going to bed I went by Granny's bedroom to say hello and give her a hug.

"Granny, I love you, but you and I aren't faring so well here lately, are we?"

"I reckon not, sonny boy. Faye says you got a hole in your chest you can stick a broom handle through."

"Ah, Granny you, know how Mom carries on. Now me and you are going to get well.

I was lying up in bed when Elie Mae brought dinner over.

"You know, Elie Mae, darling, I could get accustomed to this type of living. Me just lying up in bed - and you waiting on me hand and foot."

"Well, I'm hoping this will all end before the wedding. Look what I brought you to eat for dinner...a T-bone steak. Let me run and carry Granny's dinner to her. Miss Faye said for me to hurry back, for this has been a very busy day."

I was well into my steak when I heard Jake Nimes call my name at the front door. My bedroom was the one near to the front of the house.

"Yeah ,what cha want?" I yelled back.

"Miss Elie Mae said we could come over."

"Who is we?"

"Me and Jeff Dunn."

"Well, y'all come on back." I heard the screen slam and boots moseying my way. "You fellows pull up a chair and set down. If you would...do most of the talking while I finish my T-bone steak," I said, still gnawing.

"For one thing, Mr. Grimes was kind of dubious of Mr. Jeff Dunn. He wanted to know how long you have known him. We didn't say anything and waited for the next question" Jake said, looking over at Jeff.

I laid my knife and fork down and wiped my hands and mouth. "Let's go around the question and answer session...did the Mayor swear in Jeff Dunn as Sheriff of Silver Springs this morning?"

"Yes he did! But said for me to inform you that you would still be acting sheriff until the trial of Huey Black was over - and you didn't have to wear a star if you didn't want to."

"Well, well Sheriff Jeff Dunn, what have you got to say for yourself?" I questioned, sliding my plate to the edge of the bed.

"I'll tell you point blank, Wolf, and you, Jake, when I left Abilene, Texas, last Thursday, I was in bad shape. By the way, my dad is a Texas Ranger and he has told me time and time again I would never amount to anything. I had an idea if I got killed by you I would get my name in the newspaper. When my pa read the paper where his son went up against the world's fastest gun slinger, at least my pa could say his son didn't get shot down in Main Street by a drunken cowboy. Instead, 'My boy went out in style... by the world's fastest gun.'"

I could tell that Jeff had an attitude problem.

"Then you are saying you had no idea you could out draw me in a gun fight?" I asked.

"Yes that's right," Jeff answered bowing his head.

"This is why I want no more part of being a sheriff. You were using me to do your dirty work, Jeff, you wanted to commit suicide. You wanted to make your dad proud of you because you died. Can I suggest you make your dad proud - because you are alive and the sheriff of Silver Springs, Oklahoma?"

Jeff raised his head as if he was thinking out loud.

"You may not believe in things like this - but me and Pa had words when I left home last week - and my ma caught me just before I mounted my horse. 'Son', she said, with tears in her eyes, 'I will be praying for you, I will be praying that something good is going to happen.'"

Things grew real quiet; Jake looked at me and I smiled.

"Jeff... me and Jake believe you are going to be the best sheriff Silver Springs has ever had. And, since I am still acting sheriff, with some authority left, I want you go over to the general store and tell Mr. Grimes to fix you up with some sheriff's clothes. Get you several changings - and get you some new boots. Those you are wearing look pretty ratty. Tell him we'll take it out of your first couple of weeks pay. Then go on over to the hotel and get yourself a cheap room. Tell Clarence...I forgot his last name, but tell him the same thing. Are there any questions?" I asked.

"Now, between the two of you, one of you try to stay at the jail house and keep an eagle eye on our prisoners. Old man Huey Black has been too quiet; I don't like it. I personally know he is not going to give up without a fight and I know he still has men on the outside working for him," I commented.

"Sheriff, or Mr. Wolf, or whatever you want me to call you, I know a great deal about the law, my dad being a Texas Ranger. That was all the discussion around our supper table," Jeff informed me.

"Tell me, now, Jeff, I know you are toting a low hanging hog-leg, but can you use it?" We all started laughing.

"Well, let me put it this way, Wolf, I shore used up a lot of my pa's ammunition he didn't know about. Yes, I can hold my own shooting at bottles and tomato cans," Jeff said with a smile.

"Ha! Practice makes perfect and a man's body is much bigger than a tomato can. Who knows, you might have outdrawn me after all, Jeff."

"Wolf, I guess we'll never know, will we?"

The boys were walking out when I heard the Doctor calling, "Is anybody home?" I heard mumbling in the hall and Doctor Fletcher came walking into my room toting his black bag.

"Well, well, how is the holy one?" Doc asked, as he set his bag on the bed. "Yes, you will have a hole in ya for a while. It will mend from the inside out. Now, if you had managed to get cut, I could have sewed you up, and no hole." Doc was talking while he was removing the bandages, "Let me ask you something, Sheriff, what's all the going on up the street?"

"How would I know? I've been stuck in bed. What does it look like?"

"To me, it looks as if a bunch of men is erecting a big tent where the saloon that belonged to Huey Black once stood," the doctor stated, "I'll take a better look when I go back by."

"You don't suppose they're putting up a temporary make-shift saloon, do you? Why, there will be more drunks around here on trial day than one can shake a stick at. By the way, how does the wound look?"

"Not good, but I believe you will live if you stay off your feet until the wedding. Try to lay on your side as much as possible and let air get to the exit hole in back." As Doctor Fletcher was leaving to go visit Granny, in walked Elie Mae - mad as a wet setting hen.

"Guess what is going on up the street, Wolf Mann!"

"Now, now, Elie Mae darling, keep your drawers on and tell me what is going on up the street.

"I ain't taking them off just yet, Darling, but you'll be the first to know. They are building a saloon with a dance floor, a piano, and a bar. They are going to erect small tents out back for the whores.

"Now, Elie Mae, is this skuttlebutt or do you know for shore?"

"Well, you can ask Jeff Dunn and Jake Nimes what the dance hall girls said when they come in the diner for dinner today.  Boy, did they get an eye full!"

"Don't you think I should have been there, Darling?  It 'pears there was some important subjects discussed."

"I'm afraid not, and besides, you will get your eyes full in two more days, Baby."

"Oh, Elie Mae, couldn't you just give me, your lover to be... the man you plan to marry, a little sample of what I'm going to get on my wedding night?" I thought to myself 'I believe I can talk this girl into anything.' Elie Mae smiled and started unbuttoning three top buttons of her dress. She came closer and leaned way over in front of me to pick up the empty dishes. She slowly put both of her hands on the sides of her lovely breasts and pushed them up and together. I began to howl like a Wolf.

 "Down boy, down boy; you will have to wait."  Well, with a hole through my shoulder the size of a nickel - Elie Mae didn't have much persuading to do to get me to lie back down and behave myself.

Elie Mae sat down on the side of the bed and explained to me how she and the girls had the diner all decorated up for the wedding and my birthday party.

"Wolf darling, I think the whole town is going to turn out for the wedding."

"Do you think they are coming to see me or all the free food?"

"But, Wolf, everybody is planning on bringing a covered dish. I think the town is showing their appreciation for your getting the town's money back in the bank. But, most of all, you took Huey Black off the street - where it is safe once more."

I understood that Jeff Dunn, our new sheriff, and Jake Nimes were having a time keeping law and order up at the new temporary saloon. Word was that they hadn't had to kill anyone, yet. I think they had let three or four cowboys sleep a drunk off in jail.

# Chapter 20

I was expecting Aunt Becky Joiner in on the three o'clock train, along with her city lawyer, Frank Bedford. Mr. Grimes had paid me a visit earlier and filled me in on the Circuit Judge, who was residing in the hotel until the trial. He said the judge seemed to be a fair man and well informed of the laws that governed the Oklahoma Territory. Mr. Grimes went on to say that Judge Bob Willis was sixty-five years of age, from Ohio, and didn't stand for any hanky-panky.

It was a great day for Silver Springs, all in all. It seemed that the wedding and my birthday party was a way to get everyone out of their houses and back into town - without the fear of Huey Black's men shooting up the street and running wild. It was a family thing again. I have to admit that Silver Springs, Oklahoma, was not the place that Dad and I rode into just a little over a year ago. I guess the railroad and the stockyard made the difference. Of course, all the new businesses were certainly a big help.

I was getting bored with myself and made my way to the bathroom for a hot bath and a close shave, hoping it would make me feel better. I had already made up my mind that I would meet my Aunt Becky at the depot at three o'clock. I put on my all-black attire, including shined boots and my pearl handle pistols that Elie Mae had given back to me.

It had been a while since I visited Granny up the hall.

"Is that you, Wolf?" a weak voice came from her room as I walked up the hall nearing her door.

"I'm afraid so, Granny. I thought I would visit for a minute, if you feel up to it."

"I always have time for my favorite grandson, and I am feeling right well, you might say. I wouldn't miss the wedding tomorrow for anything in the world."

"You mean you are coming over to the wedding tomorrow at the diner?"

"I sure am, if I feel like it!"

"I sure hope you feel like it, Granny, because there's no one I'd rather have at my wedding than you."

I eased on over to the diner where everyone was busy finishing up dinner and cleaning up.

"Look who we have here...Wolf!" Mom said as I walked in the kitchen "Margie is back with us. Her father's job in California didn't work out."

"Well, glad to have you back. I'm sure you heard the big news already; Elie Mae and I are getting hitched tomorrow."

"Oh, yes, yes! I'm so happy for you two," Margie said, brushing herself off.

"Why, she has already got her eyes on our new sheriff," said Elie Mae, bringing in a load of dirty dishes."

"And what does Jeff Dunn think about this?" I asked as I pulled Elie Mae close and kissed her on the neck.

"I think he liked it, you know how Margie liked to carry on."

"Now I heard that, Elie Mae; are you saying I'm just a little forward?"

"Oh, no. How could I have ever arrived at a conclusion like that? After all, you did sit down in his lap."

"My, my, Elie Mae honey, how you do carry on! You know I slipped and almost fell. I thank the Lord that Mr. Jeff was so handy and managed to catch me."

"I think I'm going to ease over to the jail and check everything out. Then it should be time for the 3:10 train, and I hope to meet Aunt Becky Joiner."

I went through the back door of the jail and had a cup of coffee with Jeff Dunn and Jake Nimes who were all but pulling their hair out.

"What is all the commotion about, men?" I asked.

"I'll tell you, Wolf, me and Jake ain't one to bring you all our troubles, but Hugh Black's men ain't going to sit still much longer with him locked up in jail. The scuttlebutt around town is old man Huey Black has promised his men a big bonus if they will break him out of jail before the trial."

"Maybe I should have a talk with Huey Black." I poured me a refill of coffee and started toward the back of the jail.

"Well, well, Mr. Huey Black, our model prisoner. The scuttlebutt around town is some of your boys on the outside is going to try to release you from jail before the trial. Do you know anything about this?"

Huey Black swelled up like a toad frog and turned his head from me.

"You can sit there like a knot on a log if you want to, but you are in enough trouble as of now, let alone trying to break out of jail. The first shot I hear from someone trying to break you out of jail, I will personally shoot you in the head four times. Then I will drag your slimy, dead carcass outside in the street of Silver Springs and let the dogs lick your blood."

I guess I must have hit a nerve - 'cause old man Huey Black jumped up and ran at me. He grabbed the iron bars right in front of me and began to spew his venom as vulgarly as a mad man.

"I tell you what I'm gonna do to you and this town when I get out of jail. My lawyer is going to get me off on every charge that is pending against me. I'm innocent, I tell you, I'm innocent!"

"You are talking like a mad man, Mr. Black. You will hang for your crimes and you know it. You are out of money and no one will come to your rescue." I turned and walked out the cell area of the jail back to where Jeff was. "I'm going over to the depot. It's about time for the 3:10 train, and my Aunt Becky is hopefully on it.

Well, no train and no Aunt Becky. I waited, only to find out that the 3:10 was being robbed just outside of town. I had an idea who was behind this robbery, but not being able to ride I had to put this mishap on the back burner until I received my strength. I eased on into the depot and walked up to the desk as if I was going to buy a ticket. There was the same agent that I had dealings with the other day.

"Where is the train?" I shouted.

"It is being robbed," the attendant said, nervously.

"How do you know it's being robbed?" I asked, pressing the issue. "I believe you and Huey Black are working together to rob the trains...what do you have to say for yourself?"

"No! No! Sheriff, you are going to get me killed! I don't know nothing, really, I don't.

"You have been feeding information to Huey Black's men when the train is carrying the railroad's payroll, haven't you? Just like today, it is the end of the month and there is a big payroll on board."

"But they said they would kill me if didn't tell them."

"You should'a come to me or told the railroad officials before now, that you was being blackmailed by Huey Black. I'm sorry for you, sir, but as soon as the train comes, I will see if they have anyone on board to replace you. You are under arrest and going to jail."

Well, like a sheep-killing dog, the late 3:10 train finally came pulling into the station. Aunt Becky and her lawyer were the first to get off the train.

"I hear you had a little excitement back up the track a ways!"

"If you are talking about the train being robbed, you're right," Aunt Becky said, giving me a big hug and kiss. "You know how to give an easterner a Wild West welcome to make me feel right at home."

We began to laugh as I loaded Aunt Becky's trunk in to the surrey.

"Mr. Bradford, our plans are that you will be staying at the Silver Springs Hotel and Aunt Becky will be lodging in the big house with the Pittmans." I stopped by the jail house on the way to the hotel, long enough to tell Jeff to go over to the train depot and arrest the teller and put him in jail.

I thought that was simple enough. I let Mr. Frank Bedford, the lawyer, off at the hotel and headed back to our house, where Aunt Becky and I would stay. But to my surprise here came Jeff, our newly acclaimed sheriff, running from the train depot right toward me, waving both hands in the air.

"Let me see what the sheriff wants, Aunt Becky." Before turning to go to the house, I just pulled up right in the middle of the street and waited on Jeff.

"What in tar-nation do you want, Jeff?"

When he reached the surrey he was slam out of breath and could barely talk. "You need to come quickly, Wolf; the depot teller has shot himself!"

"Shot himself?" I asked.

"That's right! He is deader than a door nail. When I got over there to the depot I found him in the back, dead. It looked as if he stuck a pistol in his mouth and blew his head off, might near."

"Well you don't need me, you are the sheriff. If he is dead, you need Jerd Coggins, the undertaker. Be sure you look all around and see if he wrote a suicide note."

Slowly, things were coming together for tomorrow. The big day was all planned out; Mom and the girls had seen to that. All I needed to do was get up, dress up, and show up. I turned seventeen and was going to get married the same day. The marriage took place outside on the lawn next to the diner. It was beautifully decorated with flowers, archway and all.

I know one thing, I made one little girl happy. Of course, my day was happy as well. My Aunt Becky, the only living kin on my pa's side, was here, and my granny was able to come and sit outside. What really stole the day was when Jeff Dunn's mom and dad (the Texas Ranger) showed up from Central Texas. Even Jeff made an announcement of his and Margie's engagement. My birthday party was something I will never forget - with all the food, the big cake and all the presents. Elie Mae and I decided to spend our honeymoon in town - until after the trial of Huey Black.

The trial of Huey Black opened on the twenty-first day of July, 1877, in the unfinished saloon in Silver Springs, Oklahoma with Judge Bob Willis presiding. Although there was a packed-out crowd, there was ample room for everyone to sit comfortably. Then, there was also the July heat for us to deal with.

The chairs and most of the other furniture Mr. Charlie Cole had ordered from back East had arrived. The homemade benches constructed by the men from town were nice and comfortable and came in very handy. There were two tables that sat near the front of the courtroom. On the left sat Mr. Huey Black and his lawyer, Gus Arnold, from back East. At the right table was Frank Bedford, and Curtis Flynn, the president of Silver Springs Bank.

"Would everyone please rise," a voice intoned from somewhere near the front of the courtroom, near the judge's bench. "The Honorable Bob Willis, presiding over the Oklahoma Territory."

He appeared from a room in the back. He was wearing a black robe and walked with much dignity and authority. He took his seat behind the eye-level desk.

The judge picked up his gavel and rapped on the desk. "You may be seated," he said, clearing his throat. "We are here today to prove or disprove whether or not Huey Black robbed the Silver Springs Bank and did much damage to the bank vault." The Judge turned his attention to the table where Huey Black and his lawyer sat. "Guilty, or not guilty?" Judge Willis asked.

The lawyer for Huey Black was quick to rise. "Not guilty, Your Honor."

"Then would you please state your case to the court, Mr. Arnold?" The judge asked.

Gus Arnold arose from the table and slowly made his way over to the jury box. "First of all, Your Honor, and gentlemen of the jury, it was impossible for Mr. Huey Black to rob the Silver Springs Bank because he was out of town the night the bank was robbed. Now, I have no reason to deny the word of Mr. Huey Black, for he is a forefather of this town and served on the Town Council for over twenty years. I rest my case." He made his way back over to the table where Huey Black was and took his seat.

"Now, Counselor, it is your turn to defend your client and the bank," the judge said, looking over toward Frank Bedford.

Mr. Bedford arose from the table and walked straight toward the judge. "Now, Judge, and honorable men of this noted jury, I aim to prove, beyond any shadow of doubt, before this day is over, that Huey Black robbed the bank, killed Ruth Allen, and had Mr. Fred Mann shot to death in cold blood. Also, he swindled Wolf Mann out of his property and rustled his few cattle and horses."

Of course, Huey Black's lawyer jumped to his feet. "I protest those remarks, Your Honor, and wish to have them struck from the records of this court...my client is being tried for robbery, not murder."

The judge came down hard on his desk with his gavel. "Very well, Mr. Bedford, keep your line of questioning dealing only with bank robbery."

"Then, first, I will prove that Huey Black is a bald-face liar and there is no truth in him."

Again, Huey Black's lawyer jumped to his feet. "I object to those remarks, Your Honor, and wish to have them struck from the records of this court...my client is being tried for robbery - not whether he's a liar or not."

The judge faced Mr. Bedford. "Again, I warn you, sir, let your line of questions be about the robbery."

"I understand, Your Honor, but it was stated in this courtroom it was impossible for Mr. Huey Black to rob the Silver Springs Bank - he was out of town the night the bank was robbed. That is a bald face lie. Let me see the hands in this courtroom that saw Huey Black in town the day of the robbery."

Over a dozen hands through out the courtroom went up.

"I rest my case, Your Honor, Huey Black was in Silver Springs the night of the robbery. I now call Wolf Mann to the stand."

Glancing quickly all around, I walked to the front of the courtroom.

"Mr. Wolf, do you swear to tell the truth and nothing but the truth? Lay your hand on this Bible." I did, then sat down in a chair beside the bench.

"State your name and who you are. Then tell your story of the bank robbery," Frank Bedford said, and stepped back waiting on my answer.

"My name is Wolf Mann, and I was sheriff of Silver Springs when the bank was robbed. Now, being the sheriff, I was one of the first ones at the bank after it was robbed, along with Curtis Flynn and Mr. Grimes. The first thing I noticed was the back door of the bank was pried open. The next thing I noticed was powder burns on a mattress in a small room near the back door. Although the night of the robbery the weather was bad and it was lightning, thundering and raining, the mattress was used to muffle the sound of the explosion when the bank vault was blown open. As I began to examine the powder stains left by the blast, I also detected the strong smell of Rum-Maple tobacco prevalent on the mattress. Now, as far as I know, Huey Black is the only man in this town that uses Rum-Maple tobacco."

"I object, Your Honor! This is flimsy evidence; this proves nothing..." said Huey Black's lawyer.

"Okay... that very day I went to Huey Black's ranch with a search warrant and looked in his safe that sat in his den. There was all the money from the bank; some of the sacks were still wet from the rain that night."

"Mr. Wolf, you may step down. Your Honor, this concludes my line of questioning. Huey Black is guilty of robbing the Silver Springs Bank."

Within the next thirty minutes the twelve jurors brought in a verdict of 'guilty as charged.' In the next four days of deliberations Huey Black was convicted of two counts of murder, train robbery, land fraud, and cattle rustling. His sentence was: to hang by the neck until dead.

I left the courtroom with mixed emotions. Justice had been served; the guilty party was punished according to the law.

Elie Mae had the surrey packed and ready to go home when I reached the hotel. I tied Blackie to the back of the surrey and eased up beside my true love. Elie Mae and I soon disappeared into the Oklahoma sunset.

# ABOUT THE AUTHOR

Born in 1936, Charlie Barnett has lived his whole life within three acres of where he first saw the light of day. At the age of thirteen Charlie began publishing a monthly school comic book. Today, 62 years later, he has authored sixteen books, with many more on the way. Charlie has also penned over 200 poems that range from inspirational to southern humor.

Before retiring, Charlie spent decades as a successful entrepreneur and minister. He now enjoys writing, watching westerns, gardening, and observing butterflies and hummingbirds.

Charlie has been married to his wife, Janice, since 1958. Today they enjoy their growing family which includes: four sons, eleven grandchildren and eight great-grandchildren. Charlie is always up for a good laugh, telling stories, and speaking engagements.

## Other Great Books By Charlie Barnett

Amazing Grace

Dead But Not Buried

Devils, Daemons And Deliverance

Georgia Cowboy

Going Back To Abilene

Go West Young Man

Humorous Poems & Funny Stories

I Fell In Love With My Rapist

Just Jokes

My Mother Was An Angel

Run Johnny Run

Short Stories Told By My Granny

Standing In The Shadow

Suitcase Full Of Money

Through The Bible In Poems

Youngest Gun Slinger

Website:  www.gateswoodbooks.com

www.ingramcontent.com/pod-product-compliance
Lightning Source LLC
Chambersburg PA
CBHW070120260626
47160CB00004B/1548